NON SANZ DROICT.

William Shakespeare

THE TEMPEST

With New Dramatic Criticism and an Updated Bibliography

Edited by Robert Langbaum

GENERAL EDITOR: SYLVAN BARNET
The Signet Classic Shakespeare

A SIGNET CLASSIC

SIGNET CLASSIC
Published by the Penguin Group
Penguin Books USA Inc., 375 Hudson Street,
New York, New York 10014, U.S.A.
Penguin Books Ltd, 27 Wrights Lane,
London W8 5TZ, England
Penguin Books Australia Ltd, Ringwood,
Victoria, Australia
Penguin Books Canada Ltd, 10 Alcorn Avenue,
Toronto, Ontario, Canada M4V 3B2
Penguin Books (N.Z.) Ltd, 182–190 Wairau Road,
Auckland 10, New Zealand

Penguin Books Ltd, Registered Offices:
Harmondsworth, Middlesex, England

Published by Signet Classic, an imprint of Dutton Signet,
a division of Penguin Books USA Inc.

34 33 32 31 30

Copyright © 1964, 1987 by Robert Langbaum
Copyright © 1964, 1987 by Sylvan Barnet
All rights reserved

REGISTERED TRADEMARK—MARCA REGISTRADA

Library of Congress Catalog Card Number: 86-62301

Printed in the United States of America

Contents

Contents

Shakespeare: Prefatory Remarks

Between the record of his baptism in Stratford on 26 April 1564 and the record of his burial in Stratford on 25 April 1616, some forty documents name Shakespeare, and many others name his parents, his children, and his grandchildren. More facts are known about William Shakespeare than about any other playwright of the period except Ben Jonson. The facts should, however, be distinguished from the legends. The latter, inevitably more engaging and better known, tell us that the Stratford boy killed a calf in high style, poached deer and rabbits, and was forced to flee to London, where he held horses outside a playhouse. These traditions are only traditions; they may be true, but no evidence supports them, and it is well to stick to the facts.

Mary Arden, the dramatist's mother, was the daughter of a substantial landowner; about 1557 she married John Shakespeare, who was a glove-maker and trader in various farm commodities. In 1557 John Shakespeare was a member of the Council (the governing body of Stratford), in 1558 a constable of the borough, in 1561 one of the two town chamberlains, in 1565 an alderman (entitling him to the appellation "Mr."), in 1568 high bailiff—the town's highest political office, equivalent to mayor. After 1577, for an unknown reason he drops out of local politics. The birthday of William Shakespeare, the eldest son of this locally prominent man, is unrecorded; but the Stratford parish register records that the infant was baptized on 26 April 1564. (It is quite possible that he was born on 23 April, but this date has probably been assigned by tradition because it is the date on which, fifty-two years later, he died.) The attendance records of the Stratford grammar school of the period are not extant, but it is reasonable to assume that the son of a local official attended the school and received substantial training in Latin. The masters of the school from Shakespeare's seventh to fifteenth years held Oxford degrees; the Elizabethan curriculum excluded mathematics and the natural sciences but taught a good deal of Latin rhetoric, logic, and literature. On 27 November 1582 a marriage license was issued to Shakespeare and Anne Hathaway, eight years his senior. The couple had a child in May, 1583. Perhaps the marriage was necessary, but perhaps the couple had earlier engaged in a formal "troth plight" which would render their children legitimate even if no further ceremony were performed. In 1585 Anne Hathaway bore Shakespeare twins.

That Shakespeare was born is excellent; that he married and had children is pleasant; but that we know nothing about his departure from Stratford to London, or about the beginning of his theatrical career, is lamentable and must be admitted. We would gladly sacrifice details about his children's baptism for details about his earliest days on the stage. Perhaps the poaching episode is true (but it is first reported almost a century after Shakespeare's death), or perhaps he first left Stratford to be a schoolteacher, as another tradition holds; perhaps he was moved by

> Such wind as scatters young men through the world,
> To seek their fortunes further than at home
> Where small experience grows.

In 1592, thanks to the cantankerousness of Robert Greene, a rival playwright and a pamphleteer, we have our first reference, a snarling one, to Shakespeare as an actor and playwright. Greene warns those of his own educated friends who wrote for the theater against an actor who has presumed to turn playwright:

> There is an upstart crow, beautified with our feathers, that with his *tiger's heart wrapped in a player's hide* supposes he is as well able to bombast out a blank verse as the best of

you, and being an absolute Johannes-factotum is in his own
conceit the only Shake-scene in a country.

The reference to the player, as well as the allusion to
Aesop's crow (who strutted in borrowed plumage, as an
actor struts in fine words not his own), makes it clear that
by this date Shakespeare had both acted and written. That
Shakespeare is meant is indicated not only by "Shake-
scene" but by the parody of a line from one of Shakespeare's plays, *3 Henry VI:* "O, tiger's heart wrapped in
a woman's hide." If Shakespeare in 1592 was prominent
enough to be attacked by an envious dramatist, he probably had served an apprenticeship in the theater for at least
a few years.

In any case, by 1592 Shakespeare had acted and written,
and there are a number of subsequent references to him as
an actor: documents indicate that in 1598 he is a "principal
comedian," in 1603 a "principal tragedian," in 1608 he is
one of the "men players." The profession of actor was not
for a gentleman, and it occasionally drew the scorn of
university men who resented writing speeches for persons
less educated than themselves, but it was respectable
enough: players, if prosperous, were in effect members of
the bourgeoisie, and there is nothing to suggest that Stratford considered William Shakespeare less than a solid citizen. When, in 1596, the Shakespeares were granted a coat
of arms, the grant was made to Shakespeare's father, but
probably William Shakespeare (who the next year bought
the second-largest house in town) had arranged the matter
on his own behalf. In subsequent transactions he is occasionally styled a gentleman.

Although in 1593 and 1594 Shakespeare published two
narrative poems dedicated to the Earl of Southampton,
Venus and Adonis and *The Rape of Lucrece,* and may well
have written most or all of his sonnets in the middle nine-
ties, Shakespeare's literary activity seems to have been almost entirely devoted to the theater. (It may be significant
that the two narrative poems were written in years when
the plague closed the theaters for several months.) In 1594
he was a charter member of a theatrical company called the

Chamberlain's Men (which in 1603 changed its name to
the King's Men); until he retired to Stratford (about 1611,
apparently), he was with this remarkably stable company.
From 1599 the company acted primarily at the Globe
Theatre, in which Shakespeare held a one-tenth interest.
Other Elizabethan dramatists are known to have acted, but
no other is known also to have been entitled to a share in
the profits of the playhouse.

Shakespeare's first eight published plays did not have his
name on them, but this is not remarkable; the most popular
play of the sixteenth century, Thomas Kyd's *The Spanish
Tragedy*, went through many editions without naming Kyd,
and Kyd's authorship is known only because a book on the
profession of acting happens to quote (and attribute to
Kyd) some lines on the interest of Roman emperors in the
drama. What is remarkable is that after 1598 Shakespeare's
name commonly appears on printed plays—some of which
are not his. Another indication of his popularity comes
from Francis Meres, author of *Palladis Tamia: Wit's
Treasury* (1598): in this anthology of snippets accompa-
nied by an essay on literature, many playwrights are mentioned, but Shakespeare's name occurs more often than any
other, and Shakespeare is the only playwright whose plays
are listed.

From his acting, playwriting, and share in a theater,
Shakespeare seems to have made considerable money. He
put it to work, making substantial investments in Stratford
real estate. When he made his will (less than a month before he died), he sought to leave his property intact to his
descendants. Of small bequests to relatives and to friends
(including three actors, Richard Burbage, John Heminges,
and Henry Condell), that to his wife of the second-best bed
has provoked the most comment; perhaps it was the bed
the couple had slept in, the best being reserved for visitors.
In any case, had Shakespeare not excepted it, the bed
would have gone (with the rest of his household posses-
sions) to his daughter and her husband. On 25 April 1616
he was buried within the chancel of the church at Stratford.
An unattractive monument to his memory, placed on a wall
near the grave, says he died on 23 April. Over the grave

itself are the lines, perhaps by Shakespeare, that (more than his literary fame) have kept his bones undisturbed in the crowded burial ground where old bones were often dislodged to make way for new:

> Good friend, for Jesus' sake forbear
> To dig the dust enclosed here.
> Blessed be the man that spares these stones
> And cursed be he that moves my bones.

Thirty-seven plays, as well as some nondramatic poems, are held to constitute the Shakespeare canon. The dates of composition of most of the works are highly uncertain, but there is often evidence of a *terminus a quo* (starting point) and/or a *terminus ad quem* (terminal point) that provides a framework for intelligent guessing. For example, *Richard II* cannot be earlier than 1595, the publication date of some material to which it is indebted; *The Merchant of Venice* cannot be later than 1598, the year Francis Meres mentioned it. Sometimes arguments for a date hang on an alleged topical allusion, such as the lines about the unseasonable weather in *A Midsummer Night's Dream*, II.i.81— 117, but such an allusion (if indeed it is an allusion) can be variously interpreted, and in any case there is always the possibility that a topical allusion was inserted during a revision, years after the composition of a play. Dates are often attributed on the basis of style, and although conjectures about style usually rest on other conjectures, sooner or later one must rely on one's literary sense. There is no real proof, for example, that *Othello* is not as early as *Romeo and Juliet*, but one feels *Othello* is later, and because the first record of its performance is 1604, one is glad enough to set its composition at that date and not push it back into Shakespeare's early years. The following chronology, then, is as much indebted to informed guesswork and sensitivity as it is to fact. The dates, necessarily imprecise, indicate something like a scholarly consensus.

PLAYS

1588–93   *The Comedy of Errors*

POEMS

1593-94   *The Rape of Lucrece*
1593-1600   *Sonnets*
1600-01   *The Phoenix and the Turtle*

Shakespeare's Theater

In Shakespeare's infancy, Elizabethan actors performed wherever they could—in great halls, at court, in the courtyards of inns. The innyards must have made rather unsatisfactory theaters: on some days they were unavailable because carters bringing goods to London used them as depots; when available, they had to be rented from the innkeeper; perhaps most important, London inns were subject to the Common Council of London, which was not well disposed toward theatricals. In 1574 the Common Council required that plays and playing places in London be licensed. It asserted that

sundry great disorders and inconveniences have been found to ensue to this city by the inordinate haunting of great multitudes of people, specially youth, to plays, interludes, and shows, namely occasion of frays and quarrels, evil practices of incontinency in great inns having chambers and secret places adjoining to their open stages and galleries,

and ordered that innkeepers who wished licenses to hold performances put up a bond and make contributions to the poor.

The requirement that plays and innyard theaters be licensed, along with the other drawbacks of playing at inns, probably drove James Burbage (a carpenter-turned-actor) to rent in 1576 a plot of land northeast of the city walls and to build here—on property outside the jurisdiction of the city—England's first permanent construction designed for plays. He called it simply the Theatre. About all that is known of its construction is that it was wood. It soon had imitators, the most famous being the Globe (1599), built across the Thames (again outside the city's jurisdiction), out of timbers of the Theatre, which had been dismantled when Burbage's lease ran out.

There are three important sources of information about the structure of Elizabethan playhouses—drawings, a contract, and stage directions in plays. Of drawings, only the so-called De Witt drawing (c. 1596) of the Swan—really a friend's copy of De Witt's drawing—is of much significance. It shows a building of three tiers, with a stage jutting from a wall into the yard or center of the building. The tiers are roofed, and part of the stage is covered by a roof that projects from the rear and is supported at its front on two posts, but the groundlings, who paid a penny to stand in front of the stage, were exposed to the sky. (Performances in such a playhouse were held only in the daytime; artificial illumination was not used.) At the rear of the stage are two doors; above the stage is a gallery. The second major source of information, the contract for the Fortune, specifies that although the Globe is to be the model, the Fortune is to be square, eighty feet outside and fifty-five inside. The stage is to be forty-three feet broad, and is to extend into the middle of the yard (i.e., it is twenty-seven and a half feet deep). For patrons willing to pay more than the general admission charged of the groundlings, there were to be three galleries provided with seats. From the third chief source, stage directions, one learns that entrance to the stage was by doors, presumably spaced widely apart at the rear ("Enter one citizen at one door, and another at the other"), and that in addition to the platform stage there was occasionally some sort of curtained booth or alcove allowing for "discovery" scenes, and some sort of playing space "aloft" or "above" to represent (for example) the top of a city's walls or a room above the street. Doubtless each theater had its own peculiarities, but perhaps we can talk about a "typical" Elizabethan theater if we realize that no theater need exactly have fit the description, just as no father is the typical father with 3.7 children. This hypothetical theater is wooden, round or polygonal (in *Henry V* Shakespeare calls it a "wooden *O*"), capable of holding some eight hundred spectators standing in the yard around the projecting elevated stage and some fifteen hundred additional spectators seated in the three roofed galleries. The stage, protected by a "shadow" or "heavens" or roof, is entered by two doors; behind the doors is the "tiring house" (attiring house, i.e., dressing room), and above the doors is some sort of gallery that may sometimes hold spectators but that can be used (for example) as the bedroom from which Romeo—according to a stage direction in one text— "goeth down." Some evidence suggests that a throne can be lowered onto the platform stage, perhaps from the "shadow"; certainly characters can descend from the stage through a trap or traps into the cellar or "hell." Sometimes this space beneath the platform accommodates a sound-effects man or musician (in *Antony and Cleopatra* "music of the hautboys is under the stage") or an actor (in *Hamlet* the "Ghost cries under the stage"). Most characters simply walk on and off, but because there is no curtain in front of the platform, corpses will have to be carried off (Hamlet must lug Polonius' guts into the neighbor room), or will have to fall at the rear, where the curtain on the alcove or booth can be drawn to conceal them.

Such may have been the so-called "public theater." Another kind of theater, called the "private theater" because its much greater admission charge limited its audience to the wealthy or the prodigal, must be briefly mentioned. The private theater was basically a large room, entirely roofed and therefore artificially illuminated, with a stage at one end. In 1576 one such theater was established in Blackfriars, a Dominican priory in London that had been suppressed in 1538 and confiscated by the Crown and thus was not under the city's jurisdiction. All the actors in the Blackfriars theater were boys about eight to thirteen years old (in the public theaters similar boys played female parts; a boy Lady Macbeth played to a man Macbeth). This private theater had a precarious existence, and ceased operations in 1584. In 1596 James Burbage, who had already made theatrical history by building the Theatre, began to construct a second Blackfriars theater. He died in 1597, and for several years this second Blackfriars theater was used by a troupe of boys, but in 1608 two of Burbage's sons and five other actors (including

Shakespeare) became joint operators of the theater, using it in the winter when the open-air Globe was unsuitable. Perhaps such a smaller theater, roofed, artificially illuminated, and with a tradition of a courtly audience, exerted an influence on Shakespeare's late plays.

Performances in the private theaters may well have had intermissions during which music was played, but in the public theaters the action was probably uninterrupted, flowing from scene to scene almost without a break. Actors would enter, speak, exit, and others would immediately enter and establish (if necessary) the new locale by a few properties and by words and gestures. Here are some samples of Shakespeare's scene painting:

> This is Illyria, lady.

> Well, this is the Forest of Arden.

> This castle hath a pleasant seat; the air
> Nimbly and sweetly recommends itself
> Unto our gentle senses.

On the other hand, it is a mistake to conceive of the Elizabethan stage as bare. Although Shakespeare's Chorus in *Henry V* calls the stage an "unworthy scaffold" and urges the spectators to "eke out our performance with your mind," there was considerable spectacle. The last act of *Macbeth,* for example, has five stage directions calling for "drum and colors," and another sort of appeal to the eye is indicated by the stage direction "Enter Macduff, with Macbeth's head." Some scenery and properties may have been substantial; doubtless a throne was used, and in one play of the period we encounter this direction: "Hector takes up a great piece of rock and casts at Ajax, who tears up a young tree by the roots and assails Hector." The matter is of some importance, and will be glanced at again in the next section.

The Texts of Shakespeare

Though eighteen of his plays were published during his

lifetime, Shakespeare seems never to have supervised their publication. There is nothing unusual here; when a playwright sold a play to a theatrical company he surrendered his ownership of it. Normally a company would not publish the play, because to publish it meant to allow competitors to acquire the piece. Some plays, however, did get published: apparently treacherous actors sometimes pieced together a play for a publisher, sometimes a company in need of money sold a play, and sometimes a company allowed a play to be published that no longer drew audiences. That Shakespeare did not concern himself with publication, then, is scarcely remarkable; of his contemporaries only Ben Jonson carefully supervised the publication of his own plays. In 1623, seven years after Shakespeare's death, John Heminges and Henry Condell (two senior members of Shakespeare's company, who had performed with him for about twenty years) collected his plays—published and unpublished—into a large volume, commonly called the First Folio. (A folio is a volume consisting of sheets that have been folded once, each sheet thus making two leaves, or four pages. The eighteen plays published during Shakespeare's lifetime had been issued one play per volume in small books called quartos. Each sheet in a quarto has been folded twice, making four leaves, or eight pages.) The First Folio contains thirty-six plays; a thirty-seventh, *Pericles,* though not in the Folio, is regarded as canonical. Heminges and Condell suggest in an address "To the great variety of readers" that the republished plays are presented in better form than in the quartos: "Before you were abused with diverse stolen and surreptitious copies, maimed and deformed by the frauds and stealths of injurious impostors that exposed them; even those, are now offered to your view cured and perfect of their limbs, and all the rest absolute in their numbers, as he [i.e., Shakespeare] conceived them."

Whoever was assigned to prepare the texts for publication in the First Folio seems to have taken his job seriously and yet not to have performed it with uniform care. The sources of the texts seem to have been, in general, good unpublished copies or the best published copies.

The first play in the collection, *The Tempest,* is divided into acts and scenes, has unusually full stage directions and descriptions of spectacle, and concludes with a list of the characters, but the editor was not able (or willing) to present all of the succeeding texts so fully dressed. Later texts occasionally show signs of carelessness: in one scene of *Much Ado About Nothing* the names of actors, instead of characters, appear as speech prefixes, as they had in the quarto, which the Folio reprints; proofreading throughout the Folio is spotty and apparently was done without reference to the printer's copy; the pagination of *Hamlet* jumps from 156 to 257.

A modern editor of Shakespeare must first select his copy; no problem if the play exists only in the Folio, but a considerable problem if the relationship between a quarto and the Folio—or an early quarto and a later one —is unclear. When an editor has chosen what seems to him to be the most authoritative text or texts for his copy, he has not done with making decisions. First of all, he must reckon with Elizabethan spelling. If he is not producing a facsimile, he probably modernizes it, but ought he to preserve the old form of words that apparently were pronounced quite unlike their modern forms—"lanthorn" "alablaster"? If he preserves these forms, is he really preserving Shakespeare's forms or perhaps those of a compositor in the printing house? What is one to do when one finds "lanthorn" and "lantern" in adjacent lines? (The editors of this series in general, but not invariably, assume that words should be spelled in their modern form.) Elizabethan punctuation, too, presents problems. For example in the First Folio, the only text for the play, Macbeth rejects his wife's idea that he can wash the blood from his hand:

> no: this my Hand will rather
> The multitudinous Seas incarnardine,
> Making the Greene one, Red.

Obviously an editor will remove the superfluous capitals, and he will probably alter the spelling to "incarnadine," but will he leave the comma before "red," letting Macbeth speak of the sea as "the green one," or will he (like most modern editors) remove the comma and thus have Macbeth say that his hand will make the ocean *uniformly* red?

An editor will sometimes have to change more than spelling or punctuation. Macbeth says to his wife:

> I dare do all that may become a man,
> Who dares no more, is none.

For two centuries editors have agreed that the second line is unsatisfactory, and have emended "no" to "do": "Who dares do more is none." But when in the same play Ross says that fearful persons

> floate vpon a wilde and violent Sea
> Each way, and moue,

need "move" be emended to "none," as it often is, on the hunch that the compositor misread the manuscript? The editors of the Signet Classic Shakespeare have restrained themselves from making abundant emendations. In their minds they hear Dr. Johnson on the dangers of emending: "I have adopted the Roman sentiment, that it is more honorable to save a citizen than to kill an enemy." Some departures (in addition to spelling, punctuation, and lineation) from the copy text have of course been made, but the original readings are listed in a note following the play, so that the reader can evaluate them for himself.

The editors of the Signet Classic Shakespeare, following tradition, have added line numbers and in many cases act and scene divisions as well as indications of locale at the beginning of scenes. The Folio divided most of the plays into acts and some into scenes. Early eighteenth-century editors increased the divisions. These divisions, which provide a convenient way of referring to passages in the plays, have been retained, but when not in the text chosen as the basis for the Signet Classic text they are enclosed in square brackets [ ] to indicate that they are editorial additions. Similarly, although no play of Shakespeare's published during his lifetime was equipped with indications of locale at the heads of scene divisions, locales have here been added in square brackets for the convenience of the reader, who lacks the information afforded to spectators by costumes, properties, and gestures. The spectator can tell at a glance he is in the throne room, but without an editorial indication the reader may be puzzled for a while. It should be mentioned, incidentally, that there are a few authentic stage directions—perhaps Shakespeare's, perhaps a prompter's—that suggest locales: for example, "Enter Brutus in his orchard," and "They go up into the Senate house." It is hoped that the bracketed additions provide the reader with the sort of help provided in these two authentic directions, but it is equally hoped that the reader will remember that the stage was not loaded with scenery.

No editor during the course of his work can fail to recollect some words Heminges and Condell prefixed to the Folio:

It had been a thing, we confess, worthy to have been wished, that the author himself had lived to have set forth and overseen his own writings. But since it hath been ordained otherwise, and he by death departed from that right, we pray you do not envy his friends the office of their care and pain to have collected and published them.

Nor can an editor, after he has done his best, forget Heminges and Condell's final words: "And so we leave you to other of his friends, whom if you need can be your guides. If you need them not, you can lead yourselves, and others. And such readers we wish him."

SYLVAN BARNET
Tufts University

Introduction

The Tempest is probably the last play wholly written by Shakespeare. Generations of readers have for this reason been tempted to see it as a culmination of Shakespeare's vision, to identify Prospero with Shakespeare, and to read the famous speech in which Prospero breaks his magic wand as Shakespeare's farewell to his art. Although critics nowadays hesitate to identify Prospero with Shakespeare, those of us who love *The Tempest* cannot help feeling that it represents a culmination—that Shakespeare could not have written it without the wisdom and technique he had accumulated through writing all his other plays.

We get this impression because the characterizations, for example, are so simple—Prospero is wise, Miranda is pure, Caliban is base, Antonio is wicked. Yet these are not the simple characters of a playwright who cannot do any better. They are the simple characters of the playwright who has already created Hamlet and Macbeth and Lear. And we feel this; we feel we are in touch, through the characters of *The Tempest*, with very real and very powerful forces. Caliban, who speaks one of the most beautiful passages of poetry in the play, is enigmatic enough. But where will you come to an end of understanding Ariel? Ariel's complexity certainly does not lie in his characterization. It lies, you may say, in the poetry he speaks. But that is to beg the question.

It is the deliberate return to naïveté, after the tragic complexity, that makes us feel there is something special about the four plays of Shakespeare's final period. The special effect is most apparent in *The Tempest*, because it is the lightest in surface of the four. It is presented to us as a gorgeous bubble, which is blown up for our entertainment like the masque Prospero conjures for Ferdinand and Miranda, and which is just as easily dispelled in the end. Yet *The Tempest* contains the subject matter of tragedy, and it gives us throughout the sense of omniscience, of surveying all life, that we get only at the highest points of illumination in the tragedies. No wonder then that *The Tempest* seems the appropriate statement of age, of the man who having seen it all can teach us that the profoundest statement is the lightest and that life, when we see through it, is gay, is tragicomically gay —that the evil, the violence, the tragedy are all part of a providential design.

The Tempest was probably written during the fall and winter of 1610–1611. It was produced at court in the fall of 1611, and again during the winter of 1612–1613 as part of the festivities that preceded the marriage of the King's daughter Elizabeth to the Elector Palatine. The First Folio probably gives us the play as it was acted at court during the winter. But there is insufficient evidence to support the contention of some scholars that the play was radically revised for the wedding festivities and that the wedding masque in Act IV was inserted in honor of the betrothed couple. Some scholars have even, in their disappointment with the verse of the wedding masque, supposed that the masque was not written by Shakespeare. But Shakespeare always uses a deliberately stilted style for a play within a play; and the masque depends for its effectiveness on spectacle rather than language. Unless new external evidence turns up, there is no reason to look outside the play itself for an explanation of the wedding masque, since the masque fits in subject matter and form into the very texture of *The Tempest*.

The masque brings to a climax the theme of nature versus art that is central to *The Tempest*. For Heaven and Earth, Juno and Ceres, unite in the masque to pronounce a blessing on the union of Ferdinand and Miranda, and to connect sexual union with nature's fruitfulness as seen in its ideal aspect. Venus and her son Cupid are,

however, as representatives of lawless passion, specifically
excluded from the natural force celebrated in the masque.
This fits in with Prospero's severe warning to Ferdinand
not to "break" Miranda's "virgin knot" before marriage.
Nature is celebrated in the masque as a principle of order.
And it is shown to be, as a principle of order, inextricably
intertwined with art, civilization, idea.

There is good reason to believe that Shakespeare had
in mind, when he wrote *The Tempest*, the reports that
first reached England in September 1610 of the miraculous deliverance of the crew and passengers of a ship
that had been lost the year before in a terrible tempest
off the Bermudas—those stormy islands that Shakespeare
refers to in *The Tempest* as "the still-vexed Bermoothes."
The written accounts of the survivors (extracts from
which appear under "The Source of *The Tempest*") emphasize the providential quality of their deliverance, for
the castaways were saved by the magically beneficent
nature of the island on which they found themselves.
These so-called Bermuda pamphlets go on to see the very
storm and shipwreck as providential, since they enabled
the castaways to discover for the benefit of mankind that
the islands that mariners had shunned as inhabited by
devils were actually an island paradise.

In exclaiming over the ways of providence, the Bermuda pamphlets offer those paradoxes that are at the
heart of the tragicomic vision—the sort of paradoxes
Shakespeare uses in *The Tempest*. "Though the seas
threaten, they are merciful," says Ferdinand in the end.
And Gonzalo sums up the meaning of the play through
a series of paradoxes. "Was Milan thrust from Milan,
that his issue/ Should become kings of Naples?" he asks.

> In one voyage
> Did Claribel her husband find at Tunis,
> And Ferdinand her brother found a wife
> Where he himself was lost; Prospero his dukedom
> In a poor isle; and all of us ourselves
> When no man was his own.

                                        (V.i.208–13)

This is the essential message of tragicomedy—that we lose in order to recover something greater, that we die in order to be reborn to a better life. One of the Bermuda pamphlets speaks paradoxically of "these infortunate (yet fortunate) islands," and even calls the shipwreck and deliverance "this tragical comedy."

The Bermuda episode must have raised again for Shakespeare the perennial question that became particularly pertinent after the discovery of the New World— the question of whether nature is not superior to art, and whether man is not nobler in a state of nature than in a state of civilization. It is not surprising that Shakespeare had also in mind, when he wrote *The Tempest*, the essay "Of the Cannibals" (also extracted under "Source") in which Montaigne praises the American Indians in terms that helped establish the ideal of the Noble Savage. Gonzalo's description of his ideal commonwealth is a close paraphrase of Montaigne's essay.

The island of *The Tempest* is in the Mediterranean, somewhere between Tunis and Naples; yet it seems more magically remote and unlocated than if it had been given a specific location, even one so far as the Bermudas. By setting his island in the Mediterranean, Shakespeare is able to bring the European tradition to bear on the question of nature versus art. He can assimilate the latest ideas about the New World to traditional ideas of the Golden Age and the Garden of Eden. He can remind us of Aeneas, who lost Troy that he might found Rome. Aeneas was driven by a storm to Carthage (specifically associated here with Tunis), from whence he sailed to Italy. In fulfilling his destiny, he underwent wanderings and ordeals analogous to those of the court party in *The Tempest*, including a banquet involving harpies. It is worth mentioning, in connection with Gonzalo's enigmatic references to "widow Dido" and "widower Aeneas," that two of the Bermuda pamphlets compare Dido and Aeneas, as colonizers of new territories, to the colonists of the New World.

Shakespeare addresses himself to the question of nature versus art by ringing all possible changes on the meaning of "nature." Caliban is natural in that he is earthy and earthbound, low, material. But Ariel is just as natural in that he represents the fluid elements of water and air and also those bodiless energies of nature that strike us as "spiritual." Caliban, whose name may derive from "cannibal," is the natural man seen in one aspect. But Miranda is also natural, and the two are contrasted throughout. Both were brought up in a state of nature; and if Miranda never saw a man other than her father, Caliban never saw a woman other than his mother. Caliban is natural in the sense that nature is rudimentary and mindless; he cannot be educated. Miranda is natural in the sense that we take the Golden Age or the Garden of Eden to be our natural condition. She has been superbly educated by Prospero, but education has with her been absorbed in the natural; knowledge has not lost her the Garden.

The case of Caliban is complex, because we cannot be certain that he is human. He was begotten by a devil on the witch Sycorax, and he is spoken of either as something between an animal and a man, or as something between a sea and a land animal. All the ironic changes on the meaning of "nature" can be heard in Trinculo's remark about Caliban: "That a monster should be such a natural!"—in which "natural" means "idiot." If we take nature to be a principle of order, then the primitive Caliban is a monster, a piece of disorder or deformity.

Trinculo's remark contrasts with Miranda's, when she thinks Ferdinand must be a god, "for nothing natural/ I ever saw so noble." Ferdinand, too, and in the end Alonso think for the same reason that Miranda must be a goddess. Shakespeare would seem to be telling us that your view of the natural depends on your view of the supernatural— on whether you see behind natural phenomena the evil machinations of the witch Sycorax and her devil-god Setebos, or whether you see at work a rational and benevolent providence. He seems to be telling us that every creature can be judged by its potential metamorphoses, by what it is capable of becoming. Miranda sees all the human beings in the play as godlike. But Caliban, who constantly shifts before our eyes between human and animal, fears that he and his drunken co-conspirators will turn into apes or into barnacles, geese believed to be the product of metamorphosis from shellfish.

There is no question as to which view of nature Shakespeare adheres to. He presents here, as in the history plays and the tragedies, a grand vision of order in nature and society; only the emphasis here, far more than in his other plays, is on nature. The fact that Caliban takes the drunken butler, Stephano, for a god is a sign of how high man ranks on the scale of life. It is because we recognize the differences of degree within the human scale that we laugh at Caliban's illusion, but give our poetic faith to the illusion of Ferdinand and Miranda when they take each other for divine. Caliban's crime in conspiring against Prospero is a sin against degree—like the plot of Antonio and Sebastian against Alonso, and Antonio's usurpation of Prospero's throne. Prospero erred in attempting to educate Caliban, just as he erred in allowing Antonio to play the duke in Milan. In both cases, he blurred distinctions of degree and helped create the disorder that followed.

Caliban is only evil when judged by human standards, or when he himself aspires to get above his place. In attempting to be "free," he only exchanges masters; for a slave he is and should be, as he himself recognizes in the end. Ariel, on the other hand, is by nature a free spirit (he seems free enough even in the bondage of which he complains), and he is therefore appropriately freed in the end. There is a connection in Shakespeare's worldview between biological and social rank and moral obligation. Thus, Antonio's crime against his brother and sovereign is also spoken of as "unnatural." But Antonio is much worse than Caliban, because much higher up on the scale. For the same reason, Stephano and Trinculo seem even baser than Caliban and even more ridiculous in their aspiration to get above themselves.

With the exception of Antonio, all the characters in the play are saved in the end according to their degree. They undergo a ritual temptation and punishment. Caliban, Stephano, and Trinculo are befouled in a horse-pond for their temptation to murder Prospero; and when Stephano and Trinculo are tempted to steal the clothes left out for them as bait, all three conspirators are chased away by spirits in the shape of dogs. These punishments are appropriate to the level of their moral life.

The court party are ritualistically tempted and punished by the banquet that disappears when they start to eat of it. Antonio and Sebastian have also been tempted to murder Alonso; and Alonso has been ritualistically punished by the supposed loss of his son and by his brother's temptation to do to him what he helped Antonio do to Prospero. When Ariel, who is invisible to everyone except Prospero, accuses Alonso, Antonio, and Sebastian of being "three men of sin," his voice comes to them as an inner voice. Alonso's attack of conscience comes as a total illumination. He now understands the union of the natural and moral order:

> Methought the billows spoke and told me of it;
> The winds did sing it to me; and the thunder,
> . . . .
>   did bass my trespass.
> Therefore my son i' th' ooze is bedded.
>   (III.iii.96–100)

Since Ferdinand and Miranda start without guilt, their development is mystical rather than moral. Ferdinand's ordeal prepares him to share with Miranda the vision of heaven on earth that Prospero sets before them in the wedding masque. They themselves appear in a masque-like vision of perfection, when Prospero draws a curtain to reveal them to the court party. Note that Ferdinand repeats in his ordeal the bondage of Caliban. But bondage at the lovers' high level of existence is transformed into freedom and happiness.

Prospero himself is, I think, tempted, when he remembers Caliban's conspiracy against him, to take revenge against the court party; for Caliban's conspiracy reminds him of the conspiracy of Antonio and Alonso. It is inconsistent with Prospero's role of a providence in the play to suppose that he did not from the start plan for events to work out as they do, and that he is actually converted from some original purpose of revenge by Ariel's remark that he would pity the court party were he human. Since Prospero obviously planned the marriage of Ferdinand and Miranda, it is likely that he also planned to be reconciled with Alonso and the others and that Ariel recalls him to his purpose. The point where, at the thought of Caliban, Prospero interrupts the masque, and is shaken by emotion, is the one point where he seems fallible like the other human beings in the play. We seem to be getting, in his lapse from and return to his purpose, the repetition of a moral conversion from thoughts of revenge that took place before the play begins. All the tragic events of Prospero's earlier life are portrayed for us through such repetitions; so that the tragic events appear to us in a comic perspective, since we now see how well everything turned out.

Almost all the characters pair off. As sovereign and father, Prospero pairs off with Alonso; and as magician, he pairs off with Caliban's mother, the witch Sycorax, who practiced black magic on the island as against Prospero's white magic. Ferdinand pairs off with Miranda; Antonio with Sebastian; Stephano with Trinculo; Caliban with Ariel. In his role of providence, Prospero stands alone at the top of the design. Such symmetries are at the heart of comic technique, perhaps because they make us feel we are seeing events from above, as part of a pattern, and can therefore restrain sympathy in the confidence that all is well. The design also explains the sense in which Shakespeare is not realistic in *The Tempest*. He is dealing in simplifications like those of the mathematician. He is giving us a diagram of the order of things.

The play begins with a scene of disorder—a tempest at sea that renders meaningless the usual social order. The sailors are disrespectful to the aristocrats, who in trying to assert authority get in the way of the ship's organization. The good-humored courage of Gonzalo stands out against the irrationality of Antonio and Sebastian, who scream abuse at the sailors—though they are later in the play to think themselves very rational in plotting social disorder. The storm gives the boatswain a chance to display a natural superiority that has nothing to do with rank.

In the next scene, we learn that the tempest is an illusion created to regenerate the social order—to restore a reformed Prospero to the throne of Milan, and to lead Ferdinand and Miranda to the throne of Naples. Ariel turns the noise and confusion of the tempest into music, the music that leads Ferdinand to Miranda. The play is pervaded, as G. Wilson Knight has shown in *The Shakespearean Tempest*, by the imagery of tempest, sea, natural noise, and music. This imagery sets the play in a world where disorder is seen to be not merely at the service of order, but inextricably intertwined, indeed identical, with it. It requires only a transformation of perception to recognize order in disorder.

It is, I think, because Ariel makes music out of the natural noises of the island that there is an undersong of animal noises behind one of his songs, and the sound of the sea behind another. When Caliban says, "Be not afeard; the isle is full of noises,/ Sounds and sweet airs that give delight and hurt not," he catches the world of nature between metamorphoses, between noise and music, sleep and waking. We say he renders the magical atmosphere of the island. We mean by this that, like Ariel in his songs, Caliban in this lovely speech shows the appearances of things as fluid and ever-changing aspects of a single force—a force that is beneficent, though it may seem in certain aspects evil.

This force is represented by the sea that washes through every nook and cranny of the play, moving the characters to their destiny both by carrying them there and by washing right up into their consciousness. When Prospero tells Miranda of the "sea sorrow" that brought them to the island, he describes the sea as both threatening and loving. We were cast adrift, he says,

> To cry to th' sea that roared to us; to sigh
> To th' winds, whose pity, sighing back again,
> Did us but loving wrong.

> (I.ii.149–51)

The supposed drowning of Ferdinand is spoken of in attractive images. And when one of Alonso's courtiers suggests that Ferdinand may have made it to land, he makes us see that, by struggling against the waves, Ferdinand actually rode them to shore as you ride a fiery steed.

> I saw him beat the surges under him
> And ride upon their backs. He trod the water,
> Whose enmity he flung aside, and breasted
> The surge most swol'n that met him. His bold head
> 'Bove the contentious waves he kept, and oared
> Himself with his good arms in lusty stroke
> To th' shore . . .

> (II.i.119–25)

The passage—which is, in its complexity of implication and its metrical suppleness, a good example of Shakespeare's late style—turns violence into harmony. It is but a step away from the song in which Ariel makes drowning seem so desirable, because it is, like all aspects of existence in this play, "a sea change/ Into something rich and strange" —into the one force that moves all things. Prospero's magic is a portion of nature's; his providential design is a portion of God's.

Antonio, when he tempts Sebastian to murder the King, uses sea imagery, connecting it with the imagery of sleep and dream to signify the force of Sebastian's real desire. Antonio speaks, through his imagery, truer than he knows; for even his plot is necessary to the providential design of the play. Antonio is an effective villain, because he manipulates real, which is to say magical, forces. Prospero uses the imagery of metamorphosis when he tells Miranda how Antonio so transformed the Milanese court as to make real Antonio's appearance of being duke. The wild sounds of sea and tempest turn for Alonso into rational music that tells him of his crime. And Prospero

brings the sea imagery to a climax when he says in the
end of the court party,

> Their understanding
> Begins to swell, and the approaching tide
> Will shortly fill the reasonable shore,
> That now lies foul and muddy.
>
> (V.i.79–82)

The sea is now identified with rationality.

The most admirable characters are those who can perceive order in disorder, because they have the capacity
for wonder. When Ferdinand says "Admired Miranda,"
he is playing on the meaning of her name; he is saying,
"O wonderful woman, who is to be wondered at." And
when, during the masque, he calls Prospero "So rare a
wond'red father" (a father possessed of wonders and
therefore to be wondered at), it is a sign that he now sees
Prospero right. There is an irony in Miranda's famous
remark at the end, when she first beholds the court party:

> O, wonder!
> How many goodly creatures are there here!
> How beauteous mankind is! O brave new world
> That has such people in't!
>
> (V.i.181–84)

Nevertheless, it is the whole point of the play to make us
feel that Miranda is right—that she, in her innocence,
sees all these people as they really are, as through all
their metamorphoses they are tending to be.

It is to Caliban's credit that he exhibits a capacity for
wonder lacking in Stephano and Trinculo and in Antonio
and Sebastian. That is because Caliban is natural. His
faults do not stem from a perversion of reason, as do
those of the four witty characters who do not exhibit a
capacity for wonder. Only Gonzalo combines both wit
and wonder. In the first appearance of the court party,
we see how differently the same phenomena may strike
different people. For only Gonzalo sees that their deliver-

ance was miraculous and that the island is a paradise. To
be in the Garden of Eden is, we are to understand, a
matter of perception. Antonio and Sebastian are with their
witty quibbling—their quibble, for example, over the few
miles that separate modern Tunis from ancient Carthage
—merely destructive.

The effect of wonder is created in *The Tempest* through
a combination of several genres—tragicomedy, pastoral,
romance, and masque. Antonio's temptation of Sebastian
has been compared to the temptation of Macbeth by Lady
Macbeth; it is the stuff of tragedy. Our view of it, however, is comic, because we know that Ariel is watching
over the scene and has brought it about as part of Prospero's design. The whole action is comic in this sense.
The abbreviation of time (*The Tempest* and *The Comedy
of Errors* are the only plays in which Shakespeare observes the classical unity of time) enables us to see even
Prospero's tragedy in Milan as, in retrospect, for the
best. The comic perspective does not, however, make us
laugh. It makes us marvel.

Not only the tragedy, but the comedy, too, is dissolved
in wonder. Bernard Knox has, in the essay reprinted in
this volume, connected *The Tempest* with Roman comedies about slaves. Nevertheless, Caliban and Ariel are
too marvelous to be laughed at as we laugh at the slaves
in Roman comedies. Stephano and Trinculo seem a kind
of comic relief, just because we do so little laughing at
the main action of *The Tempest*. Through Prospero's eyes,
The Tempest shows us life as God must see it. God could
not view life tragically, because He knows that all is for
the best. God also knows, as Prospero knows of Ferdinand, that the ordeals He sets for us are for our own good
and are not so hard or serious as we think them. Neither,
however, could God laugh at us as we laugh at the characters in comedies; for He would not ridicule us, or be
dazzled by our wit.

Prospero's view of life is set forth in the famous speech
in which he says, after dispelling the wedding masque,
"We are such stuff/ As dreams are made on." He is, I
think, recovering his perspective in this speech after the

relapse into thoughts of revenge. The speech is, like Miranda's exclamations, an expression of the marvelous quality of life. Prospero implies, in consoling Ferdinand for the disappearance of the masque, that if life is as illusory as the masque, it is also as gorgeously illusory. He implies also that there is a reality behind life just as there is Prospero behind the masque.

In his detachment from the appearances of life, Prospero regains an innocence of vision analogous to Miranda's. It is the vision of pastoral, the genre that deals with man and nature in their unfallen state. By swiftly recapitulating all the facts of life, tragicomedy leads us to see through life with the eyes of Miranda who never left the Garden. Tragicomedy uses to this end the devices of romance. For romance deals in marvelous events and solves its problems through metamorphoses and recognition scenes—through, in other words, transformations of perception. When Alonso recognizes Prospero and Ferdinand, both of whom he had thought dead, he recognizes their magical preciousness and thus really *sees* them for the first time. The same is true of the crew's response to the ship, when it is magically restored to them. The recognized objects are transformed through the transformed eyes of the beholders; so that more is restored than has been lost.

The masque, with its emphasis on spectacle and surprise, subordinates all other effects to the effect of wonder. "The fringed curtains of thine eye advance," says Prospero to Miranda when the spectacle of Ferdinand is about to break upon her. It is as though a theater curtain were to be raised; as, indeed, it is raised or drawn when the spectacle of the lovers breaks upon the court party. All the scenes that offer the characters illumination are masquelike and illusory. Yet it is through these illusions that the characters come to understand reality. We all found ourselves, says Gonzalo in the end, "when no man was his own."

Art is just such an experience of enchantment. The speech in which Prospero breaks his magic wand is not so much Shakespeare's farewell to his art as it is his comment on the relation between art and life. For in breaking his wand and taking himself and the others back to Italy, Prospero seems to be saying that the enchanted island is no abiding place, but rather a place through which we pass in order to renew and strengthen our sense of reality.

In spite of its fantastic elements, *The Tempest*, as F. R. Leavis has pointed out, never confuses but rather clarifies our sense of reality. That is no small part of its achievement—though it is characteristic of our time that Leavis prefers *The Winter's Tale* just because it is less realistic than *The Tempest*. With its bias against realism, and its interest in a symbolic art, our time is better equipped than any time since Shakespeare's to appreciate the last plays. The seventeenth and eighteenth centuries liked best of all Shakespeare's early comedies. The nineteenth century liked the tragedies best, and on the whole we still do. But it may be that the last plays—and especially *The Tempest*, which is as I see it the best of them—will in future have most to say to us. Certainly, the interest in them has in the last generation risen steadily.

ROBERT LANGBAUM
University of Virginia

The Tempest

The Scene: An uninhabited island.

Names of the Actors

Alonso, King of Naples
Sebastian, his brother
Prospero, the right Duke of Milan
Antonio, his brother, the usurping Duke of Milan
Ferdinand, son to the King of Naples
Gonzalo, an honest old councilor
Adrian and Francisco, lords
Caliban, a savage and deformed slave
Trinculo, a jester
Stephano, a drunken butler
Master of a ship
Boatswain
Mariners
Miranda, daughter to Prospero
Ariel, an airy spirit
Iris ⎫
Ceres ⎪
Juno ⎬ [presented by] spirits
Nymphs ⎪
Reapers ⎭
[Other Spirits attending on Prospero]

The Tempest

ACT I

Scene I. [*On a ship at sea.*]

A tempestuous noise of thunder and lightning heard. Enter a Shipmaster and a Boatswain.

Master. Boatswain!

Boatswain. Here, master. What cheer?

Master. Good,°1 speak to th' mariners! Fall to't yarely,° or we run ourselves aground. Bestir, bestir!
Exit.

Enter Mariners.

Boatswain. Heigh, my hearts! Cheerly, cheerly, my hearts! Yare, yare! Take in the topsail! Tend to th' master's whistle! Blow till thou burst thy wind, if room enough!°   5

Enter Alonso, Sebastian, Antonio, Ferdinand, Gonzalo, and others.

Alonso. Good boatswain, have care. Where's the master? Play the men.°   10

Boatswain. I pray now, keep below.

1 The degree sign (°) indicates a footnote, which is keyed to the text by line number. Text references are printed in *italic* type; the annotation follows in roman type.
I.i.3. *Good* good fellow   4 *yarely* briskly   7–8 *Blow till . . . room enough* the storm can blow and split itself as long as there is open sea without rocks to maneuver in   10 *Play the men* act like men

37

Antonio. Where is the master, bos'n?

Boatswain. Do you not hear him? You mar our labor. Keep your cabins; you do assist the storm.

15 *Gonzalo.* Nay, good, be patient.

Boatswain. When the sea is. Hence! What cares these roarers for the name of king? To cabin! Silence! Trouble us not!

Gonzalo. Good, yet remember whom thou hast
20 aboard.

Boatswain. None that I more love than myself. You are a councilor; if you can command these elements to silence and work the peace of the present,° we will not hand° a rope more. Use your authority.
25 If you cannot, give thanks you have lived so long, and make yourself ready in your cabin for the mischance of the hour, if it so hap. Cheerly, good hearts! Out of our way, I say. *Exit.*

Gonzalo. I have great comfort from this fellow. Me-
30 thinks he hath no drowning mark upon him; his complexion is perfect gallows.° Stand fast, good Fate, to his hanging! Make the rope of his destiny our cable, for our own doth little advantage.° If he be not born to be hanged, our case is miserable.
Exit [with the rest].

Enter Boatswain.

35 *Boatswain.* Down with the topmast! Yare! Lower, lower! Bring her to try with main course!° (*A cry within.*) A plague upon this howling! They are louder than the weather or our office.°

23 *work the peace of the present* restore the present to peace (since as a councilor his job is to quell disorder) 24 *hand* handle 30–31 *no drowning mark . . . gallows* (alluding to the proverb, "He that's born to be hanged need fear no drowning") 33 *doth little advantage* gives us little advantage 36 *Bring her to try with main course* heave to, under the mainsail 37–38 *They are louder . . . office* these passengers make more noise than the tempest or than we do at our work

Enter Sebastian, Antonio, and Gonzalo.

Yet again? What do you here? Shall we give o'er°
and drown? Have you a mind to sink?   40

Sebastian. A pox o' your throat, you bawling, blas-
phemous, incharitable dog!

Boatswain. Work you, then.

Antonio. Hang, cur! Hang, you whoreson, insolent
noisemaker! We are less afraid to be drowned than   45
thou art.

Gonzalo. I'll warrant him for° drowning, though the
ship were no stronger than a nutshell and as leaky
as an unstanched° wench.

Boatswain. Lay her ahold, ahold! Set her two   50
courses!° Off to sea again! Lay her off!°

Enter Mariners wet.

Mariners. All lost! To prayers, to prayers! All lost!
[*Exeunt.*]

Boatswain. What, must our mouths be cold?

Gonzalo. The King and Prince at prayers! Let's assist
them,
For our case is as theirs.

Sebastian.   I am out of patience.   55

Antonio. We are merely° cheated of our lives by
drunkards.
This wide-chopped° rascal—would thou mightst lie
drowning
The washing of ten tides!°

39 *give o'er* give up trying to run the ship   47 *warrant him for*
guarantee him against   49 *unstanched* wide-open   50–51 *Lay her
ahold.... courses* (the ship is still being blown dangerously to shore,
so the boatswain orders that the foresail be set in addition to the
mainsail; but the ship still moves toward shore)   51 *Lay her off* i.e.,
away from the shore   56 *merely* completely   57 *wide-chopped* big-
mouthed   58 *ten tides* (pirates were hanged on the shore and left
there until three tides had washed over them)

Gonzalo.   He'll be hanged yet,
Though every drop of water swear against it
And gape at wid'st to glut him.

60   *A confused noise within:* "Mercy on us!"
"We split, we split!" "Farewell, my wife and chil-
    dren!"
"Farewell, brother!" "We split, we split, we split!"
                                 [Exit Boatswain.]

Antonio. Let's all sink wi' th' King.

Sebastian.   Let's take leave of him.
                           Exit [with Antonio].

Gonzalo. Now would I give a thousand furlongs of
65   sea for an acre of barren ground—long heath,°
brown furze, anything. The wills above be done,
but I would fain die a dry death.   *Exit.*

Scene II. *[The island. In front of Prospero's cell.]*

Enter Prospero and Miranda.

Miranda. If by your art, my dearest father, you have
Put the wild waters in this roar, allay them.
The sky, it seems, would pour down stinking pitch
But that the sea, mounting to th' welkin's cheek,°
5   Dashes the fire out. O, I have suffered
With those that I saw suffer! A brave° vessel
(Who had no doubt some noble creature in her)
Dashed all to pieces! O, the cry did knock

---

65 *heath* heather   I.ii.4 *welkin's cheek* face of the sky   6 *brave* fine,
gallant (the word often has this meaning in the play)

Against my very heart! Poor souls, they perished!
Had I been any god of power, I would   *10*
Have sunk the sea within the earth or ere
It should the good ship so have swallowed and
The fraughting° souls within her.

Prospero.   Be collected.
No more amazement.° Tell your piteous heart
There's no harm done.

Miranda.   O, woe the day!

Prospero.   No harm.   *15*
I have done nothing but in care of thee,
Of thee my dear one, thee my daughter, who
Art ignorant of what thou art, naught knowing
Of whence I am, nor that I am more better
Than Prospero, master of a full poor cell,   *20*
And thy no greater father.°

Miranda.   More to know
Did never meddle° with my thoughts.

Prospero.   'Tis time
I should inform thee farther. Lend thy hand
And pluck my magic garment from me. So.
                    [*Lays down his robe.*]
Lie there, my art. Wipe thou thine eyes; have
   comfort.   *25*
The direful spectacle of the wrack, which touched
The very virtue° of compassion in thee,
I have with such provision° in mine art
So safely ordered that there is no soul—
No, not so much perdition° as an hair   *30*
Betid° to any creature in the vessel
Which thou heard'st cry, which thou saw'st sink.
   Sit down;
For thou must now know farther.

---

13 *fraughting* forming her freight   14 *amazement* consternation
21 *thy no greater father* i.e., thy father, no greater than the Prospero
just described   22 *meddle* mingle   27 *virtue* essence   28 *provision*
foresight   30 *perdition* loss   31 *Betid* happened

Miranda.   You have often
  Begun to tell me what I am; but stopped
35 And left me to a bootless inquisition,
  Concluding, "Stay; not yet."

Prospero.   The hour's now come;
  The very minute bids thee ope thine ear.
  Obey, and be attentive. Canst thou remember
  A time before we came unto this cell?
40 I do not think thou canst, for then thou wast not
  Out° three years old.

Miranda.   Certainly, sir, I can.

Prospero. By what? By any other house or person?
  Of anything the image tell me that
  Hath kept with thy remembrance.

Miranda.   'Tis far off,
45 And rather like a dream than an assurance
  That my remembrance warrants.° Had I not
  Four or five women once that tended me?

Prospero. Thou hadst, and more, Miranda. But how
     is it
  That this lives in thy mind? What seest thou else
50 In the dark backward and abysm of time?
  If thou rememb'rest aught ere thou cam'st here,
  How thou cam'st here thou mayst.

Miranda.   But that I do not.

Prospero. Twelve year since, Miranda, twelve year
     since,
  Thy father was the Duke of Milan° and
  A prince of power.

55 *Miranda.*   Sir, are not you my father?

Prospero. Thy mother was a piece° of virtue, and
  She said thou wast my daughter; and thy father
  Was Duke of Milan; and his only heir

41 *Out* fully   46 *remembrance warrants* memory guarantees   54
Milan (pronounced "Mílan")   56 *piece* masterpiece

And princess, no worse issued.°

Miranda.   O the heavens!
What foul play had we that we came from thence?   60
Or blessèd was't we did?

Prospero.   Both, both, my girl!
By foul play, as thou say'st, were we heaved thence,
But blessedly holp° hither.

Miranda.   O, my heart bleeds
To think o' th' teen that I have turned you to,°
Which is from° my remembrance! Please you,
   farther.   65

Prospero. My brother and thy uncle, called
   Antonio—
I pray thee mark me—that a brother should
Be so perfidious!—he whom next thyself
Of all the world I loved, and to him put
The manage of my state,° as at that time   70
Through all the signories° it was the first,
And Prospero the prime duke, being so reputed
In dignity, and for the liberal arts
Without a parallel. Those being all my study,
The government I cast upon my brother   75
And to my state grew stranger, being transported
And rapt in secret studies. Thy false uncle—
Dost thou attend me?

Miranda.   Sir, most heedfully.

Prospero. Being once perfected° how to grant suits,
How to deny them, who t' advance, and who   80
To trash for overtopping,° new-created
The creatures that were mine, I say—or changed
   'em,

---

59 *no worse issued* of no meaner lineage than he   63 *holp* helped
64 *teen that I have turned you to* sorrow I have caused you to remember   65 *from* out of   70 *manage of my state* management of
my domain   71 *signories* lordships (of Italy)   79 *perfected* grown
skillful   81 *trash for overtopping* (1) check the speed of (as of
hounds) (2) cut down to size (as of overtall trees) the aspirants
for political favor who are growing too bold

Or else new-formed 'em°—having both the key°
Of officer and office, set all hearts i' th' state
To what tune pleased his ear, that now he was
The ivy which had hid my princely trunk
And sucked my verdure out on't. Thou attend'st
    not?

Miranda. O, good sir, I do.

Prospero.   I pray thee mark me.
I thus neglecting worldly ends, all dedicated
To closeness° and the bettering of my mind—
With that which, but by being so retired,
O'erprized all popular rate, in my false brother
Awaked an evil nature,° and my trust,
Like a good parent,° did beget of him
A falsehood in its contrary as great
As my trust was, which had indeed no limit,
A confidence sans bound. He being thus lorded—
Not only with what my revenue° yielded
But what my power might else exact, like one
Who having into truth—by telling of it,°
Made such a sinner of his memory
To° credit his own lie, he did believe
He was indeed the Duke, out o' th' substitution
And executing th' outward face of royalty
With all prerogative.° Hence his ambition
    growing—
Dost thou hear?

81–83 *new-created/The creatures . . . new-formed 'em* i.e., he re-created my following—either exchanging my adherents for his own, or else transforming my adherents into different people   83 *key* (a pun leading to the musical metaphor)   90 *closeness* se-clusion   91–93 *With that . . . evil nature* i.e., with that dedication to the mind which, were it not that it kept me from exercising the duties of my office would surpass in value all ordinary estimate, I awakened evil in my brother's nature   94 *good parent* (alluding to the proverb cited by Miranda in line 120)   98 *revenue* (pronounced "revènue")   99–100 *like one/Who having . . . of it* i.e., like one who really had these things—by repeatedly saying he had them (*into* = unto)   102 *To* as to   103–05 *out o' th' substitution . . . all prerogative* i.e., as a result of his acting as my substitute and per-forming the outward functions of royalty with all its prerogatives

Miranda.   Your tale, sir, would cure deafness.

Prospero. To have no screen between this part he
  played
  And him he played it for, he needs will be
  Absolute Milan.° Me (poor man) my library
  Was dukedom large enough. Of temporal royalties   110
  He thinks me now incapable; confederates
  (So dry° he was for sway) wi' th' King of Naples
  To give him annual tribute, do him homage,
  Subject his coronet to his crown, and bend
  The dukedom, yet unbowed (alas, poor Milan!),   115
  To most ignoble stooping.

Miranda.   O the heavens!

Prospero. Mark his condition,° and th' event;° then
  tell me
  If this might be a brother.

Miranda.   I should sin
  To think but nobly of my grandmother.
  Good wombs have borne bad sons.

Prospero.   Now the condition.   120
  This King of Naples, being an enemy
  To me inveterate, hearkens my brother's suit;
  Which was, that he, in lieu o' th' premises°
  Of homage and I know not how much tribute,
  Should presently extirpate me and mine   125
  Out of the dukedom and confer fair Milan,
  With all the honors, on my brother. Whereon,
  A treacherous army levied, one midnight
  Fated to th' purpose, did Antonio open
  The gates of Milan; and, i' th' dead of darkness, 130
  The ministers° for th' purpose hurried thence
  Me and thy crying self.

Miranda.   Alack, for pity!

---

109 *Absolute Milan* Duke of Milan in fact   112 *dry* thirsty
117 *condition* terms of his pact with Naples   117 *event* outcome
123 *in lieu o' th' premises* in return for the guarantees   131 *ministers* agents

I, not rememb'ring how I cried out then,
Will cry it o'er again; it is a hint°
That wrings mine eyes to't.

155 *Prospero.*   Hear a little further,
And then I'll bring thee to the present business
Which now's upon's; without the which this story
Were most impertinent.°

Miranda.   Wherefore did they not
That hour destroy us?

Prospero.   Well demanded, wench.
My tale provokes that question. Dear, they durst
140   not,
So dear the love my people bore me; nor set
A mark so bloody on the business; but,
With colors fairer, painted their foul ends.
In few,° they hurried us aboard a bark;
145 Bore us some leagues to sea, where they prepared
A rotten carcass of a butt,° not rigged,
Nor tackle, sail, nor mast; the very rats
Instinctively have quit it. There they hoist us,
To cry to th' sea that roared to us; to sigh
150 To th' winds, whose pity, sighing back again,
Did us but loving wrong.

Miranda.   Alack, what trouble
Was I then to you!

Prospero.   O, a cherubin
Thou wast that did preserve me! Thou didst smile,
Infusèd with a fortitude from heaven,
155 When I have decked° the sea with drops full salt,
Under my burden groaned; which° raised in me
An undergoing stomach,° to bear up
Against what should ensue.

Miranda.   How came we ashore?

---

134 *hint* occasion 138 *impertinent* inappropriate 144 *few* few
words 146 *butt* tub 155 *decked* covered (wept salt tears into the
sea) 156 *which* i.e., Miranda's smile 157 *undergoing stomach*
spirit of endurance

Prospero. By providence divine.
Some food we had, and some fresh water, that   *160*
A noble Neapolitan, Gonzalo,
Out of his charity, who being then appointed
Master of this design, did give us, with
Rich garments, linens, stuffs, and necessaries
Which since have steaded° much. So, of his gentle-   *165*
     ness,
Knowing I loved my books, he furnished me
From mine own library with volumes that
I prize above my dukedom.

Miranda.   Would I might
But ever see that man!

Prospero.   Now I arise.
Sit still, and hear the last of our sea sorrow.   *170*
Here in this island we arrived; and here
Have I, thy schoolmaster, made thee more profit
Than other princess' can,° that have more time
For vainer hours, and tutors not so careful.

Miranda. Heavens thank you for't! And now I pray
     you, sir—   *175*
For still 'tis beating in my mind—your reason
For raising this sea storm?

Prospero.   Know thus far forth.
By accident most strange, bountiful Fortune
(Now my dear lady)° hath mine enemies
Brought to this shore; and by my prescience   *180*
I find my zenith° doth depend upon
A most auspicious star, whose influence
If now I court not, but omit,° my fortunes
Will ever after droop. Here cease more questions.
Thou art inclined to sleep. 'Tis a good dullness,   *185*
And give it way. I know thou canst not choose.
                    [*Miranda sleeps.*]

165 *steaded* been of use   173 *princess' can* princesses can have
179 *Now my dear lady* i.e., formerly my foe, now my patroness
181 *zenith* apex of fortune   183 *omit* neglect

Come away,° servant, come! I am ready now.
Approach, my Ariel! Come!

Enter Ariel.

Ariel. All hail, great master! Grave sir, hail! I come
190   To answer thy best pleasure; be't to fly,
To swim, to dive into the fire, to ride
On the curled clouds. To thy strong bidding task°
Ariel and all his quality.°

Prospero.   Hast thou, spirit,
Performed, to point,° the tempest that I bade thee?

195 *Ariel.* To every article.
I boarded the King's ship. Now on the beak,°
Now in the waist,° the deck,° in every cabin,
I flamed amazement.° Sometime I'd divide
And burn in many places; on the topmast,
200   The yards, and boresprit° would I flame distinctly,°
Then meet and join. Jove's lightnings, the precursors
O' th' dreadful thunderclaps, more momentary
And sight-outrunning were not. The fire and cracks
Of sulfurous roaring the most mighty Neptune
205   Seem to besiege, and make his bold waves tremble;
Yea, his dread trident shake.

Prospero.   My brave spirit!
Who was so firm, so constant, that this coil°
Would not infect his reason?

Ariel.   Not a soul
But felt a fever of the mad and played
210   Some tricks of desperation. All but mariners
Plunged in the foaming brine and quit the vessel,
Then all afire with me. The King's son Ferdinand,

187 *Come away* i.e., come from where you are; come here   192 *task* tax to the utmost   193 *quality* cohorts (Ariel is leader of a band of spirits)   194 *to point* in every detail   196 *beak* prow   197 *waist* amidships   197 *deck* poop   198 *flamed amazement* struck terror by appearing as (St. Elmo's) fire   200 *boresprit* bowsprit   200 *distinctly* in different places   207 *coil* uproar

With hair up-staring° (then like reeds, not hair),
Was the first man that leapt; cried "Hell is empty,
And all the devils are here!"

Prospero.   Why, that's my spirit! 215
But was not this nigh shore?

Ariel.   Close by, my master.

Prospero. But are they, Ariel, safe?

Ariel.   Not a hair perished.
On their sustaining° garments not a blemish,
But fresher than before; and as thou bad'st me,
In troops I have dispersed them 'bout the isle.   220
The King's son have I landed by himself,
Whom I left cooling of the air with sighs
In an odd angle of the isle, and sitting,
His arms in this sad knot.
                    [*Illustrates with a gesture.*]

Prospero.   Of the King's ship,
The mariners, say how thou hast disposed,   225
And all the rest o' th' fleet.

Ariel.   Safely in harbor
Is the King's ship; in the deep nook where once
Thou call'dst me up at midnight to fetch dew
From the still-vexed Bermoothes,° there she's hid;
The mariners all under hatches stowed,   230
Who, with a charm joined to their suff'red° labor,
I have left asleep. And for the rest o' th' fleet,
Which I dispersed, they all have met again,
And are upon the Mediterranean flote°
Bound sadly home for Naples,   235
Supposing that they saw the King's ship wracked
And his great person perish.

Prospero.   Ariel, thy charge
Exactly is performed; but there's more work.

213 *up-staring* standing on end   218 *sustaining* buoying them up
229 *Bermoothes* Bermudas   231 *suff'red* undergone   234 *flote* sea

What is the time o' th' day?

Ariel.   Past the mid season.°

Prospero. At least two glasses.° The time 'twixt six
240   and now
Must by us both be spent most preciously.

Ariel. Is there more toil? Since thou dost give me
pains,°
Let me remember° thee what thou hast promised,
Which is not yet performed me.

Prospero.   How now? Moody?
What is't thou canst demand?

245 *Ariel.*   My liberty.

Prospero. Before the time be out? No more!

Ariel.   I prithee,
Remember I have done thee worthy service,
Told thee no lies, made thee no mistakings, served
Without or grudge or grumblings. Thou did
promise
To bate me° a full year.

250 *Prospero.*   Dost thou forget
From what a torment I did free thee?

Ariel.   No.

Prospero. Thou dost; and think'st it much to tread
the ooze
Of the salt deep,
To run upon the sharp wind of the North,
255   To do me business in the veins° o' th' earth
When it is baked° with frost.

Ariel.   I do not, sir.

Prospero. Thou liest, malignant thing! Hast thou
forgot

---

239 *mid season* noon   240 *two glasses* two o'clock   242 *pains* hard
tasks   243 *remember* remind   250 *bate me* reduce my term of
service   255 *veins* streams   256 *baked* caked

The foul witch Sycorax,° who with age and envy°
Was grown into a hoop? Hast thou forgot her?

Ariel. No, sir.

Prospero.   Thou hast. Where was she born? Speak!
    Tell me!   260

Ariel. Sir, in Argier.°

Prospero.   O, was she so? I must
    Once in a month recount what thou hast been,
    Which thou forget'st. This damned witch Sycorax,
    For mischiefs manifold, and sorceries terrible
    To enter human hearing, from Argier,   265
    Thou know'st, was banished. For one thing she did
    They would not take her life. Is not this true?

Ariel. Ay, sir.

Prospero. This blue-eyed° hag was hither brought
        with child
    And here was left by th' sailors. Thou, my slave,   270
    As thou report'st thyself, wast then her servant.
    And, for thou wast a spirit too delicate
    To act her earthy and abhorred commands,
    Refusing her grand hests,° she did confine thee,
    By help of her more potent ministers,°   275
    And in her most unmitigable rage,
    Into a cloven pine; within which rift
    Imprisoned thou didst painfully remain
    A dozen years; within which space she died
    And left thee there, where thou didst vent thy
        groans   280
    As fast as millwheels strike. Then was this island
    (Save for the son that she did litter here,
    A freckled whelp, hagborn) not honored with
    A human shape.

258 *Sycorax* (name not found elsewhere; probably derived from
Greek *sys*, "sow," and *korax*, which means both "raven"—see line
322—and "hook"—hence perhaps "hoop")   258 *envy* malice   261
Argier Algiers   269 *blue-eyed* (referring to the livid color of the
eyelid, a sign of pregnancy)   274 *hests* commands   275 *her more
potent ministers* her agents, spirits more powerful than thou

Ariel.   Yes, Caliban her son.

283 *Prospero.* Dull thing, I say so! He, that Caliban
    Whom now I keep in service. Thou best know'st
    What torment I did find thee in; thy groans
    Did make wolves howl and penetrate the breasts
    Of ever-angry bears. It was a torment
290 To lay upon the damned, which Sycorax
    Could not again undo. It was mine art,
    When I arrived and heard thee, that made gape
    The pine, and let thee out.

Ariel.   I thank thee, master.

Prospero. If thou more murmur'st, I will rend an oak
295 And peg thee in his° knotty entrails till
    Thou hast howled away twelve winters.

Ariel.   Pardon, master.
    I will be correspondent° to command
    And do my spriting gently.°

Prospero.   Do so; and after two days
    I will discharge thee.

Ariel.   That's my noble master!
300 What shall I do? Say what? What shall I do?

Prospero. Go make thyself like a nymph o' th' sea. Be
        subject
    To no sight but thine and mine, invisible
    To every eyeball else.° Go take this shape
    And hither come in't. Go! Hence with diligence!
                        Exit [Ariel].
305 Awake, dear heart, awake! Thou hast slept well.
    Awake!

Miranda. The strangeness of your story put
    Heaviness in me.

295 *his* its   297 *correspondent* obedient   298 *do my spriting gently*
render graciously my services as a spirit   302–03 *invisible/To
every eyeball else* (Ariel is invisible to everyone in the play except
Prospero; Henslowe's *Diary*, an Elizabethan stage account, lists
"a robe for to go invisible")

Prospero.   Shake it off. Come on.
  We'll visit Caliban, my slave, who never
  Yields us kind answer.

Miranda.   'Tis a villain, sir,
  I do not love to look on.

Prospero.   But as 'tis,   *310*
  We cannot miss° him. He does make our fire,
  Fetch in our wood, and serves in offices
  That profit us. What, ho! Slave! Caliban!
  Thou earth, thou! Speak!

Caliban. (Within)   There's wood enough within.

Prospero. Come forth, I say! There's other business *315*
    for thee.
  Come, thou tortoise! When?°

            Enter Ariel like a water nymph.

  Fine apparition! My quaint° Ariel,
  Hark in thine ear.   [*Whispers.*]

Ariel.   My lord, it shall be done. *Exit.*

Prospero. Thou poisonous slave, got by the devil
    himself
  Upon thy wicked dam, come forth!   *320*

            Enter Caliban.

Caliban. As wicked dew as e'er my mother brushed
  With raven's feather from unwholesome fen
  Drop on you both! A southwest blow on ye
  And blister you all o'er!

Prospero. For this, be sure, tonight thou shalt have
    cramps,   *325*
  Side-stitches that shall pen thy breath up. Urchins°
  Shall, for that vast of night that they may work,°

311 *miss* do without   316 *When* (expression of impatience)   317
quaint ingenious   326 *Urchins* goblins in the shape of hedgehogs
327 *vast of night . . . work* (the long, empty stretch of night during
which malignant spirits are allowed to be active)

All exercise on thee; thou shalt be pinched
As thick as honeycomb, each pinch more stinging
Than bees that made 'em.

330 *Caliban.*   I must eat my dinner.
This island's mine by Sycorax my mother,
Which thou tak'st from me. When thou cam'st first,
Thou strok'st me and made much of me; wouldst
    give me
Water with berries in't; and teach me how
335 To name the bigger light, and how the less,
That burn by day and night. And then I loved thee
And showed thee all the qualities o' th' isle,
The fresh springs, brine pits, barren place and
    fertile.
Cursed be I that did so! All the charms
340 Of Sycorax—toads, beetles, bats, light on you!
For I am all the subjects that you have,
Which first was mine own king; and here you sty
    me
In this hard rock, whiles you do keep from me
The rest o' th' island.

Prospero.   Thou most lying slave,
Whom stripes° may move, not kindness! I have
345   used thee
(Filth as thou art) with humane care, and lodged
    thee
In mine own cell till thou didst seek to violate
The honor of my child.

Caliban. O ho, O ho! Would't had been done!
350   Thou didst prevent me; I had peopled else
This isle with Calibans.

Miranda.°   Abhorrèd slave,
Which any print of goodness wilt not take,
Being capable of all ill!° I pitied thee,

---

345 *stripes* lashes   351 (many editors transfer this speech to Prospero as inappropriate to Miranda)   353 *capable of all ill* susceptible only to evil impressions

Took pains to make thee speak, taught thee each
    hour
One thing or other. When thou didst not, savage,   *355*
Know thine own meaning, but wouldst gabble like
A thing most brutish, I endowed thy purposes
With words that made them known. But thy vile
    race,
Though thou didst learn, had that in't which good
    natures
Could not abide to be with. Therefore wast thou   *360*
Deservedly confined into this rock, who hadst
Deserved more than a prison.

Caliban. You taught me language, and my profit on't
Is, I know how to curse. The red plague rid° you
For learning me your language!

Prospero.   Hagseed, hence!   *365*
Fetch us in fuel. And be quick, thou'rt best,°
To answer other business. Shrug'st thou, malice?
If thou neglect'st or dost unwillingly
What I command, I'll rack thee with old° cramps,
Fill all thy bones with aches,° make thee roar   *370*
That beasts shall tremble at thy din.

Caliban.   No, pray thee.
[*Aside*] I must obey. His art is of such pow'r
It would control my dam's god, Setebos,
And make a vassal of him.

Prospero.   So, slave; hence!   *Exit Caliban.*

*Enter Ferdinand; and Ariel (invisible), playing
    and singing.*

Ariel's song.

Come unto these yellow sands,   *375*

364 *rid* destroy   366 *thou'rt best* you'd better   369 *old* plenty of
(with an additional suggestion, "such as old people have")   370
aches (pronounced "aitches")

               And then take hands.
           Curtsied when you have and kissed
              The wild waves whist,°
           Foot it featly° here and there;
380   And, sweet sprites, the burden bear.
              Hark, hark!
                 Burden, dispersedly.° Bow, wow!
           The watchdogs bark.
                 [*Burden, dispersedly.*] Bow, wow!
385   Hark, hark! I hear
           The strain of strutting chanticleer
              Cry cock-a-diddle-dow.

Ferdinand. Where should this music be? I' th' air or
           th' earth?
           It sounds no more; and sure it waits upon
390   Some god o' th' island. Sitting on a bank,
           Weeping again the King my father's wrack,
           This music crept by me upon the waters,
           Allaying both their fury and my passion°
           With its sweet air. Thence I have followed it,
395   Or it hath drawn me rather; but 'tis gone.
           No, it begins again.

                      Ariel's song.

           Full fathom five thy father lies;
              Of his bones are coral made;
           Those are pearls that were his eyes;
400   Nothing of him that doth fade
           But doth suffer a sea change
           Into something rich and strange.
           Sea nymphs hourly ring his knell:
                      Burden. Ding-dong.
405   Hark! Now I hear them—ding-dong bell.

377–78 *kissed/The wild waves whist* i.e., when you have, through
the harmony of kissing in the dance, kissed the wild waves into
silence (?); when you have kissed in the dance, the wild waves being
silenced (?)   379 *featly* nimbly   382 *Burden, dispersedly* (an undersong, coming from all parts of the stage; it imitates the barking
of dogs and perhaps in the end the crowing of a cock)   393 *passion*
grief

Ferdinand. The ditty does remember my drowned
     father.
  This is no mortal business, nor no sound
  That the earth owes.° I hear it now above me.

Prospero. The fringèd curtains of thine eye advance°
  And say what thou seest yond.

Miranda.   What is't? A spirit? 410
  Lord, how it looks about! Believe me, sir,
  It carries a brave form. But 'tis a spirit.

Prospero. No, wench; it eats, and sleeps, and hath
     such senses
  As we have, such. This gallant which thou seest
  Was in the wrack; and, but he's something stained 415
  With grief (that's beauty's canker), thou mightst
     call him
  A goodly person. He hath lost his fellows
  And strays about to find 'em.

Miranda.   I might call him
  A thing divine; for nothing natural
  I ever saw so noble.

Prospero.   [*Aside*] It goes on, I see,   420
  As my soul prompts it. Spirit, fine spirit, I'll free
     thee
  Within two days for this.

Ferdinand.   Most sure, the goddess
  On whom these airs attend! Vouchsafe my prayer
  May know if you remain° upon this island,
  And that you will some good instruction give   425
  How I may bear me° here. My prime request,
  Which I do last pronounce, is (O you wonder!)
  If you be maid or no?

Miranda.   No wonder, sir,
  But certainly a maid.

---

408 *owes* owns 409 *advance* raise 423–24 *Vouchsafe my prayer
. . . remain* may my prayer induce you to inform me whether you
dwell 426 *bear me* conduct myself

Ferdinand.   My language? Heavens!
430 I am the best of them that speak this speech,
Were I but where 'tis spoken.

Prospero.   How? The best?
What wert thou if the King of Naples heard thee?

Ferdinand. A single° thing, as I am now, that won-
ders
To hear thee speak of Naples. He does hear me;
435 And that he does I weep. Myself am Naples,
Who with mine eyes, never since at ebb, beheld
The King my father wracked.

Miranda.   Alack, for mercy!

Ferdinand. Yes, faith, and all his lords, the Duke of
Milan
And his brave son° being twain.°

Prospero.   [*Aside*] The Duke of Milan
440 And his more braver daughter could control° thee,
If now 'twere fit to do't. At the first sight
They have changed eyes.° Delicate Ariel,
I'll set thee free for this. [*To Ferdinand*] A word,
good sir.
I fear you have done yourself some wrong.° A
word!

445 *Miranda.* Why speaks my father so ungently? This
Is the third man that e'er I saw; the first
That e'er I sighed for. Pity move my father
To be inclined my way!

Ferdinand.   O, if a virgin,
And your affection not gone forth, I'll make you
The Queen of Naples.

450 *Prospero.*   Soft, sir! One word more.
[*Aside*] They are both in either's pow'rs. But this
swift business

433 *single* (1) solitary (2) helpless 439 *son* (the only time Antonio's son is mentioned) 439 *twain* two (of these lords) 440
control refute 442 *changed eyes* i.e., fallen in love 444 *done
yourself some wrong* said what is not so

I must uneasy make, lest too light winning
Make the prize light. [*To Ferdinand*] One word
  more! I charge thee
That thou attend me. Thou dost here usurp
The name thou ow'st° not, and hast put thyself   *455*
Upon this island as a spy, to win it
From me, the lord on't.

Ferdinand.   No, as I am a man!

Miranda. There's nothing ill can dwell in such a
  temple.
If the ill spirit have so fair a house,
Good things will strive to dwell with't.

Prospero.   Follow me.   *460*
[*To Miranda*] Speak not you for him; he's a traitor.
  [*To Ferdinand*] Come!
I'll manacle thy neck and feet together;
Sea water shalt thou drink; thy food shall be
The fresh-brook mussels, withered roots, and husks
Wherein the acorn cradled. Follow!

Ferdinand.   No.   *465*
I will resist such entertainment till
Mine enemy has more pow'r.
                He draws, and is charmed from moving.

Miranda.   O dear father,
Make not too rash a trial of him, for
He's gentle and not fearful.°

Prospero.   What, I say,
My foot my tutor?° [*To Ferdinand*] Put thy sword
  up, traitor—   *470*
Who mak'st a show but dar'st not strike, thy con-
  science
Is so possessed with guilt! Come, from thy ward!°
For I can here disarm thee with this stick°
And make thy weapon drop.

455 *ow'st* ownest   469 *gentle and not fearful* of noble birth and
no coward   470 *My foot my tutor* am I to be instructed by my inferior   472 *ward* fighting posture   473 *stick* i.e., his wand

Miranda.   Beseech you, father!

Prospero. Hence! Hang not on my garments.

475 *Miranda.*   Sir, have pity.
I'll be his surety.

Prospero.   Silence! One word more
Shall make me chide thee, if not hate thee. What,
An advocate for an impostor? Hush!
Thou think'st there is no more such shapes as he,
480 Having seen but him and Caliban. Foolish wench!
To th' most of men this is a Caliban,
And they to him are angels.

Miranda.   My affections
Are then most humble. I have no ambition
To see a goodlier man.

Prospero. [*To Ferdinand*] Come on, obey!
485 Thy nerves° are in their infancy again
And have no vigor in them.

Ferdinand.   So they are.
My spirits, as in a dream, are all bound up.
My father's loss, the weakness which I feel,
The wrack of all my friends, nor this man's threats
490 To whom I am subdued, are but light to me,
Might I but through my prison once a day
Behold this maid. All corners else o' th' earth
Let liberty make use of. Space enough
Have I in such a prison.

Prospero. [*Aside*] It works. [*To Ferdinand*] Come on.
[*To Ariel*] Thou hast done well, fine Ariel! [*To*
495 *Ferdinand*] Follow me.
[*To Ariel*] Hark what thou else shalt do me.

Miranda.   Be of comfort.
My father's of a better nature, sir,
Than he appears by speech. This is unwonted
Which now came from him.

485 *nerves* sinews

Prospero.   Thou shalt be as free
As mountain winds; but then° exactly do   500
All points of my command.

Ariel.   To th' syllable.

Prospero. [*To Ferdinand*] Come, follow. [*To Miranda*] Speak not for him.   *Exeunt.*

ACT II

Scene I. [*Another part of the island.*]

*Enter Alonso, Sebastian, Antonio, Gonzalo,
Adrian, Francisco, and others.*

Gonzalo. Beseech you, sir, be merry. You have cause
(So have we all) of joy; for our escape
Is much beyond our loss. Our hint of° woe
Is common; every day some sailor's wife,
The master of some merchant,° and the merchant,   5
Have just our theme of woe. But for the miracle,
I mean our preservation, few in millions
Can speak like us. Then wisely, good sir, weigh
Our sorrow with° our comfort.

Alonso.   Prithee, peace.

Sebastian. [*Aside to Antonio*] He receives comfort   10
like cold porridge.°

Antonio. [*Aside to Sebastian*] The visitor° will not
give him o'er so.°

Sebastian. Look, he's winding up the watch of his
wit; by and by it will strike.   15

500 *then* till then   II.i.3 *hint of* occasion for   5 *master of some
merchant* captain of some merchant ship   9 *with* against   10–11 *He
receives comfort like cold porridge* ("He" is Alonso; pun on
"peace," since porridge contained peas)   12 *visitor* spiritual comforter   13 *give him o'er so* release him so easily

Gonzalo. Sir—

Sebastian. [*Aside to Antonio*] One. Tell.°

Gonzalo. When every grief is entertained, that's°
offered
Comes to th' entertainer—

20 *Sebastian.* A dollar.

Gonzalo. Dolor comes to him, indeed. You have
spoken truer than you purposed.

Sebastian. You have taken it wiselier° than I meant
you should.

25 *Gonzalo.* Therefore, my lord—

Antonio. Fie, what a spendthrift is he of his tongue!

Alonso. I prithee, spare.°

Gonzalo. Well, I have done. But yet—

Sebastian. He will be talking.

30 *Antonio.* Which, of he or Adrian, for a good wager,
first° begins to crow?

Sebastian. The old cock.°

Antonio. The cock'rel.°

Sebastian. Done! The wager?

33 *Antonio.* A laughter.°

Sebastian. A match!

Adrian. Though this island seem to be desert—

Antonio. Ha, ha, ha!

Sebastian. So, you're paid.

17 *One. Tell* he has struck one; keep count   18 *that's* that which is
23 *wiselier* i.e., understood my pun   27 *spare* spare your words
30–31 *Which, of he or Adrian . . . first* let's wager which of the two,
Gonzalo or Adrian, will first   32 *old cock* i.e., Gonzalo   33
cock'rel young cock; i.e., Adrian   35 *laughter* the winner will have
the laugh on the loser

Adrian. Uninhabitable and almost inaccessible—   40

Sebastian. Yet—

Adrian. Yet—

Antonio. He could not miss't.

Adrian. It must needs be of subtle, tender, and delicate temperance.°   45

Antonio. Temperance was a delicate wench.

Sebastian. Ay, and a subtle, as he most learnedly
delivered.

Adrian. The air breathes upon us here most sweetly.

Sebastian. As if it had lungs, and rotten ones.   50

Antonio. Or as 'twere perfumed by a fen.

Gonzalo. Here is everything advantageous to life.

Antonio. True; save means to live.

Sebastian. Of that there's none, or little.

Gonzalo. How lush and lusty the grass looks! How   55
green!

Antonio. The ground indeed is tawny.

Sebastian. With an eye° of green in't.

Antonio. He misses not much.

Sebastian. No; he doth but mistake the truth totally.   60

Gonzalo. But the rarity of it is—which is indeed almost beyond credit—

Sebastian. As many vouched rarities are.

Gonzalo. That our garments, being, as they were,
drenched in the sea, hold, notwithstanding, their   65
freshness and glosses, being rather new-dyed than
stained with salt water.

45 *temperance* climate (in the next line, a girl's name) 58 *eye*
spot (also perhaps Gonzalo's eye)

Antonio. If but one of his pockets could speak, would it not say he lies?°

70 *Sebastian.* Ay, or very falsely pocket up his report.°

Gonzalo. Methinks our garments are now as fresh as when we put them on first in Afric, at the marriage of the King's fair daughter Claribel to the King of Tunis.

75 *Sebastian.* 'Twas a sweet marriage, and we prosper well in our return.

Adrian. Tunis was never graced before with such a paragon to° their queen.

Gonzalo. Not since widow Dido's time.

80 *Antonio.* Widow? A pox o' that! How came that "widow" in? Widow Dido!

Sebastian. What if he had said "widower Aeneas"° too? Good Lord, how you take it!

Adrian. "Widow Dido," said you? You make me
85 study of that. She was of Carthage, not of Tunis.

Gonzalo. This Tunis, sir, was Carthage.

Adrian. Carthage?

Gonzalo. I assure you, Carthage.

Antonio. His word is more than the miraculous
90 harp.°

Sebastian. He hath raised the wall and houses too.

Antonio. What impossible matter will he make easy next?

68–69 *If but . . . he lies* i.e., the inside of Gonzalo's pockets are stained   70 *Ay, or . . . his report* unless the pocket were, like a false knave, to receive without resentment the imputation that it is unstained   78 *to* for   81–82 *Widow Dido . . . "widower Aeneas"* (the point of the joke is that Dido was a widow, but one doesn't ordinarily think of her that way; and the same with Aeneas)   89–90 *miraculous harp* (of Amphion, which only raised the *walls* of Thebes; whereas Gonzalo has rebuilt the whole ancient city of Carthage by identifying it mistakenly with modern Tunis)

Sebastian. I think he will carry this island home in his
    pocket and give it his son for an apple.   95

Antonio. And, sowing the kernels of it in the sea,
    bring forth more islands.

Gonzalo. Ay!

Antonio. Why, in good time.°

Gonzalo. [*To Alonso*] Sir, we were talking that our   100
    garments seem now as fresh as when we were at
    Tunis at the marriage of your daughter, who is now
    Queen.

Antonio. And the rarest that e'er came there.

Sebastian. Bate,° I beseech you, widow Dido.   105

Antonio. O, widow Dido? Ay, widow Dido!

Gonzalo. Is not, sir, my doublet as fresh as the first
    day I wore it? I mean, in a sort.°

Antonio. That "sort" was well fished for.

Gonzalo. When I wore it at your daughter's marriage.   110

Alonso. You cram these words into mine ears against
    The stomach of my sense.° Would I had never
    Married my daughter there! For, coming thence,
    My son is lost; and, in my rate,° she too,
    Who is so far from Italy removed   115
    I ne'er again shall see her. O thou mine heir
    Of Naples and of Milan, what strange fish
    Hath made his meal on thee?

Francisco.   Sir, he may live.
    I saw him beat the surges under him
    And ride upon their backs. He trod the water,   120
    Whose enmity he flung aside, and breasted

99 *Why, in good time* (hearing Gonzalo reaffirm his false statement
about Tunis and Carthage, Antonio suggests that Gonzalo will indeed, at the first opportunity, carry this island home in his pocket)
105 *Bate* except   108 *in a sort* so to speak   111–12 *against/The
stomach of my sense* i.e., though my mind (or feelings) have no
appetite for them   114 *rate* opinion

The surge most swol'n that met him. His bold head
'Bove the contentious waves he kept, and oared
Himself with his good arms in lusty stroke
To th' shore, that o'er his° wave-worn basis
125   bowed,°
As stooping to relieve him. I not doubt
He came alive to land.

Alonso.   No, no, he's gone.

Sebastian. [*To Alonso*] Sir, you may thank yourself for
      this great loss,
That would not bless our Europe with your
      daughter,
130   But rather loose her to an African,
Where she, at least, is banished from your eye
Who hath cause to wet the grief on't.

Alonso.   Prithee, peace.

Sebastian. You were kneeled to and importuned
      otherwise
By all of us; and the fair soul herself
135   Weighed, between loathness and obedience, at
Which end o' th' beam should bow.° We have lost
      your son,
I fear, forever. Milan and Naples have
Moe° widows in them of this business' making
Than we bring men to comfort them.
The fault's your own.

140 *Alonso.*   So is the dear'st° o' th' loss.

Gonzalo. My Lord Sebastian,
The truth you speak doth lack some gentleness,
And time to speak it in. You rub the sore
When you should bring the plaster.

Sebastian.   Very well.

---

125 *his* its   125 *wave-worn basis bowed* (the image is of a guardian
cliff on the shore)   135-36 *Weighed, between . . . should bow*
(Claribel's unwillingness to marry was outweighed by her obedience
to her father)   138 *Moe* more   140 *dear'st* (intensifies the meaning of the noun)

Antonio. And most chirurgeonly.°   *145*

Gonzalo. [*To Alonso*] It is foul weather in us all, good
  sir,
  When you are cloudy.

Sebastian. [*Aside to Antonio*] Foul weather?

Antonio. [*Aside to Sebastian*]   Very foul.

Gonzalo. Had I plantation° of this isle, my lord—

Antonio. He'd sow't with nettle seed.

Sebastian.   Or docks, or mallows.

Gonzalo. And were the king on't, what would I do?   *150*

Sebastian. Scape being drunk for want of wine.

Gonzalo. I' th' commonwealth I would by contraries°
Execute all things. For no kind of traffic°
Would I admit; no name of magistrate;
Letters° should not be known; riches, poverty,   *155*
And use of service,° none; contract, succession,°
Bourn,° bound of land, tilth,° vineyard, none;
No use of metal, corn, or wine, or oil;
No occupation; all men idle, all;
And women too, but innocent and pure;   *160*
No sovereignty.

Sebastian.   Yet he would be king on't.

Antonio. The latter end of his commonwealth forgets
  the beginning.

Gonzalo. All things in common nature should pro-
  duce
  Without sweat or endeavor. Treason, felony,   *165*
Sword, pike, knife, gun, or need of any engine°
Would I not have; but nature should bring forth,
Of it° own kind, all foison,° all abundance,

145 *chirurgeonly* like a surgeon 148 *plantation* colonization (Antonio then puns by taking the word in its other sense) 152 *contraries* in contrast to the usual customs 153 *traffic* trade 155 *Letters* learning 156 *service* servants 156 *succession* inheritance 157 *Bourn* boundary 157 *tilth* agriculture 166 *engine* weapon 168 *it* its 168 *foison* abundance

To feed my innocent people.

170 *Sebastian.* No marrying 'mong his subjects?

Antonio. None, man, all idle—whores and knaves.

Gonzalo. I would with such perfection govern, sir,
T' excel the Golden Age.

Sebastian. [*Loudly*]   Save his Majesty!

Antonio. [*Loudly*] Long live Gonzalo!

Gonzalo.   And—do you mark me, sir?

Alonso. Prithee, no more. Thou dost talk nothing to
175   me.

Gonzalo. I do well believe your Highness; and did
it to minister occasion° to these gentlemen, who
are of such sensible° and nimble lungs that they
always use to laugh at nothing.

180 *Antonio.* 'Twas you we laughed at.

Gonzalo. Who in this kind of merry fooling am nothing to you; so you may continue, and laugh at
nothing still.

Antonio. What a blow was there given!

185 *Sebastian.* And° it had not fall'n flatlong.°

Gonzalo. You are gentlemen of brave mettle; you
would lift the moon out of her sphere if she would
continue in it five weeks without changing.

Enter Ariel [*invisible*] *playing solemn music.*

Sebastian. We would so, and then go a-batfowling.°

190 *Antonio.* Nay, good my lord, be not angry.

177 *minister occasion* afford opportunity   178 *sensible* sensitive
185 *And* if   185 *flatlong* with the flat of the sword   189 *We would
so, and then go a-batfowling* we would use the moon for a lantern in
order to hunt birds at night by attracting them with a light and
beating them down with bats; i.e., in order to gull simpletons
like you (?)

Gonzalo. No, I warrant you; I will not adventure my
    discretion so weakly.° Will you laugh me asleep?
    For I am very heavy.

Antonio. Go sleep, and hear us.
    [*All sleep except Alonso, Sebastian, and Antonio.*]

Alonso. What, all so soon asleep? I wish mine eyes   195
    Would, with themselves, shut up my thoughts. I
       find
    They are inclined to do so.

Sebastian.   Please you, sir,
    Do not omit° the heavy offer of it.
    It seldom visits sorrow; when it doth,
    It is a comforter.

Antonio.   We two, my lord,   200
    Will guard your person while you take your rest,
    And watch your safety.

Alonso.   Thank you. Wondrous heavy.
                    [*Alonso sleeps. Exit Ariel.*]

Sebastian. What a strange drowsiness possesses them!

Antonio. It is the quality o' th' climate.

Sebastian.   Why
    Doth it not then our eyelids sink? I find not   205
    Myself disposed to sleep.

Antonio.   Nor I: my spirits are nimble.
    They fell together all, as by consent.
    They dropped as by a thunderstroke. What might,
    Worthy Sebastian—O, what might?—No more!
    And yet methinks I see it in thy face,   210
    What thou shouldst be. Th' occasion speaks° thee,
       and
    My strong imagination sees a crown
    Dropping upon thy head.

191–92 *adventure my discretion so weakly* risk my reputation for
good sense because of your weak wit   198 *omit* neglect   211 *speaks*
speaks to

Sebastian.   What? Art thou waking?

Antonio. Do you not hear me speak?

Sebastian.   I do; and surely
215   It is a sleepy language, and thou speak'st
        Out of thy sleep. What is it thou didst say?
        This is a strange repose, to be asleep
        With eyes wide open; standing, speaking, moving,
        And yet so fast asleep.

Antonio.   Noble Sebastian,
220   Thou let'st thy fortune sleep—die, rather; wink'st°
        Whiles thou art waking.

Sebastian.   Thou dost snore distinctly;
        There's meaning in thy snores.

Antonio. I am more serious than my custom. You
        Must be so too, if heed° me; which to do
        Trebles thee o'er.°

225 *Sebastian.*   Well, I am standing water.

Antonio. I'll teach you how to flow.

Sebastian.   Do so. To ebb
        Hereditary sloth instructs me.

Antonio.   O,
        If you but knew how you the purpose cherish
        Whiles thus you mock it; how, in stripping it,
230   You more invest it!° Ebbing men, indeed,
        Most often do so near the bottom run
        By their own fear or sloth.

Sebastian.   Prithee, say on.
        The setting of thine eye and cheek proclaim
        A matter° from thee; and a birth, indeed,
        Which throes thee much° to yield.

                                        Thus, sir:
235 *Antonio.*

220 *wink'st* dost shut thine eyes   224 *if heed* if you heed   225
Trebles thee o'er makes thee three times what thou now art   229–
30 *in stripping . . . invest it* in stripping the purpose off you, you
clothe yourself with it all the more   234 *matter* matter of importance   235 *throes thee much* costs thee much pain

Although this lord of weak remembrance,° this
Who shall be of as little memory°
When he is earthed,° hath here almost persuaded
(For he's a spirit of persuasion, only
Professes to persuade°) the King his son's alive,   240
'Tis as impossible that he's undrowned
As he that sleeps here swims.

Sebastian.   I have no hope
That he's undrowned.

Antonio.   O, out of that no hope
What great hope have you! No hope that way is
Another way so high a hope that even   245
Ambition cannot pierce a wink beyond,
But doubt discovery there.° Will you grant with me
That Ferdinand is drowned?

Sebastian.   He's gone.

Antonio.   Then tell me,
Who's the next heir of Naples?

Sebastian.   Claribel.

Antonio. She that is Queen of Tunis; she that dwells   250
   Ten leagues beyond man's life;° she that from
      Naples
   Can have no note—unless the sun were post;°
   The man i' th' moon's too slow—till newborn chins
   Be rough and razorable;° she that from whom
   We all were sea-swallowed,° though some cast°
      again,   255

236 *remembrance* memory   237 *of as little memory* as little remembered   238 *earthed* buried   239–40 *only/Professes to persuade* his only profession is to persuade   246–47 *Ambition cannot . . . discovery there* the eye of ambition can reach no farther, but must even doubt the reality of what it discerns thus far   251 *ten leagues beyond man's life* it would take a lifetime to get within ten leagues of the place   252 *post* messenger   253–54 *till newborn chins/Be rough and razorable* till babies just born be ready to shave   254–55 *she that . . . were sea-swallowed* she who is separated from Naples by so dangerous a sea that we were ourselves swallowed up by it   255 *cast* cast upon the shore (with a suggestion of its theatrical meaning that leads to the next metaphor)

And, by that destiny, to perform an act
Whereof what's past is prologue, what to come,
In yours and my discharge.

Sebastian.   What stuff is this? How say you?
'Tis true my brother's daughter's Queen of Tunis;
260 So is she heir of Naples; 'twixt which regions
There is some space.

Antonio.   A space whose ev'ry cubit
Seems to cry out "How shall that Claribel
Measure us back to Naples? Keep in Tunis,
And let Sebastian wake!" Say this were death
265 That now hath seized them, why, they were no
worse
Than now they are. There be that can rule Naples
As well as he that sleeps; lords that can prate
As amply and unnecessarily
As this Gonzalo; I myself could make
270 A chough° of as deep chat. O, that you bore
The mind that I do! What a sleep were this
For your advancement! Do you understand me?

Sebastian. Methinks I do.

Antonio.   And how does your content
Tender° your own good fortune?

Sebastian.   I remember
You did supplant your brother Prospero.

275 *Antonio.*   True.
And look how well my garments sit upon me,
Much feater° than before. My brother's servants
Were then my fellows; now they are my men.

Sebastian. But, for your conscience—

280 *Antonio.* Ay, sir, where lies that? If 'twere a kibe,°
'Twould put me to my slipper; but I feel not
This deity in my bosom. Twenty consciences

270 *chough* jackdaw (a bird that can be taught to speak a few
words)   274 *Tender* regard (i.e., do you like your good fortune)
277 *feater* more becomingly   280 *kibe* chilblain on the heel

That stand 'twixt me and Milan, candied be they
And melt, ere they molest! Here lies your brother,
No better than the earth he lies upon—
If he were that which now he's like, that's dead°—   285
Whom I with this obedient steel (three inches
     of it)
Can lay to bed forever; whiles you, doing thus,
To the perpetual wink° for aye might put
This ancient morsel, this Sir Prudence, who   290
Should not upbraid our course. For all the rest,
They'll take suggestion as a cat laps milk;
They'll tell the clock° to any business that
We say befits the hour.

Sebastian.   Thy case, dear friend,
Shall be my precedent. As thou got'st Milan,   295
I'll come by Naples. Draw thy sword. One stroke
Shall free thee from the tribute which thou payest,
And I the King shall love thee.

Antonio.   Draw together;
And when I rear my hand, do you the like,
To fall it on Gonzalo.   [*They draw.*]

Sebastian.   O, but one word!   300

Enter Ariel [invisible] with music and song.

Ariel. My master through his art foresees the danger
That you, his friend, are in, and sends me forth
(For else his project dies) to keep them living.
                    Sings in Gonzalo's ear.

               While you here do snoring lie,
               Open-eyed conspiracy
                    His time doth take.   305
               If of life you keep a care,
               Shake off slumber and beware.
                    Awake, awake!

286 *that's dead* that is, if he were dead   289 *wink* eye-shut   293
tell the clock say yes

Antonio. Then let us both be sudden.

310 *Gonzalo.* [*Wakes*]   Now good angels
     Preserve the King!   [*The others wake.*]

Alonso. Why, how now? Ho, awake! Why are you
     drawn?
     Wherefore this ghastly looking?

Gonzalo.   What's the matter?

Sebastian. Whiles we stood here securing your repose,
315   Even now, we heard a hollow burst of bellowing
     Like bulls, or rather lions. Did't not wake you?
     It struck mine ear most terribly.

Alonso.   I heard nothing.

Antonio. O, 'twas a din to fright a monster's ear,
     To make an earthquake! Sure it was the roar
     Of a whole herd of lions.

320 *Alonso.*   Heard you this, Gonzalo?

Gonzalo. Upon mine honor, sir, I heard a humming,
     And that a strange one too, which did awake me.
     I shaked you, sir, and cried. As mine eyes opened,
     I saw their weapons drawn. There was a noise,
325   That's verily.° 'Tis best we stand upon our guard,
     Or that we quit this place. Let's draw our weapons.

Alonso. Lead off this ground, and let's make further
     search
     For my poor son.

Gonzalo.   Heavens keep him from these beasts!
     For he is, sure, i' th' island.

Alonso.   Lead away.

330 *Ariel.* Prospero my lord shall know what I have done.
     So, King, go safely on to seek thy son.   *Exeunt.*

325 *verily* the truth

Scene II. [*Another part of the island.*]

Enter Caliban with a burden of wood. A noise of
   thunder heard.

Caliban. All the infections that the sun sucks up
  From bogs, fens, flats, on Prosper fall, and make
    him
  By inchmeal° a disease! His spirits hear me,
  And yet I needs must curse. But they'll nor pinch,
  Fright me with urchin shows,° pitch me i' th' mire,   *5*
  Nor lead me, like a firebrand,° in the dark
  Out of my way, unless he bid 'em. But
  For every trifle are they set upon me;
  Sometime like apes that mow° and chatter at me,
  And after bite me; then like hedgehogs which   *10*
  Lie tumbling in my barefoot way and mount
  Their pricks at my footfall; sometime am I
  All wound with adders, who with cloven tongues
  Do hiss me into madness.

Enter Trinculo.

             Lo, now, lo!
  Here comes a spirit of his, and to torment me   *15*
  For bringing wood in slowly. I'll fall flat.
  Perchance he will not mind me.   [*Lies down.*]

Trinculo. Here's neither bush nor shrub to bear off°
  any weather at all, and another storm brewing; I
  hear it sing i' th' wind. Yond same black cloud,   *20*
  yond huge one, looks like a foul bombard° that
  would shed his liquor. If it should thunder as it

II.ii.3 *By inchmeal* inch by inch   5 *urchin shows* impish apparitions
6 *like a firebrand* in the form of a will-o'-the-wisp   9 *mow* make
faces   18 *bear off* ward off   21 *bombard* large leather jug

did before, I know not where to hide my head.
Yond same cloud cannot choose but fall by pail-
fuls. What have we here? A man or a fish? Dead
or alive? A fish! He smells like a fish; a very ancient and fishlike smell; a kind of not of the new-
est Poor John.° A strange fish! Were I in England
now, as once I was, and had but this fish painted,°
not a holiday fool there but would give a piece of
silver. There would this monster make a man;° any
strange beast there makes a man. When they will
not give a doit° to relieve a lame beggar, they will
lay out ten to see a dead Indian. Legged like a man!
And his fins like arms! Warm, o' my troth! I do
now let loose my opinion, hold it no longer. This
is no fish, but an islander, that hath lately suffered
by a thunderbolt. [*Thunder.*] Alas, the storm is
come again! My best way is to creep under his
gaberdine; there is no other shelter hereabout. Misery acquaints a man with strange bedfellows. I will
here shroud till the dregs of the storm be past.
　　　　　[*Creeps under Caliban's garment.*]

Enter Stephano, singing, [a bottle in his hand.]

Stephano.　I shall no more to sea, to sea;
　　　　　Here shall I die ashore.

This is a very scurvy tune to sing at a man's fu-
neral. Well, here's my comfort.　　　　　*Drinks.*

The master, the swabber, the boatswain, and I,
　　The gunner, and his mate,
Loved Mall, Meg, and Marian, and Margery,
　　But none of us cared for Kate.
　　For she had a tongue with a tang,
　　Would cry to a sailor "Go hang!"
She loved not the savor of tar nor of pitch;

28 *Poor John* dried hake　29 *painted* i.e., as a sign hung outside
a booth at a fair　31 *make a man* (pun: make a man's fortune)
33 *doit* smallest coin

Yet a tailor might scratch her where'er she did itch.
Then to sea, boys, and let her go hang!　　　*55*

This is a scurvy tune too; but here's my comfort.
　　　　　　　　　　　　　　　　Drinks.

Caliban. Do not torment me! O!

Stephano. What's the matter? Have we devils here?
Do you put tricks upon 's with savages and men
of Inde, ha? I have not scaped drowning to be　　*60*
afeard now of your four legs. For it hath been
said, "As proper a man as ever went on four legs
cannot make him give ground"; and it shall be said
so again, while Stephano breathes at' nostrils.°

Caliban. The spirit torments me. O!　　　*65*

Stephano. This is some monster of the isle, with four
legs, who hath got, as I take it, an ague. Where the
devil should he learn our language? I will give him
some relief, if it be but for that. If I can recover°
him, and keep him tame, and get to Naples with　*70*
him, he's a present for any emperor that ever trod
on neat's leather.°

Caliban. Do not torment me, prithee; I'll bring my
wood home faster.

Stephano. He's in his fit now and does not talk after　*75*
the wisest. He shall taste of my bottle; if he have
never drunk wine afore, it will go near to remove
his fit. If I can recover him and keep him tame, I
will not take too much° for him. He shall pay for
him that hath him, and that soundly.　　*80*

Caliban. Thou dost me yet but little hurt. Thou wilt
anon;° I know it by thy trembling.° Now Prosper
works upon thee.

Stephano. Come on your ways, open your mouth;

64 *at' nostrils* at the nostrils　69 *recover* cure　72 *neat's leather*
cowhide　79 *not take too much* too much will not be enough
82 *anon* soon　82 *trembling* (Trinculo is shaking with fear)

85   here is that which will give language to you, cat.°
     Open your mouth. This will shake your shaking, I
     can tell you, and that soundly. [*Gives Caliban
     drink.*] You cannot tell who's your friend. Open
     your chaps° again.

90   *Trinculo.* I should know that voice. It should be—
     but he is drowned; and these are devils. O, defend
     me!

     Stephano. Four legs and two voices—a most delicate
     monster! His forward voice now is to speak well
95   of his friend; his backward voice is to utter foul
     speeches and to detract. If all the wine in my bottle
     will recover him, I will help his ague. Come! [*Gives
     drink.*] Amen! I will pour some in thy other
     mouth.

100 *Trinculo.* Stephano!

     Stephano. Doth thy other mouth call me? Mercy,
     mercy! This is a devil, and no monster. I will leave
     him; I have no long spoon.°

     Trinculo. Stephano! If thou beest Stephano, touch me
105 and speak to me; for I am Trinculo—be not afeard
     —thy good friend Trinculo.

     Stephano. If thou beest Trinculo, come forth. I'll pull
     thee by the lesser legs. If any be Trinculo's legs,
     these are they. [*Draws him out from under Cali-
110 ban's garment.*] Thou art very Trinculo indeed!
     How cam'st thou to be the siege° of this moon-
     calf?° Can he vent Trinculos?

     Trinculo. I took him to be killed with a thunder-
     stroke. But art thou not drowned, Stephano? I
115 hope now thou art not drowned. Is the storm over-
     blown? I hid me under the dead mooncalf's gaber-
     dine for fear of the storm. And art thou living,

85 *cat* (alluding to the proverb "Liquor will make a cat talk")
89 *chaps* jaws   103 *long spoon* (alluding to the proverb "He who
sups with [i.e., from the same dish as] the devil must have a long
spoon")   111 *siege* excrement   111–12 *mooncalf* monstrosity

Stephano? O Stephano, two Neapolitans scaped!

Stephano. Prithee do not turn me about; my stomach
  is not constant.   *120*

Caliban. [*Aside*] These be fine things, and if° they be
    not sprites.
  That's a brave god and bears celestial liquor.
  I will kneel to him.

Stephano. How didst thou scape? How cam'st thou
  hither? Swear by this bottle how thou cam'st   *125*
  hither. I escaped upon a butt of sack which the
  sailors heaved o'erboard—by this bottle which I
  made of the bark of a tree with mine own hands
  since I was cast ashore.

Caliban. I'll swear upon that bottle to be thy true   *130*
  subject, for the liquor is not earthly.

Stephano. Here! Swear then how thou escap'dst.

Trinculo. Swum ashore, man, like a duck. I can swim
  like a duck, I'll be sworn.

Stephano. Here, kiss the book. [*Gives him drink.*]   *135*
  Though thou canst swim like a duck, thou art made
  like a goose.

Trinculo. O Stephano, hast any more of this?

Stephano. The whole butt, man. My cellar is in a
  rock by th' seaside, where my wine is hid. How   *140*
  now, mooncalf? How does thine ague?

Caliban. Hast thou not dropped from heaven?

Stephano. Out o' th' moon, I do assure thee. I was the
  Man i' th' Moon when time was.°

Caliban. I have seen thee in her, and I do adore thee.   *145*
  My mistress showed me thee, and thy dog, and
  thy bush.°

121 *and if* if   144 *when time was* once upon a time   146–47 *thee,
and thy dog, and thy bush* (the Man in the Moon was banished
there, according to legend, for gathering brushwood with his dog
on Sunday)

Stephano. Come, swear to that; kiss the book. [*Gives
him drink.*] I will furnish it anon with new con-
150 tents. Swear. [*Caliban drinks.*]

Trinculo. By this good light, this is a very shallow
monster! I afeard of him? A very weak monster!
The Man i' th' Moon? A most poor credulous
monster! Well drawn,° monster, in good sooth!

155 *Caliban.* I'll show thee every fertile inch o' th' island;
and I will kiss thy foot. I prithee, be my god.

Trinculo. By this light, a most perfidious and drunken
monster! When's god's asleep, he'll rob his bottle.

Caliban. I'll kiss thy foot. I'll swear myself thy sub-
160 ject.

Stephano. Come on then. Down, and swear!

Trinculo. I shall laugh myself to death at this puppy-
headed monster. A most scurvy monster! I could
find in my heart to beat him—

165 *Stephano.* Come, kiss.

Trinculo. But that the poor monster's in drink. An
abominable monster!

Caliban. I'll show thee the best springs; I'll pluck thee
berries;
I'll fish for thee, and get thee wood enough.
170 A plague upon the tyrant that I serve!
I'll bear him no more sticks, but follow thee,
Thou wondrous man.

Trinculo. A most ridiculous monster, to make a wonder of a poor drunkard!

Caliban. I prithee let me bring thee where crabs°
175 grow;
And I with my long nails will dig thee pignuts,°
Show thee a jay's nest, and instruct thee how

154 *Well drawn* a good pull at the bottle   175 *crabs* crab apples
176 *pignuts* earthnuts

To snare the nimble marmoset. I'll bring thee
To clust'ring filberts, and sometimes I'll get thee
Young scamels° from the rock. Wilt thou go with
me?   180

Stephano. I prithee now, lead the way without any
more talking. Trinculo, the King and all our company else being drowned, we will inherit here.
Here, bear my bottle. Fellow Trinculo, we'll fill
him by and by again.   185

                            Caliban sings drunkenly.

Caliban. Farewell, master; farewell, farewell!

Trinculo. A howling monster! A drunken monster!

Caliban.

    No more dams° I'll make for fish,
      Nor fetch in firing
      At requiring,   190
    Nor scrape trenchering,° nor wash dish.
      'Ban, 'Ban, Ca—Caliban
    Has a new master. Get a new man!

Freedom, high day! High day, freedom! Freedom,
high day, freedom!   193

Stephano. O brave monster! Lead the way.   *Exeunt.*

ACT III

Scene I. [*In front of Prospero's cell.*]

Enter Ferdinand, bearing a log.

Ferdinand. There be some sports are painful, and
their labor
    Delight in them sets off;° some kinds of baseness

---

180 *scamels* (perhaps a misprint for "seamels" or "seamews," a
kind of sea bird)   188 *dams* (to catch fish and keep them)   191
trenchering trenchers, wooden plates   III.i.2 *sets off* cancels

Are nobly undergone, and most poor matters
Point to rich ends. This my mean task
Would be as heavy to me as odious, but
The mistress which I serve quickens° what's dead
And makes my labors pleasures. O, she is
Ten times more gentle than her father's crabbed;
And he's composed of harshness. I must remove
Some thousands of these logs and pile them up,
Upon a sore injunction.° My sweet mistress
Weeps when she sees me work, and says such baseness
Had never like executor. I forget;°
But these sweet thoughts do even refresh my labors,
Most busiest when I do it.°

Enter Miranda; and Prospero [behind, unseen].

Miranda.   Alas, now pray you,
Work not so hard! I would the lightning had
Burnt up those logs that you are enjoined to pile!
Pray set it down and rest you. When this burns,
'Twill weep° for having wearied you. My father
Is hard at study; pray now rest yourself;
He's safe for these three hours.

Ferdinand.   O most dear mistress,
The sun will set before I shall discharge
What I must strive to do.

Miranda.   If you'll sit down,
I'll bear your logs the while. Pray give me that;
I'll carry it to the pile.

Ferdinand.   No, precious creature,
I had rather crack my sinews, break my back,
Than you should such dishonor undergo
While I sit lazy by.

6 *quickens* brings to life   11 *sore injunction* severe command
13 *forget* i.e., my task   15 *Most busiest when I do it* i.e., my
thoughts are busiest when I am (the Folio's *busie lest* has been
variously emended; *it* may refer to "task," line 4, the understood
object in line 13)   19 *weep* i.e., exude resin

Miranda.   It would become me
As well as it does you; and I should do it
With much more ease; for my good will is to it,   50
And yours it is against.

Prospero. [*Aside*]   Poor worm, thou art infected!
This visitation° shows it.

Miranda.   You look wearily.

Ferdinand. No, noble mistress, 'tis fresh morning with
    me
When you are by at night.° I do beseech you,
Chiefly that I might set it in my prayers,   55
What is your name?

Miranda.   Miranda. O my father,
I have broke your hest° to say so!

Ferdinand.   Admired Miranda!°
Indeed the top of admiration, worth
What's dearest to the world! Full many a lady
I have eyed with best regard, and many a time   60
Th' harmony of their tongues hath into bondage
Brought my too diligent ear. For several virtues
Have I liked several women; never any
With so full soul but some defect in her
Did quarrel with the noblest grace she owed,°   65
And put it to the foil.° But you, O you,
So perfect and so peerless, are created
Of every creature's best.

Miranda.   I do not know
One of my sex; no woman's face remember,
Save, from my glass, mine own. Nor have I seen   50
More that I may call men than you, good friend,
And my dear father. How features are abroad
I am skilless° of; but, by my modesty

32 *visitation* (1) visit (2) attack of plague (referring to metaphor
of "infected")   34 *at night* i.e., even at night when I am very
tired   37 *hest* command   37 *Admired Miranda* ("admired" means
"to be wondered at"; the Latin "Miranda" means "wonderful")
45 *owed* owned   46 *put it to the foil* defeated it   53 *skilless*
ignorant

(The jewel in my dower), I would not wish
55 Any companion in the world but you;
Nor can imagination form a shape,
Besides yourself, to like of.° But I prattle
Something too wildly, and my father's precepts
I therein do forget.

Ferdinand.   I am, in my condition,
60 A prince, Miranda; I do think, a king
(I would not so), and would no more endure
This wooden slavery than to suffer
The fleshfly blow my mouth. Hear my soul speak!
The very instant that I saw you, did
65 My heart fly to your service; there resides,
To make me slave to it; and for your sake
Am I this patient log-man.

Miranda.   Do you love me?

Ferdinand. O heaven, O earth, bear witness to this
          sound,
And crown what I profess with kind event°
70 If I speak true! If hollowly, invert
What best is boded me° to mischief! I,
Beyond all limit of what else i' th' world,
Do love, prize, honor you.

Miranda.   I am a fool
To weep at what I am glad of.

Prospero.   [*Aside*] Fair encounter
75 Of two most rare affections! Heavens rain grace
On that which breeds between 'em!

Ferdinand.   Wherefore weep you?

Miranda. At mine unworthiness, that dare not offer
What I desire to give, and much less take
What I shall die to want.° But this is trifling;°
80 And all the more it seeks to hide itself,

57 *like of* like   69 *event* outcome   71 *What best is boded me* whatever good fortune fate has in store for me   79 *to want* if I lack
79 *trifling* i.e., to speak in riddles like this

The bigger bulk it shows. Hence, bashful cunning,
And prompt me, plain and holy innocence!
I am your wife, if you will marry me;
If not, I'll die your maid. To be your fellow°
You may deny me; but I'll be your servant,   85
Whether you will or no.

Ferdinand.   My mistress, dearest,
And I thus humble ever.

Miranda.   My husband then?

Ferdinand. Ay, with a heart as willing
As bondage e'er of freedom.° Here's my hand.

Miranda. And mine, with my heart in't; and now
farewell   90
Till half an hour hence.

Ferdinand.   A thousand thousand!
                    *Exeunt [Ferdinand and Miranda
                         in different directions].*

Prospero. So glad of this as they I cannot be,
Who are surprised withal;° but my rejoicing
At nothing can be more. I'll to my book;
For yet ere suppertime must I perform   95
Much business appertaining.°   *Exit.*

Scene II. [*Another part of the island.*]

Enter Caliban, Stephano, and Trinculo.

Stephano. Tell not me! When the butt is out, we will
drink water; not a drop before. Therefore bear up
and board 'em!° Servant monster, drink to me.

Trinculo. Servant monster? The folly of this island!

---

84 *fellow* equal   89 *of freedom* i.e., to win freedom   93 *withal* by
it   96 *appertaining* i.e., to my plan   III.ii.2–3 *bear up and board
'em* i.e., drink up

5   They say there's but five upon this isle; we are three
    of them. If th' other two be brained like us, the
    state totters.

    Stephano. Drink, servant monster, when I bid thee;
    thy eyes are almost set in thy head.

10 *Trinculo.* Where should they be set else? He were a
    brave monster indeed if they were set in his tail.

    Stephano. My man-monster hath drowned his tongue
    in sack. For my part, the sea cannot drown me. I
    swam, ere I could recover the shore, five-and-thirty
15 leagues off and on, by this light. Thou shalt be my
    lieutenant, monster, or my standard.°

    Trinculo. Your lieutenant, if you list;° he's no stan-
    dard.

    Stephano. We'll not run,° Monsieur Monster.

20 *Trinculo.* Nor go° neither; but you'll lie° like dogs,
    and yet say nothing neither.

    Stephano. Mooncalf, speak once in thy life, if thou
    beest a good mooncalf.

    Caliban. How does thy honor? Let me lick thy shoe.
25 I'll not serve him; he is not valiant.

    Trinculo. Thou liest, most ignorant monster; I am in
    case° to justle° a constable. Why, thou deboshed°
    fish thou, was there ever man a coward that hath
    drunk so much sack as I today? Wilt thou tell a
30 monstrous lie, being but half a fish and half a
    monster?

    Caliban. Lo, how he mocks me! Wilt thou let him,
    my lord?

---

16 *standard* standard-bearer, ensign (pun since Caliban is so drunk
he cannot stand)   17 *if you list* if it please you (with pun on
"list" as pertaining to a ship that leans over to one side)   19-20
run, lie (with puns on secondary meanings: "make water," "ex-
crete")   20 *go* walk   27 *case* fit condition   27 *justle* jostle   27 *de-
boshed* debauched

Trinculo. "Lord" quoth he? That a monster should
  be such a natural!°   35

Caliban. Lo, lo, again! Bite him to death, I prithee.

Stephano. Trinculo, keep a good tongue in your head.
  If you prove a mutineer—the next tree!° The poor
  monster's my subject, and he shall not suffer in-
  dignity.   40

Caliban. I thank my noble lord. Wilt thou be pleased
  to hearken once again to the suit I made to thee?

Stephano. Marry,° will I. Kneel and repeat it; I will
  stand, and so shall Trinculo.

               Enter Ariel, invisible.

Caliban. As I told thee before, I am subject to a
  tyrant,   45
  A sorcerer, that by his cunning hath
  Cheated me of the island.

Ariel. Thou liest.

Caliban.   Thou liest, thou jesting monkey
  thou!
  I would my valiant master would destroy thee.
  I do not lie.   50

Stephano. Trinculo, if you trouble him any more in's
  tale, by this hand, I will supplant some of your
  teeth.

Trinculo. Why, I said nothing.

Stephano. Mum then, and no more. Proceed.   55

Caliban. I say by sorcery he got this isle;
  From me he got it. If thy greatness will
  Revenge it on him—for I know thou dar'st,
  But this thing° dare not—

---

35 *natural* idiot 38 *the next tree* i.e., you will be hanged 43
Marry (an expletive, from "By the Virgin Mary") 59 *this thing*
i.e., Trinculo

60 *Stephano.* That's most certain.

Caliban. Thou shalt be lord of it, and I'll serve thee.

Stephano. How now shall this be compassed?
    Canst thou bring me to the party?

Caliban. Yea, yea, my lord! I'll yield him thee asleep,
65   Where thou mayst knock a nail into his head.

Ariel. Thou liest; thou canst not.

Caliban. What a pied° ninny's this! Thou scurvy
    patch!°
    I do beseech thy greatness, give him blows
    And take his bottle from him. When that's gone,
    He shall drink naught but brine, for I'll not show
70   him
    Where the quick freshes° are.

Stephano. Trinculo, run into no further danger! Inter-
    rupt the monster one word further and, by this
    hand, I'll turn my mercy out o' doors and make a
75   stockfish° of thee.

Trinculo. Why, what did I? I did nothing. I'll go far-
    ther off.

Stephano. Didst thou not say he lied?

Ariel. Thou liest.

80 *Stephano.* Do I so? Take thou that! [*Strikes Trin-
    culo.*] As you like this, give me the lie another time.

Trinculo. I did not give the lie. Out o' your wits, and
    hearing too? A pox o' your bottle! This can sack
    and drinking do. A murrain° on your monster, and
85   the devil take your fingers!

Caliban. Ha, ha, ha!

Stephano. Now forward with your tale. [*To Trinculo*]
    Prithee, stand further off.

67 *pied* (referring to Trinculo's parti-colored jester's costume)
67 *patch* clown   71 *quick freshes* living springs of fresh water
75 *stockfish* dried cod, softened by beating   84 *murrain* plague
(that infects cattle)

Caliban. Beat him enough. After a little time
 I'll beat him too.

Stephano. Stand farther. Come, proceed. 90

Caliban. Why, as I told thee, 'tis a custom with him
 I' th' afternoon to sleep. There thou mayst brain
  him,
 Having first seized his books, or with a log
 Batter his skull, or paunch° him with a stake,
 Or cut his wezand° with thy knife. Remember 95
 First to possess his books; for without them
 He's but a sot,° as I am, nor hath not
 One spirit to command. They all do hate him
 As rootedly as I. Burn but his books.
 He has brave utensils° (for so he calls them) 100
 Which, when he has a house, he'll deck withal.
 And that most deeply to consider is
 The beauty of his daughter. He himself
 Calls her a nonpareil. I never saw a woman
 But only Sycorax my dam and she; 105
 But she as far surpasseth Sycorax
 As great'st does least.

Stephano. Is it so brave a lass?

Caliban. Ay, lord. She will become thy bed, I
  warrant,
 And bring thee forth brave brood.

Stephano. Monster, I will kill this man. His daughter 110
 and I will be King and Queen—save our Graces!—
 and Trinculo and thyself shall be viceroys. Dost
 thou like the plot, Trinculo?

Trinculo. Excellent.

Stephano. Give me thy hand. I am sorry I beat thee; 115
 but while thou liv'st, keep a good tongue in thy
 head.

94 *paunch* stab in the belly   95 *wezand* windpipe   97 *sot* fool
100 *brave utensils* fine furnishings (pronounced "útensils")

Caliban. Within this half hour will he be asleep.
   Wilt thou destroy him then?

Stephano.   Ay, on mine honor.

120 *Ariel.* This will I tell my master.

Caliban. Thou mak'st me merry; I am full of pleasure.
   Let us be jocund. Will you troll the catch°
   You taught me but whilere?°

Stephano. At thy request, monster, I will do reason,
125   any reason.° Come on, Trinculo, let us sing. *Sings.*

            Flout 'em and scout° 'em
            And scout 'em and flout 'em!
            Thought is free.

Caliban. That's not the tune.
            Ariel plays the tune on a tabor° and pipe.

130 *Stephano.* What is this same?

Trinculo. This is the tune of our catch, played by the
   picture of Nobody.°

Stephano. If thou beest a man, show thyself in thy
   likeness. If thou beest a devil, take't as thou list.

135 *Trinculo.* O, forgive me my sins!

Stephano. He that dies pays all debts. I defy thee.
   Mercy upon us!

Caliban. Art thou afeard?

Stephano. No, monster, not I.

140 *Caliban.* Be not afeard; the isle is full of noises,
            Sounds and sweet airs that give delight and hurt
            not.

122 *troll the catch* sing the round   123 *but whilere* just now
124-25 *reason, any reason* i.e., anything within reason   126 *scout*
jeer at   129 s.d. *tabor* small drum worn at the side   132 *Nobody*
(alluding to the picture of No-body—a man all head, legs, and arms,
but without trunk—on the title page of the anonymous comedy
No-body and Some-body)

Sometimes a thousand twangling instruments
Will hum about mine ears; and sometime voices
That, if I then had waked after long sleep,
Will make me sleep again; and then, in dreaming,   145
The clouds methought would open and show riches
Ready to drop upon me, that, when I waked,
I cried to dream again.

Stephano. This will prove a brave kingdom to me,
where I shall have my music for nothing.   150

Caliban. When Prospero is destroyed.

Stephano. That shall be by and by; I remember the
story.

Trinculo. The sound is going away; let's follow it, and
after do our work.   155

Stephano. Lead, monster; we'll follow. I would I
could see this taborer; he lays it on.

Trinculo. [*To Caliban*] Wilt come?° I'll follow Stephano.   *Exeunt.*

Scene III. [*Another part of the island.*]

*Enter Alonso, Sebastian, Antonio, Gonzalo,
Adrian, Francisco, etc.*

Gonzalo. By'r Lakin,° I can go no further, sir;
My old bones aches. Here's a maze trod indeed
Through forthrights and meanders.° By your
      patience,
I needs must rest me.

Alonso.   Old lord, I cannot blame thee,
Who am myself attached° with weariness   5

158 *Wilt come* (Caliban lingers because the other two are being
distracted from his purpose by the music)   III.iii.1 *By'r Lakin*
by our Lady   3 *forthrights and meanders* straight and winding paths
5 *attached* seized

To th' dulling of my spirits. Sit down and rest.
Even here I will put off my hope, and keep it
No longer for my flatterer. He is drowned
Whom thus we stray to find; and the sea mocks
10 Our frustrate search on land. Well, let him go.

Antonio. [*Aside to Sebastian*] I am right glad that
he's so out of hope.
Do not for one repulse forgo the purpose
That you resolved t' effect.

Sebastian. [*Aside to Antonio*] The next advantage
Will we take throughly.°

Antonio. [*Aside to Sebastian*] Let it be tonight;
15 For, now they are oppressed with travel, they
Will not nor cannot use such vigilance
As when they are fresh.

Sebastian. [*Aside to Antonio*] I say tonight. No more.

*Solemn and strange music; and Prosper on the top°
(invisible). Enter several strange Shapes, bringing
in a banquet; and dance about it with gentle actions of salutations; and, inviting the King etc. to
eat, they depart.*

Alonso. What harmony is this? My good friends,
hark!

Gonzalo. Marvelous sweet music!

Alonso. Give us kind keepers,° heavens! What were
20 these?

Sebastian. A living drollery.° Now I will believe
That there are unicorns; that in Arabia

14 *throughly* thoroughly   17 s.d. *the top* upper stage (or perhaps a
playing area above it)   20 *kind keepers* guardian angels   21 *drollery* puppet show

There is one tree, the phoenix' throne; one phoenix
At this hour reigning there.

Antonio.   I'll believe both;
And what does else want credit,° come to me,   25
And I'll be sworn 'tis true. Travelers ne'er did lie,
Though fools at home condemn 'em.

Gonzalo.   If in Naples
I should report this now, would they believe me
If I should say I saw such islanders?
(For certes these are people of the island)   80
Who, though they are of monstrous shape, yet note,
Their manners are more gentle, kind, than of
Our human generation you shall find
Many—nay, almost any.

Prospero.   [*Aside*] Honest lord,
Thou hast said well; for some of you there present   85
Are worse than devils.

Alonso.   I cannot too much muse°
Such shapes, such gesture, and such sound, ex-
          pressing
(Although they want the use of tongue) a kind
     Of excellent dumb discourse.

Prospero.   [*Aside*] Praise in departing.°

Francisco. They vanished strangely.

Sebastian.   No matter, since   40
They have left their viands behind; for we have
          stomachs.
Will't please you taste of what is here?

Alonso.   Not I.

Gonzalo. Faith, sir, you need not fear. When we were
          boys,
Who would believe that there were mountaineers

25 *credit* believing   36 *muse* wonder at   39 *Praise in departing*
save your praise for the end

Dewlapped° like bulls, whose throats had hanging
45   at 'em
Wallets of flesh? Or that there were such men
Whose heads stood in their breasts? Which now
      we find
Each putter-out of five for one° will bring us
Good warrant of.

Alonso.   I will stand to, and feed;
50   Although my last, no matter, since I feel
The best is past. Brother, my lord the Duke,
Stand to, and do as we.

Thunder and lightning. Enter Ariel, like a harpy;
claps his wings upon the table; and with a
quaint device° the banquet vanishes.

Ariel. You are three men of sin, whom destiny—
That hath to instrument° this lower world
55   And what is in't——the never-surfeited sea
Hath caused to belch up you and on this island,
Where man doth not inhabit, you 'mongst men
Being most unfit to live. I have made you mad;
And even with suchlike valor° men hang and
      drown
Their proper selves.
                    [*Alonso, Sebastian, etc. draw their swords.*]
60   You fools! I and my fellows
Are ministers of Fate. The elements,
Of whom your swords are tempered,° may as well
Wound the loud winds, or with bemocked-at stabs
Kill the still-closing° waters, as diminish
One dowle° that's in my plume.° My fellow min-
65   isters

45 *Dewlapped* with skin hanging from the neck (like mountaineers
with goiter)   48 *putter-out of five for one* traveler who insures
himself by depositing a sum of money to be repaid fivefold if he
returns safely (i.e., any ordinary traveler will confirm nowadays
those reports we used to think fanciful)   52 s.d. *quaint device*
ingenious device (of stage mechanism)   54 *to instrument* as its instrument   59 *suchlike valor* i.e., the courage that comes of madness
62 *tempered* composed   64 *still-closing* ever closing again (as
soon as wounded)   65 *dowle* bit of down   65 *plume* plumage

Are like invulnerable. If you could hurt,°
Your swords are now too massy° for your strengths
And will not be uplifted. But remember
(For that's my business to you) that you three
From Milan did supplant good Prospero;　　　　　　70
Exposed unto the sea, which hath requit it,°
Him and his innocent child; for which foul deed
The pow'rs, delaying, not forgetting, have
Incensed the seas and shores, yea, all the creatures,
Against your peace. Thee of thy son, Alonso,　　　75
They have bereft; and do pronounce by me
Ling'ring perdition (worse than any death
Can be at once) shall step by step attend
You and your ways; whose wraths to guard you from,
Which here, in this most desolate isle, else falls　　80
Upon your heads, is nothing but heart's sorrow°
And a clear life ensuing.

*He vanishes in thunder; then, to soft music, enter
the Shapes again, and dance with mocks and
mows,° and carrying out the table.*

Prospero. Bravely the figure of this harpy hast thou
Performed, my Ariel; a grace it had, devouring.°
Of my instruction hast thou nothing bated°　　　　85
In what thou hadst to say. So, with good life°
And observation strange,° my meaner ministers°
Their several kinds have done.° My high charms work,
And these, mine enemies, are all knit up
In their distractions. They now are in my pow'r;　　90
And in these fits I leave them, while I visit

66 *If you could hurt* even if you could hurt us　67 *massy* heavy
71 *requit it* avenged that crime　81 *nothing but heart's sorrow* only
repentance (will protect you from the wrath of these powers)
82 s.d. *mocks and mows* mocking gestures and grimaces　84 *devouring* i.e., in making the banquet disappear　85 *bated* omitted　86
good life good lifelike acting　87 *observation strange* remarkable
attention to my wishes　87 *meaner ministers* i.e., inferior to Ariel
88 *Their several kinds have done* have acted the parts their natures
suited them for

Young Ferdinand, whom they suppose is drowned,
And his and mine loved darling.   [*Exit above.*]

Gonzalo. I' th' name of something holy, sir, why
    stand you
In this strange stare?

95 *Alonso.*   O, it is monstrous, monstrous!
Methought the billows spoke and told me of it;
The winds did sing it to me; and the thunder,
That deep and dreadful organ pipe, pronounced
The name of Prosper; it did bass my trespass.°
100 Therefore my son i' th' ooze is bedded; and
I'll seek him deeper than e'er plummet sounded
And with him there lie mudded.   *Exit.*

Sebastian.   But one fiend at a time,
I'll fight their legions o'er!°

Antonio.   I'll be thy second.
                    Exeunt [Sebastian and Antonio].

Gonzalo. All three of them are desperate; their great
    guilt,
105 Like poison given to work a great time after,
Now 'gins to bite the spirits. I do beseech you,
That are of suppler joints, follow them swiftly
And hinder them from what this ecstasy°
May now provoke them to.

Adrian.   Follow, I pray you.
                            Exeunt omnes.

---

99 *bass my trespass* i.e., made me understand my trespass by turning it into music for which the thunder provided the bass part
103 *o'er* one after another to the last   108 *ecstasy* madness

ACT IV

Scene I. [*In front of Prospero's cell.*]

Enter Prospero, Ferdinand, and Miranda.

Prospero. If I have too austerely punished you,
Your compensation makes amends; for I
Have given you here a third of mine own life,
Or that for which I live; who once again
I tender to thy hand. All thy vexations   5
Were but my trials of thy love, and thou
Hast strangely° stood the test. Here, afore heaven,
I ratify this my rich gift. O Ferdinand,
Do not smile at me that I boast her off,°
For thou shalt find she will outstrip all praise   10
And make it halt° behind her.

Ferdinand.   I do believe it
Against an oracle.°

Prospero. Then, as my gift, and thine own acquisition
Worthily purchased, take my daughter. But
If thou dost break her virgin-knot before   15
All sanctimonious° ceremonies may
With full and holy rite be minist'red,

IV.i.7 *strangely* wonderfully   9 *boast her off* (includes perhaps idea
of showing her off)   11 *halt* limp   12 *Against an oracle* though an
oracle should declare otherwise   16 *sanctimonious* holy

No sweet aspersion° shall the heavens let fall
To make this contract grow;° but barren hate,
20   Sour-eyed disdain, and discord shall bestrew
The union of your bed with weeds so loathly
That you shall hate it both. Therefore take heed,
As Hymen's lamps shall light you.°

Ferdinand.   As I hope
For quiet days, fair issue, and long life,
25   With such love as 'tis now, the murkiest den,
The most opportune° place, the strong'st sug-
          gestion
Our worser genius can,° shall never melt
Mine honor into lust, to take away
The edge° of that day's celebration
When I shall think or Phoebus' steeds are foun-
30   dered°
Or Night kept chained below.°

Prospero.   Fairly spoke.
Sit then and talk with her; she is thine own.
What, Ariel!° My industrious servant, Ariel!

                    Enter Ariel.

Ariel. What would my potent master? Here I am.

Prospero. Thou and thy meaner fellows your last
35   service
Did worthily perform; and I must use you
In such another trick. Go bring the rabble,°
O'er whom I give thee pow'r, here to this place.
Incite them to quick motion; for I must

18 *aspersion* blessing (like rain on crops)   19 *grow* become fruitful   23 *As Hymen's lamps shall light you* i.e., as earnestly as you
pray that the torch of the god of marriage shall burn without smoke
(a good omen for wedded happiness)   26 *opportune* (pronounced
"oppórtune")   27 *Our worser genius can* our evil spirit can offer
29 *edge* keen enjoyment   30 *foundered* lamed   30–31 *or Phoebus'
steeds . . . below* i.e., that either day will never end or night
will never come   33 *What, Ariel* (summoning Ariel)   37 *rabble*
"thy meaner fellows"

Bestow upon the eyes of this young couple   40
Some vanity of° mine art. It is my promise,
And they expect it from me.

Ariel.   Presently?

Prospero. Ay, with a twink.

Ariel. Before you can say "Come" and "Go,"
And breathe twice and cry, "So, so,"
Each one, tripping on his toe,   45
Will be here with mop and mow.°
Do you love me, master? No?

Prospero. Dearly, my delicate Ariel. Do not approach
Till thou dost hear me call.

Ariel.   Well; I conceive.°   *Exit.*   50

Prospero. Look thou be true.° Do not give dalliance
Too much the rein; the strongest oaths are straw
To th' fire i' th' blood. Be more abstemious,
Or else good night your vow!

Ferdinand.   I warrant you, sir.
The white cold virgin snow upon my heart°   55
Abates the ardor of my liver.°

Prospero.   Well.
Now come, my Ariel; bring a corollary°
Rather than want a spirit. Appear, and pertly!
No tongue! All eyes! Be silent.   *Soft music.*

Enter Iris.°

Iris. Ceres, most bounteous lady, thy rich leas°   60
Of wheat, rye, barley, fetches,° oats, and peas;

41 *vanity of* illusion conjured up by   47 *mop and mow* gestures and
grimaces   50 *conceive* understand   51 *be true* (Prospero appears
to have caught the lovers in an embrace)   55 *The white cold . . .
heart* her pure white breast on mine (?)   56 *liver* (supposed seat
of sexual passion)   57 *corollary* surplus (of spirits)   59 s.d. *Iris*
goddess of the rainbow and Juno's messenger   60 *leas* meadows
61 *fetches* vetch (a kind of forage)

Thy turfy mountains, where live nibbling sheep,
And flat meads thatched with stover,° them to
keep;
Thy banks with pionèd and twillèd brims,°
65 Which spongy April at thy hest betrims
To make cold nymphs chaste crowns; and thy
broom groves,
Whose shadow the dismissèd bachelor loves,
Being lasslorn; thy pole-clipt vineyard;°
And thy sea-marge, sterile and rocky-hard,
Where thou thyself dost air°—the queen o' th'
70 sky,°
Whose wat'ry arch and messenger am I,
Bids thee leave these, and with her sovereign grace,

Juno descends.°

Here on this grass plot, in this very place,
To come and sport; her peacocks fly amain.°
73 Approach, rich Ceres, her to entertain.

Enter Ceres.

Ceres. Hail, many-colored messenger, that ne'er
Dost disobey the wife of Jupiter,
Who, with thy saffron wings, upon my flow'rs
Diffusest honey drops, refreshing show'rs,
80 And with each end of thy blue bow dost crown
My bosky° acres and my unshrubbed down,
Rich scarf to my proud earth. Why hath thy queen
Summoned me hither to this short-grassed green?

Iris. A contract of true love to celebrate

63 *meads thatched with stover* (meadows covered with a kind of
grass used for winter fodder)   64 *pionèd and twillèd brims* (obscure; may refer to the trenched and ridged edges of banks that
have been repaired after the erosions of winter)   68 *pole-clipt
vineyard* i.e., vineyard whose vines grow neatly around (embrace)
poles (though possibly the word is "poll-clipped," i.e., pruned)
70 *air* take the air   70 *queen o' th' sky* Juno   72 s.d. (this direction seems to come too soon, but the machine may have lowered
her very slowly)   74 *amain* swiftly (peacocks, sacred to Juno, drew
her chariot)   81 *bosky* shrubbed

And some donation freely to estate°   *85*
On the blessed lovers.

Ceres.   Tell me, heavenly bow,
If Venus or her son, as thou dost know,
Do now attend the Queen? Since they did plot
The means that dusky Dis my daughter got,°
Her and her blind boy's scandaled° company   *90*
I have forsworn.

Iris.   Of her society
Be not afraid; I met her Deity
Cutting the clouds towards Paphos,° and her son
Dove-drawn with her. Here thought they to have
    done
Some wanton charm upon this man and maid,   *95*
Whose vows are, that no bed-right shall be paid
Till Hymen's torch be lighted. But in vain;
Mars's hot minion is returned again;°
Her waspish-headed son° has broke his arrows,
Swears he will shoot no more, but play with
    sparrows   *100*
And be a boy right out.°

[*Juno alights.*]

Ceres.   Highest queen of state,
Great Juno, comes; I know her by her gait.

Juno. How does my bounteous sister? Go with me
To bless this twain, that they may prosperous be
And honored in their issue.   *105*

They sing.

Juno.   Honor, riches, marriage blessing,

85 *estate* bestow 89 *dusky Dis my daughter got* (alluding to the
abduction of Proserpine by Pluto [Dis], god of the underworld)
90 *scandaled* scandalous 93 *Paphos* (in Cyprus, center of Venus'
cult) 98 *Mars's hot minion is returned again* i.e., Mars's lustful mistress (Venus) is on her way back to Paphos 99 *waspish-headed
son* (Cupid is irritable and stings with his arrows) 101 *a boy right
out* an ordinary boy

Long continuance, and increasing,
Hourly joys be still° upon you!
Juno sings her blessings on you.

110 [Ceres.]   Earth's increase, foison° plenty,
Barns and garners never empty,
Vines with clust'ring bunches growing,
Plants with goodly burden bowing;
Spring come to you at the farthest
115   In the very end of harvest.°
Scarcity and want shall shun you,
Ceres' blessing so is on you.

Ferdinand. This is a most majestic vision, and
Harmonious charmingly. May I be bold
To think these spirits?

120 *Prospero.*   Spirits, which by mine art
I have from their confines called to enact
My present fancies.

Ferdinand.   Let me live here ever!
So rare a wond'red° father and a wise
Makes this place Paradise.

Juno and Ceres whisper, and send Iris on employment.

Prospero.   Sweet now, silence!
125 Juno and Ceres whisper seriously.
There's something else to do. Hush and be mute,
Or else our spell is marred.

Iris. You nymphs, called Naiades, of the windring°
brooks,
With your sedged crowns and ever-harmless looks,
130 Leave your crisp° channels, and on this green land
Answer your summons; Juno does command.
Come, temperate nymphs, and help to celebrate
A contract of true love; be not too late.

108 *still* ever   110 *foison* abundance   114-15 *Spring come to you
... harvest* i.e., may there be no winter in your lives   123 *wond'red*
possessed of wonders; i.e., both wonderful and wonder-working,
and therefore to be wondered at   128 *windring* winding and wan-
dering (?)   130 *crisp* rippling

Enter certain Nymphs.

You sunburned sicklemen, of August weary,
Come hither from the furrow and be merry.　　　135
Make holiday; your rye-straw hats put on,
And these fresh nymphs encounter everyone
In country footing.°

Enter certain Reapers, properly habited. They
join with the Nymphs in a graceful dance; to-
wards the end whereof Prospero starts sud-
denly and speaks;° after which, to a strange,
hollow, and confused noise, they heavily°
vanish.

Prospero. [*Aside*] I had forgot that foul conspiracy
Of the beast Caliban and his confederates　　　140
Against my life. The minute of their plot
Is almost come. [*To the Spirits*] Well done!
Avoid!° No more!

Ferdinand. This is strange. Your father's in some
passion
That works him strongly.

Miranda.　　　　　　　　Never till this day
Saw I him touched with anger so distempered.°　　　145

Prospero. You do look, my son, in a movèd sort,°
As if you were dismayed; be cheerful, sir.
Our revels now are ended. These our actors,
As I foretold you, were all spirits and
Are melted into air, into thin air;　　　150
And, like the baseless fabric of this vision,
The cloud-capped towers, the gorgeous palaces,
The solemn temples, the great globe itself,
Yea, all which it inherit,° shall dissolve,

138 *footing* dance　138 s.d. *speaks* (breaking the spell, which depends on silence)　138 s.d. *heavily* reluctantly　142 *Avoid* begone
145 *distempered* violent　146 *movèd sort* troubled state　154 *it*
inherit occupy it

133   And, like this insubstantial pageant faded,
       Leave not a rack° behind. We are such stuff
       As dreams are made on, and our little life
       Is rounded with a sleep. Sir, I am vexed.
       Bear with my weakness; my old brain is troubled.
160   Be not disturbed with my infirmity.
       If you be pleased, retire into my cell
       And there repose. A turn or two I'll walk
       To still my beating mind.

Ferdinand, Miranda.   We wish your peace.
                      Exit [Ferdinand with Miranda].

Prospero. Come with a thought! I thank thee, Ariel.°
    Come.

Enter Ariel.

Ariel. Thy thoughts I cleave to. What's thy pleasure?

165 *Prospero.*   Spirit,
       We must prepare to meet with Caliban.

Ariel. Ay, my commander. When I presented° Ceres,
    I thought to have told thee of it, but I feared
    Lest I might anger thee.

Prospero. Say again, where didst thou leave these
170   varlets?°

Ariel. I told you, sir, they were red-hot with drinking;
    So full of valor that they smote the air
    For breathing in their faces, beat the ground
    For kissing of their feet; yet always bending°
175   Towards their project. Then I beat my tabor;
    At which like unbacked° colts they pricked their
        ears,
    Advanced° their eyelids, lifted up their noses
    As they smelt music. So I charmed their ears

156 *rack* wisp of cloud   164 *I thank thee, Ariel* (for the masque?)
167 *presented* acted the part of (?) introduced (?)   170 *varlets*
ruffians   174 *bending* directing their steps   176 *unbacked* unbroken
177 *Advanced* lifted up

That calflike they my lowing followed through
Toothed briers, sharp furzes, pricking goss,° and
    thorns,   *180*
Which ent'red their frail shins. At last I left them
I' th' filthy mantled° pool beyond your cell,
There dancing up to th' chins, that the foul lake
O'erstunk their feet.

Prospero.   This was well done, my bird.
Thy shape invisible retain thou still.
The trumpery° in my house, go bring it hither   *185*
For stale° to catch these thieves.

Ariel.   I go, I go.   *Exit.*

Prospero. A devil, a born devil, on whose nature
Nurture can never stick; on whom my pains,
Humanely taken, all, all lost, quite lost!   *190*
And as with age his body uglier grows,
So his mind cankers. I will plague them all,
Even to roaring.

    Enter Ariel, loaden with glistering apparel, etc.

        Come, hang them on this line.°

*[Prospero and Ariel remain, invisible.] Enter
    Caliban, Stephano, and Trinculo, all wet.*

Caliban. Pray you tread softly, that the blind mole
    may not
Hear a foot fall. We now are near his cell.   *195*

Stephano. Monster, your fairy, which you say is a
    harmless fairy, has done little better than played
    the Jack° with us.

Trinculo. Monster, I do smell all horse piss, at which
    my nose is in great indignation.   *200*

180 *goss* gorse   182 *filthy mantled* covered with filthy scum   186
trumpery (the "glistering apparel" mentioned in the next stage
direction)   187 *stale* decoy   193 *line* lime tree (linden)   198
Jack (1) knave (2) jack-o'-lantern, will-o'-the-wisp

Stephano. So is mine. Do you hear, monster? If I
should take a displeasure against you, look you—

Trinculo. Thou wert but a lost monster.

Caliban. Good my lord, give me thy favor still.
205 Be patient, for the prize I'll bring thee to
Shall hoodwink° this mischance. Therefore speak
 softly.
All's hushed as midnight yet.

Trinculo. Ay, but to lose our bottles in the pool—

Stephano. There is not only disgrace and dishonor in
210 that, monster, but an infinite loss.

Trinculo. That's more to me than my wetting. Yet this
is your harmless fairy, monster.

Stephano. I will fetch off my bottle, though I be o'er
ears° for my labor.

215 *Caliban.* Prithee, my king, be quiet. Seest thou here?
This is the mouth o' th' cell. No noise, and enter.
Do that good mischief which may make this island
Thine own forever, and I, thy Caliban,
For aye thy footlicker.

220 *Stephano.* Give me thy hand. I do begin to have
bloody thoughts.

Trinculo. O King Stephano! O peer!° O worthy
Stephano, look what a wardrobe here is for thee!

Caliban. Let it alone, thou fool! It is but trash.

225 *Trinculo.* O, ho, monster! We know what belongs to
a frippery.° O King Stephano!

Stephano. Put off that gown, Trinculo! By this hand,
I'll have that gown!

206 *hoodwink* put out of sight 213–14 *o'er ears* i.e., over my ears
in water 222 *peer* (alluding to the song "King Stephen was and a
worthy peer;/His breeches cost him but a crown," quoted in *Othello*
II. iii) 226 *frippery* old-clothes shop; i.e., we are good judges of
castoff clothes

Trinculo. Thy Grace shall have it.

Caliban. The dropsy drown this fool! What do you
    mean   230
To dote thus on such luggage?° Let't alone,
And do the murder first. If he awake,
From toe to crown he'll fill our skins with pinches,
Make us strange stuff.

Stephano. Be you quiet, monster. Mistress line, is not   235
this my jerkin?° [*Takes it down.*] Now is the jerkin
under the line.° Now, jerkin, you are like to lose
your hair and prove a bald jerkin.°

Trinculo. Do, do!° We steal by line and level,° and't
like° your Grace.   240

Stephano. I thank thee for that jest. Here's a garment
for't. Wit shall not go unrewarded while I am king
of this country. "Steal by line and level" is an excellent pass of pate.° There's another garment for't.

Trinculo. Monster, come put some lime° upon your   245
fingers, and away with the rest.

Caliban. I will have none on't. We shall lose our time
And all be turned to barnacles,° or to apes
With foreheads villainous low.

Stephano. Monster, lay-to your fingers; help to bear   250
this away where my hogshead of wine is, or I'll turn
you out of my kingdom. Go to, carry this.

Trinculo. And this.

Stephano. Ay, and this.

---

231 *luggage* useless encumbrances   236 *jerkin* kind of jacket   237
under the line pun: (1) under the lime tree (2) under the equator
238 *bald jerkin* (sailors proverbially lost their hair from fevers con-
tracted while crossing the equator)   239 *Do, do* fine, fine   239 *by
line and level* by plumb line and carpenter's level; i.e., according to
rule (with pun on "line")   239–40 *and't like* if it please   244 *pass
of pate* sally of wit   245 *lime* birdlime (which is sticky; thieves have
sticky fingers)   248 *barnacles* kind of geese supposed to have developed from shellfish

*A noise of hunters heard. Enter divers Spirits in
shape of dogs and hounds, hunting them about;
Prospero and Ariel setting them on.*

255 *Prospero.* Hey, Mountain, hey!

Ariel. Silver! There it goes, Silver!

Prospero. Fury, Fury! There, Tyrant, there! Hark,
hark!

[*Caliban, Stephano, and Trinculo are driven out.*]

Go, charge my goblins that they grind their joints
With dry convulsions,° shorten up their sinews
With agèd° cramps, and more pinch-spotted make
260 them
Than pard or cat o' mountain.°

Ariel.   Hark, they roar!

Prospero. Let them be hunted soundly. At this hour
Lies at my mercy all mine enemies.
Shortly shall all my labors end, and thou
265 Shalt have the air at freedom. For a little,
Follow, and do me service.   *Exeunt.*

ACT V

Scene I. [*In front of Prospero's cell.*]

Enter Prospero in his magic robes, and Ariel.

Prospero. Now does my project gather to a head.
My charms crack not, my spirits obey, and time
Goes upright with his carriage.° How's the day?

Ariel. On the sixth hour, at which time, my lord,

259 *dry convulsions* (such as come when the joints are dry from
old age)   260 *agèd* i.e., such as old people have   261 *pard or cat
o' mountain* leopard or catamount V.i.2–3 *time/ Goes upright with
his carriage* time does not stoop under his burden (because there is
so little left to do)

You said our work should cease.

Prospero.   I did say so   9
When first I raised the tempest. Say, my spirit,
How fares the King and 's followers?

Ariel.   Confined together
In the same fashion as you gave in charge,
Just as you left them——all prisoners, sir,
In the line grove which weather-fends° your cell.   10
They cannot budge till your release.° The King,
His brother, and yours abide all three distracted,
And the remainder mourning over them,
Brimful of sorrow and dismay; but chiefly
Him that you termed, sir, the good old Lord
   Gonzalo.   15
His tears runs down his beard like winter's drops
From eaves of reeds.° Your charm so strongly
   works 'em,
That if you now beheld them, your affections
Would become tender.

Prospero.   Dost thou think so, spirit?

Ariel. Mine would, sir, were I human.

Prospero.   And mine shall.   20
Hast thou, which art but air, a touch, a feeling
Of their afflictions, and shall not myself,
One of their kind, that relish all as sharply,
Passion° as they, be kindlier moved than thou art?
Though with their high wrongs I am struck to th'
   quick,
                                                       25
Yet with my nobler reason 'gainst my fury
Do I take part. The rarer action is
In virtue than in vengeance. They being penitent,
The sole drift of my purpose doth extend
Not a frown further. Go, release them, Ariel.   30
My charms I'll break, their senses I'll restore,
And they shall be themselves.

10 *weather-fends* protects from the weather   11 *till your release*
until released by you   17 *eaves of reeds* i.e., a thatched roof   24
Passion (verb)

Ariel.   I'll fetch them, sir.
                                              Exit.

Prospero. Ye elves of hills, brooks, standing lakes,
    and groves,
  And ye that on the sands with printless foot
35 Do chase the ebbing Neptune, and do fly him°
  When he comes back; you demi-puppets that
  By moonshine do the green sour ringlets° make,
  Whereof the ewe not bites; and you whose pastime
  Is to make midnight mushrumps,° that rejoice
40 To hear the solemn curfew; by whose aid
  (Weak masters° though ye be) I have bedimmed
  The noontide sun, called forth the mutinous winds,
  And 'twixt the green sea and the azured vault
  Set roaring war; to the dread rattling thunder
45 Have I given fire and rifted Jove's stout oak
  With his own bolt; the strong-based promontory
  Have I made shake and by the spurs° plucked up
  The pine and cedar; graves at my command
  Have waked their sleepers, oped, and let 'em forth
50 By my so potent art. But this rough magic
  I here abjure; and when I have required°
  Some heavenly music (which even now I do)
  To work mine end upon their senses that°
  This airy charm is for, I'll break my staff,
55 Bury it certain fathoms in the earth,
  And deeper than did ever plummet sound
  I'll drown my book.   *Solemn music.*

*Here enters Ariel before; then Alonso, with a
frantic gesture, attended by Gonzalo; Sebastian
and Antonio in like manner, attended by Adrian
and Francisco. They all enter the circle which
Prospero had made, and there stand charmed;
which Prospero observing, speaks.*

35 *fly him* fly with him   37 *green sour ringlets* ("fairy rings," little
circles of rank grass supposed to be formed by the dancing of fairies)
39 *mushrumps* mushrooms   41 *masters* masters of supernatural
power   47 *spurs* roots   51 *required* asked for   53 *their senses that*
the senses of those whom

A solemn air, and° the best comforter
To an unsettled fancy, cure thy brains,
Now useless, boiled within thy skull! There stand,   60
For you are spell-stopped.
Holy Gonzalo, honorable man,
Mine eyes, ev'n sociable to the show of thine,
Fall fellowly drops.° The charm dissolves apace;
And as the morning steals upon the night,   65
Melting the darkness, so their rising senses
Begin to chase the ignorant fumes that mantle
Their clearer reason. O good Gonzalo,
My true preserver, and a loyal sir
To him thou follow'st, I will pay thy graces   70
Home° both in word and deed. Most cruelly
Didst thou, Alonso, use me and my daughter.
Thy brother was a furtherer in the act.
Thou art pinched for't now, Sebastian. Flesh and
     blood,
You, brother mine, that entertained ambition,   75
Expelled remorse° and nature;° whom, with
     Sebastian
(Whose inward pinches therefore are most strong),
Would here have killed your king, I do forgive thee,
Unnatural though thou art. Their understanding
Begins to swell, and the approaching tide   80
Will shortly fill the reasonable shore,
That now lies foul and muddy. Not one of them
That yet looks on me or would know me. Ariel,
Fetch me the hat and rapier in my cell.
I will discase° me, and myself present   85
As I was sometime Milan. Quickly, spirit!
Thou shalt ere long be free.
          [Exit Ariel and returns immediately.]

     Ariel sings and helps to attire him.

58 *and* which is   63-64 *sociable to the show . . . drops* associating
themselves with the (tearful) appearance of your eyes, shed tears
in sympathy   70-71 *pay thy graces/ Home* repay thy favors
thoroughly   76 *remorse* pity   76 *nature* natural feeling   85 *discase*
disrobe

Where the bee sucks, there suck I;
In a cowslip's bell I lie;
90   There I couch when owls do cry.
On the bat's back I do fly
After summer merrily.
Merrily, merrily shall I live now
Under the blossom that hangs on the bough.

Prospero. Why, that's my dainty Ariel! I shall miss
95   thee,
But yet thou shalt have freedom; so, so, so.
To the King's ship, invisible as thou art!
There shalt thou find the mariners asleep
Under the hatches. The master and the boatswain
100   Being awake, enforce them to this place,
And presently,° I prithee.

Ariel. I drink the air before me, and return
Or ere your pulse twice beat.   *Exit.*

Gonzalo. All torment, trouble, wonder, and amazement
105   Inhabits here. Some heavenly power guide us
Out of this fearful country!

Prospero.   Behold, sir King,
The wrongèd Duke of Milan, Prospero.
For more assurance that a living prince
Does now speak to thee, I embrace thy body,
110   And to thee and thy company I bid
A hearty welcome.

Alonso.   Whe'r° thou be'st he or no,
Or some enchanted trifle° to abuse me,
As late I have been, I not know. Thy pulse
Beats, as of flesh and blood; and, since I saw thee,
115   Th' affliction of my mind amends, with which,
I fear, a madness held me. This must crave°
(And if this be at all)° a most strange story.
Thy dukedom I resign and do entreat

101 *presently* immediately   111 *Whe'r* whether   112 *trifle* apparition   116 *crave* require (to account for it)   117 *And if this be at
all* if this is really happening

Thou pardon me my wrongs. But how should Prospero
Be living and be here?

Prospero.   First, noble friend,   120
Let me embrace thine age, whose honor cannot
Be measured or confined.

Gonzalo.   Whether this be
Or be not, I'll not swear.

Prospero.   You do yet taste
Some subtleties° o' th' isle, that will not let you
Believe things certain. Welcome, my friends all.   125
[*Aside to Sebastian and Antonio*] But you, my
   brace of lords, were I so minded,
I here could pluck his Highness' frown upon you,
And justify° you traitors. At this time
I will tell no tales.

Sebastian. [*Aside*] The devil speaks in him.

Prospero.   No.
For you, most wicked sir, whom to call brother   130
Would even infect my mouth, I do forgive
Thy rankest fault—all of them; and require
My dukedom of thee, which perforce I know
Thou must restore.

Alonso.   If thou beest Prospero,
Give us particulars of thy preservation;   135
How thou hast met us here, whom three hours
   since
Were wracked upon this shore; where I have lost
(How sharp the point of this remembrance is!)
My dear son Ferdinand.

Prospero.   I am woe° for't, sir.

Alonso. Irreparable is the loss, and patience   140
Says it is past her cure.

---

124 *subtleties* deceptions (referring to pastries made to look like
something else—e.g., castles made out of sugar)   128 *justify* prove
139 *woe* sorry

Prospero.   I rather think
You have not sought her help, of whose soft grace
For the like loss I have her sovereign aid
And rest myself content.

Alonso.   You the like loss?

145 *Prospero.* As great to me, as late,° and supportable°
To make the dear° loss, have I means much weaker
Than you may call to comfort you; for I
Have lost my daughter.

Alonso.   A daughter?
O heavens, that they were living both in Naples,
150 The King and Queen there! That they were, I wish
Myself were mudded in that oozy bed
Where my son lies. When did you lose your
    daughter?

Prospero. In this last tempest. I perceive these lords
At this encounter do so much admire°
155 That they devour their reason, and scarce think
Their eyes do offices° of truth, their words
Are natural breath. But, howsoev'r you have
Been justled from your senses, know for certain
That I am Prospero, and that very duke
160 Which was thrust forth of Milan, who most strangely
Upon this shore, where you were wracked, was
    landed
To be the lord on't. No more yet of this;
For 'tis a chronicle of day by day,
Not a relation for a breakfast, nor
165 Befitting this first meeting. Welcome, sir;
This cell's my court. Here have I few attendants,
And subjects none abroad.° Pray you look in.
My dukedom since you have given me again,
I will requite you with as good a thing,
170 At least bring forth a wonder to content ye

---

145 *As great to me, as late* as great to me as your loss, and as recent
145 *supportable* (pronounced "súpportable")   146 *dear* (intensifies the meaning of the noun)   154 *admire* wonder   156 *do offices*
perform services   167 *abroad* i.e., on the island

As much as me my dukedom.

Here Prospero discovers° Ferdinand and Miranda playing at chess.

Miranda. Sweet lord, you play me false.

Ferdinand.   No, my dearest love,
I would not for the world.

Miranda. Yes, for a score of kingdoms you should
      wrangle,
And I would call it fair play.°

Alonso.   If this prove   *175*
A vision of the island, one dear son
Shall I twice lose.

Sebastian.   A most high miracle!

Ferdinand. Though the seas threaten, they are merciful.
I have cursed them without cause.   [*Kneels.*]

Alonso.   Now all the blessings
Of a glad father compass thee about!   *180*
Arise, and say how thou cam'st here.

Miranda.   O, wonder!
How many goodly creatures are there here!
How beauteous mankind is! O brave new world
That has such people in't!

Prospero.   'Tis new to thee.

Alonso. What is this maid with whom thou wast at
      play?   *185*
Your eld'st° acquaintance cannot be three hours.
Is she the goddess that hath severed us
And brought us thus together?

Ferdinand.   Sir, she is mortal;

171 s.d. *discovers* reveals (by opening a curtain at the back of the
stage)   174–75 *for a score of kingdoms . . . play* i.e., if we were
playing for stakes just short of the world, you would protest as now;
but then, the issue being important, I would call it fair play so much
do I love you (?)   186 *eld'st* longest

But by immortal providence she's mine.
190 I chose her when I could not ask my father
For his advice, nor thought I had one. She
Is daughter to this famous Duke of Milan,
Of whom so often I have heard renown
But never saw before; of whom I have
195 Received a second life; and second father
This lady makes him to me.

Alonso.   I am hers.
But, O, how oddly will it sound that I
Must ask my child forgiveness!

Prospero.   There, sir, stop.
Let us not burden our remembrance with
A heaviness that's gone.

200 *Gonzalo.*   I have inly wept,
Or should have spoke ere this. Look down, you gods,
And on this couple drop a blessèd crown!
For it is you that have chalked forth the way
Which brought us hither.

Alonso.   I say amen, Gonzalo.

205 *Gonzalo.* Was Milan thrust from Milan that his issue
Should become kings of Naples? O, rejoice
Beyond a common joy, and set it down
With gold on lasting pillars. In one voyage
Did Claribel her husband find at Tunis,
210 And Ferdinand her brother found a wife
Where he himself was lost; Prospero his dukedom
In a poor isle; and all of us ourselves
When no man was his own.

Alonso. [*To Ferdinand and Miranda*] Give me your
hands.
Let grief and sorrow still° embrace his heart
That doth not wish you joy.

213 *Gonzalo.*   Be it so! Amen!

214 *still* forever

*Enter Ariel, with the Master and Boatswain
amazedly following.*

O, look, sir; look, sir! Here is more of us!
I prophesied if a gallows were on land,
This fellow could not drown. Now, blasphemy,
That swear'st grace o'erboard,° not an oath on
    shore?
Hast thou no mouth by land? What is the news?   *220*

Boatswain. The best news is that we have safely found
Our king and company; the next, our ship,
Which, but three glasses° since, we gave out split,
Is tight and yare° and bravely rigged as when
We first put out to sea.

Ariel.   [*Aside to Prospero*] Sir, all this service   *225*
Have I done since I went.

Prospero.   [*Aside to Ariel*] My tricksy spirit!

Alonso. These are not natural events; they strengthen
From strange to stranger. Say, how came you hither?

Boatswain. If I did think, sir, I were well awake,
I'd strive to tell you. We were dead of sleep   *230*
And (how we know not) all clapped under hatches;
Where, but even now, with strange and several°
    noises
Of roaring, shrieking, howling, jingling chains,
And moe° diversity of sounds, all horrible,
We were awaked; straightway at liberty;   *235*
Where we, in all our trim, freshly beheld
Our royal, good, and gallant ship, our master
Cap'ring to eye° her. On a trice, so please you,
Even in a dream, were we divided from them
And were brought moping° hither.

Ariel. [*Aside to Prospero*]   Was't well done?   *240*

219 *That swear'st grace o'erboard* that (at sea) swearest enough to
cause grace to be withdrawn from the ship   223*glasses* hours   224
yare shipshape   232 *several* various   234 *moe* more   238 *Cap'ring
to eye* dancing to see   240 *moping* in a daze

Prospero. [*Aside to Ariel*] Bravely, my diligence.
   Thou shalt be free.

Alonso. This is as strange a maze as e'er men trod,
   And there is in this business more than nature
   Was ever conduct° of. Some oracle
   Must rectify our knowledge.

243 *Prospero.*   Sir, my liege,
   Do not infest your mind with beating on
   The strangeness of this business. At picked leisure,
   Which shall be shortly, single I'll resolve you
   (Which to you shall seem probable) of every
250 These happened accidents;° till when, be cheerful
   And think of each thing well. [*Aside to Ariel*]
      Come hither, spirit.
   Set Caliban and his companions free.
   Untie the spell. [*Exit Ariel.*] How fares my gracious
      sir?
   There are yet missing of your company
255 Some few odd lads that you remember not.

   *Enter Ariel, driving in Caliban, Stephano, and
   Trinculo, in their stolen apparel.*

Stephano. Every man shift for all the rest, and let no
   man take care for himself; for all is but fortune.
   Coragio,° bully-monster, *coragio!*

Trinculo. If these be true spies which I wear in my
260   head, here's a goodly sight.

Caliban. O Setebos,° these be brave spirits indeed!
   How fine my master is! I am afraid
   He will chastise me.

Sebastian.   Ha, ha!
   What things are these, my Lord Antonio?
   Will money buy 'em?

244 *conduct* conductor   248–50 *single I'll resolve . . . accidents*
I myself will solve the problems (and my story will make sense to
you) concerning each and every incident that has happened   258
Coragio courage (Italian)   261 *Setebos* the god of Caliban's mother

Antonio.   Very like. One of them   265
Is a plain fish and no doubt marketable.

Prospero. Mark but the badges° of these men, my
lords,
Then say if they be true.° This misshapen knave,
His mother was a witch, and one so strong
That could control the moon, make flows and ebbs,   270
And deal in her command without her power.°
These three have robbed me, and this demi-devil
(For he's a bastard one) had plotted with them
To take my life. Two of these fellows you
Must know and own; this thing of darkness I   275
Acknowledge mine.

Caliban.   I shall be pinched to death.

Alonso. Is not this Stephano, my drunken butler?

Sebastian. He is drunk now. Where had he wine?

Alonso. And Trinculo is reeling ripe. Where should
they
Find this grand liquor that hath gilded 'em?   280
How cam'st thou in this pickle?

Trinculo. I have been in such a pickle, since I saw
you last, that I fear me will never out of my bones.
I shall not fear flyblowing.°

Sebastian. Why, how now, Stephano?   285

Stephano. O, touch me not! I am not Stephano, but
a cramp.

Prospero. You'd be king o' the isle, sirrah?

Stephano. I should have been a sore° one then.

Alonso. This is a strange thing as e'er I looked on.   290

267 *badges* (worn by servants to indicate to whose service they
belong; in this case, the stolen clothes are badges of their rascality)
268 *true* honest   271 *deal in her command without her power* i.e.,
dabble in the moon's realm without the moon's legitimate authority
284 *flyblowing* (pickling preserves meat from flies)   289 *sore* (1)
tyrannical (2) aching

Prospero. He is as disproportioned in his manners
As in his shape. Go, sirrah, to my cell;
Take with you your companions. As you look
To have my pardon, trim it handsomely.

295 *Caliban.* Ay, that I will; and I'll be wise hereafter,
And seek for grace. What a thrice-double ass
Was I to take this drunkard for a god
And worship this dull fool!

Prospero.   Go to! Away!

Alonso. Hence, and bestow your luggage where you
    found it.

300 *Sebastian.* Or stole it rather.
                [*Exeunt Caliban, Stephano, and Trinculo.*]

Prospero. Sir, I invite your Highness and your train
To my poor cell, where you shall take your rest
For this one night; which, part of it, I'll waste°
With such discourse as, I not doubt, shall make it
305 Go quick away—the story of my life,
And the particular accidents° gone by
Since I came to this isle. And in the morn
I'll bring you to your ship, and so to Naples,
Where I have hope to see the nuptial
310 Of these our dear-beloved solemnizèd;°
And thence retire me to my Milan, where
Every third thought shall be my grave.

Alonso.   I long
To hear the story of your life, which must
Take° the ear strangely.

Prospero.   I'll deliver° all;
315 And promise you calm seas, auspicious gales,
And sail so expeditious that shall catch°
Your royal fleet far off. [*Aside to Ariel*] My Ariel,
    chick,
That is thy charge. Then to the elements

303 *waste* spend   306 *accidents* incidents   310 *solemnizèd* (pronounced (solémnizèd")   314 *Take* captivate   314 *deliver* tell   316 *catch* catch up with

Be free, and fare thou well! [*To the others*] Please
you, draw near.   *Exeunt omnes.*

EPILOGUE

Spoken by Prospero

Now my charms are all o'erthrown,
And what strength I have's mine own,
Which is most faint. Now 'tis true
I must be here confined by you,
Or sent to Naples. Let me not,   *5*
Since I have my dukedom got
And pardoned the deceiver, dwell
In this bare island by your spell;
But release me from my bands°
With the help of your good hands.°   *10*
Gentle breath° of yours my sails
Must fill, or else my project fails,
Which was to please. Now I want°
Spirits to enforce, art to enchant;
And my ending is despair   *15*
Unless I be relieved by prayer,°
Which pierces so that it assaults
Mercy itself and frees all faults.
As you from crimes would pardoned be,
Let your indulgence set me free.   *Exit.*   *20*

FINIS

Epi. 9 *bands* bonds   10 *hands* i.e., applause to break the spell   11
Gentle breath i.e., favorable comment   13 *want* lack   16 *prayer*
i.e., this petition

Textual Note

The Tempest was first printed in the Folio of 1623, the
First Folio. The Folio text has been carefully edited and
punctuated, and it has unusually complete stage directions
that are probably Shakespeare's own. *The Tempest* is perhaps the finest text in the Folio, which may be why the
Folio editors placed it first in the volume.

The present division into acts and scenes is that of the
Folio. The present edition silently modernizes spelling and
punctuation, regularizes speech prefixes, translates into
English the Folio's Latin designations of act and scene,
and makes certain changes in lineation in the interest
either of meter, meaning, or a consistent format. Other
departures from the Folio are listed below, including
changes in lineation that bear upon the meaning. The
reading of the present text is given first, in italics, and
then the reading of the Folio (F) in roman.

The Scene: an uninhabited island . . . Names of the Actors [appears
at end of play in F]

I.i.38 s.d. *Enter Sebastian, Antonio, and Gonzalo* [in F occurs after
"plague," line 37]

I.ii.173 *princess'* Princesse   201 *lightnings* Lightning   271 *wast* was
282 *she* he   380 *the burden bear* beare/ the burthen

II.i.5 *master* Masters   38–39 *Antonio . . . Sebastian* [speakers reversed in F]

III.i.2 *sets* set   15 *busiest* busie lest   93 *withal* with all

III.ii.126 *scout* cout

III.iii.17 *Sebastian: I say tonight. No more* [appears in F after stage direction]   29 *islanders* Islands

IV.i.9 *off* of   13 *gift* guest   124 s.d. *Juno and....employment* [follows line 127 in F]   193 *them on* on them   231 *Let't* let's

V.i.60 *boiled* boile   72 *Didst* Did   75 *entertained* entertaine   82 *lies* ly   199 *remembrance* remembrances

The Source of "The Tempest"

There is no known source for the plot of *The Tempest*. As far as we know, *The Tempest* and *Love's Labor's Lost* are Shakespeare's two original plots. Attempts have been made to locate the source of *The Tempest* in the German comedy, *Die Schöne Sidea*, by Jakob Ayrer, who died in 1605;[1] in certain scenarios of the Italian *commedia dell' arte*;[2] in two Spanish romances.[3] The differences, however, between these plots and the plot of *The Tempest* seem more significant than the similarities. The things these plots have in common with each other and with the plot of *The Tempest* are folk-tale motifs that have long been the common property of storytellers and playwrights.[4]

If there is no source for *The Tempest*, there are documents that are relevant to it. The names of many of the characters probably derive from Thomas' *History of Italy*

[1] See H. H. Furness' Variorum Edition of *The Tempest*. Philadelphia: Lippincott, 1897, pp. 324–43, which includes a translation of Ayrer's comedy.

[2] See H. D. Gray, "The Sources of *The Tempest*," *Modern Language Notes*, XXXV (1920), 321–30.

[3] Antonio de Eslava's *Noches de Invierno* (1609), Chap. IV. (See Hardin Craig, *Interpretation of Shakespeare*. Columbia, Missouri: Lucas Brothers, 1948, pp. 344–45. And Diego Ortuñez de Calahorra's *Espejo de Príncipes y Caballeros* (1562; English translation, 1578–1601). (See Joseph de Perott, "The Probable Source of the Plot of Shakespeare's *Tempest*," *Publications of the Clark University Library*, I [1903–1905], 209–16.)

[4] See W. W. Newell, "Sources of Shakespeare's *Tempest*," *Journal of American Folk-Lore*, XVI (1905), 234–57.

(1549), and the name "Setebos" derives from Robert Eden's *History of Travaile* (1577), which mentions the "great devill Setebos" worshiped by the Patagonians. Shakespeare paraphrases a passage from John Florio's translation (1603) of Montaigne's essay on the American Indians, "Of the Caniballes" (Caliban's name may derive from "cannibal"); and he paraphrases a speech of the witch, Medea, in Ovid's *Metamorphoses*—using Arthur Golding's translation (1567), which he apparently checked against the Latin original. There is good reason to believe that Shakespeare had in mind, and may even have had on his desk, when he wrote *The Tempest*, certain reports that appeared in 1610 of a tempest and a shipwreck that took place off the Bermudas in 1609. I shall print—in modernized spelling and punctuation, and with some indication of their relevance—extracts from Montaigne, Ovid, and the so-called "Bermuda pamphlets." These last require a word of explanation.

On June 2, 1609, a fleet of nine ships set sail from Plymouth for Virginia, carrying more than five hundred colonists. On July 24, a tempest off the Bermudas separated from the rest of the fleet the flagship, the *Sea-Venture*, which carried the admiral, Sir George Somers, and the new governor of the colony, Sir Thomas Gates. In the course of the next several weeks, the other ships straggled into the port at Jamestown, but the occupants of the *Sea-Venture* were given up for lost. Then, miraculously, almost a year later, on May 23, 1610, the castaways arrived in Jamestown in two small ships they had built for the journey. Their deliverance, when the news of it reached London in September, was regarded as providential. But the beneficent hand of providence emerged even more clearly when the reports of the shipwreck began to appear. For the reports showed the stormy Bermudas, which mariners had shunned as an "Ile of Divels," to be actually an island paradise.

Since Shakespeare was closely connected with the leaders of the Virginia Company (e.g., the Earls of Southampton and Pembroke) that had sponsored the expedition, he would have had good reason to read the reports of the shipwreck that appeared in 1610. The first to appear was *A Discovery of the Barmudas, otherwise called the Ile of Divels,* by Sylvester Jourdain,[5] who was with Somers. A month later there appeared *The True Declaration of the estate of the Colonie in Virginia,* which was the report of the Virginia Company.[6] Most important for our purposes is a long letter by William Strachey, who was also with Somers, which is dated July 15, 1610, but which doubtless came over to London with Gates in September. Strachey's letter was not published until 1625, in *Purchas His Pilgrimes.*[7] But it seems to have circulated in manuscript among the leaders of the Virginia Company, and we may be reasonably sure that Shakespeare read it, since it bears most closely of all the reports on *The Tempest.* It is called *A true repertory of the wracke, and redemption of Sir Thomas Gates Knight; upon, and from the Ilands of the Bermudas: his comming to Virginia, and the estate of that Colonie then, and after.*

William Strachey: from *True Repertory of the Wrack,* 1610.

[Description of the tempest]

A dreadful storm and hideous began to blow from out the northeast, which swelling and roaring as it were by fits, some hours with more violence than others, at length did beat all light from heaven; which like an hell of darkness turned black upon us, so much the more fuller of horror, as in such cases horror and fear use to overrun the troubled and overmastered senses of all, which (taken up with amazement) the ears lay so sensible to the terrible cries and murmurs of the winds, and distraction of our

5 Facsimile edition, ed. J. Q. Adams. New York: Scholars' Facsimiles and Reprints, 1940.
6 Reprinted in *Tracts and Other Papers,* collected by Peter Force. Washington: Force, 1844, Vol. III.
7 Glasgow: MacLehose; New York: Macmillan, 1906, Vol. XIX.

company, as who was most armed and best prepared was
not a little shaken.

For four and twenty hours the storm in a restless tumult
had blown so exceedingly, as we could not apprehend in
our imaginations any possibility of greater violence, yet
did we still find it, not only more terrible, but more constant, fury added to fury, and one storm urging a second
more outrageous than the former; whether it so wrought
upon our fears or indeed met with new forces. Sometimes
strikes [shrieks?] in our ship amongst women and passengers not used to such hurly and discomforts made us look
one upon the other with troubled hearts and panting
bosoms; our clamors drowned in the winds, and the winds
in thunder. Prayers might well be in the heart and lips,
but drowned in the outcries of the officers. Nothing heard
that could give comfort, nothing seen that might encour-
age hope . . . . It could not be said to rain, the waters like
whole rivers did flood in the air. . . . Here the glut of water
(as if throttling the wind erewhile) was no sooner a little
emptied and qualified, but instantly the winds (as having
gotten their mouths now free and at liberty) spake more
loud and grew tumultuous and malignant. . . . There was
not a moment in which the sudden splitting or instant
oversetting of the ship was not expected.

Howbeit this was not all. It pleased God to bring a
greater affliction yet upon us; for in the beginning of the
storm we had received likewise a mighty leak. And the
ship . . . was grown five foot suddenly deep with water
above her ballast, and we almost drowned within whilst
we sat looking when to perish from above. This, imparting
no less terror than danger, ran through the whole ship
with much fright and amazement, startled and turned the
blood, and took down the braves of the most hardy mariner of them all, insomuch as he that before happily felt
not the sorrow of others, now began to sorrow for himself
when he saw such a pond of water so suddenly broken in,
and which he knew could not (without present avoiding)
but instantly sink him. . . .

Once, so huge a sea brake upon the poop and quarter

upon us, as it covered our ship from stern to stem, like a garment or a vast cloud, it filled her brim full for a while within, from the hatches up to the spar deck . . . . with much clamor encouraged and called upon others; who gave her now up, rent in pieces and absolutely lost. ["All lost!" . . . . "We split, we split!" I.i.52,61]

[St. Elmo's fire; Ariel: "I flamed amazement." I.ii.198]

During all this time, the heavens looked so black upon us that it was not possible the elevation of the pole might be observed; nor a star by night, not sunbeam by day was to be seen. Only upon the Thursday night, Sir George Somers, being upon the watch, had an apparition of a little round light, like a faint star, trembling, and streaming along with a sparkling blaze, half the height upon the mainmast, and shooting sometimes from shroud to shroud, tempting to settle as it were upon any of the four shrouds. And for three or four hours together, or rather more, half the night it kept with us; running sometimes along the mainyard to the very end, and then returning. At which, Sir George Somers called divers about him and showed them the same, who observed it with much wonder and carefulness. But upon a sudden, toward the morning watch, they lost the sight of it and knew not what way it made. The superstitious seamen make many constructions of this sea fire, which nevertheless is usual in storms: the same (it may be) which the Grecians were wont in the Mediterranean to call Castor and Pollux, of which, if one only appeared without the other, they took it for an evil sign of great tempest. The Italians, and such, who lie open to the Adriatic and Tyrrhene Sea, call it (a sacred Body) *Corpo sancto;* the Spaniards call it Saint Elmo, and have an authentic and miraculous legend for it. Be it what it will, we laid other foundations of safety or ruin, then in the rising or falling of it, could it have served us now miraculously to have taken our height by, it might have struck amazement, and a reverence in our devotions, according to the due of a miracle. But it did not light us any whit the more to our known way, who ran now (as do hoodwinked men) at all adventures, sometimes north, and northeast, then north and by west, and sometimes half the compass.

[*Providence*]

... Sir George Somers, when no man dreamed of such happiness, had discovered and cried land. ... We were enforced to run her ashore as near the land as we could, which brought us within three-quarters of a mile of shore. ...

We found it to be the dangerous and dreaded island, or rather islands of the Bermuda; whereof let me give your Ladyship a brief description before I proceed to my narration. And that the rather, because they be so terrible to all that ever touched on them, and such tempests, thunders, and other fearful objects are seen and heard about them, that they be called commonly the Devil's Islands, and are feared and avoided of all sea travelers alive above any other place in the world. Yet it pleased our merciful God to make even this hideous and hated place both the place of our safety and means of our deliverance.

And hereby also, I hope to deliver the world from a foul and general error: it being counted of most that they can be no habitation for men, but rather given over to devils and wicked spirits. Whereas indeed we find them now by experience to be as habitable and commodious as most countries of the same climate and situation; insomuch as if the entrance into them were as easy as the place itself is contenting, it had long ere this been inhabited as well as other islands. Thus shall we make it appear that Truth is the daughter of Time, and that men ought not to deny everything which is not subject to their own sense. [Gonzalo's speech on travelers' tales, III.iii.43–49.]

[*Caliban: "I'll not show him/ Where the quick freshes are." III.ii.70–71*]

Sure it is that there are no rivers nor running springs

of fresh water to be found upon any of them. When we came first, we digged and found certain gushings and soft bubblings which, being either in bottoms or on the side of hanging ground, were only fed with rain water which nevertheless soon sinketh into the earth and vanisheth away, or emptieth itself out of sight into the sea without any channel above or upon the superficies of the earth. For according as their rains fell, we had wells and pits (which we digged) either half full, or absolute exhausted and dry, howbeit some low bottoms (which the continual descent from the hills filled full, and in those flats could have no passage away) we found to continue as fishing ponds [Caliban: "dams . . . for fish" (?). II.ii.188], or standing pools, continually summer and winter full of fresh water.

[*Caliban: "I'll get thee/ Young scamels from the rock"* (?). *II.ii.179–80*]

A kind of webfooted fowl there is, of the bigness of an English green plover, or seamew, which all the summer we saw not, and in the darkest nights of November and December (for in the night they only feed) they would come forth, but not fly far from home, and hovering in the air, and over the sea, made a strange hollow and harsh howling . . . which birds with a light bough in a dark night (as in our lowbelling [similar to "a-batfowling," II.i.189]) we caught. I have been at the taking of three hundred in an hour, and we might have laden our boats. Our men found a pretty way to take them, which was by standing on the rocks or sands by the seaside, and hollowing, laughing, and making the strangest outcry that possibly they could. With the noise whereof the birds would come flocking to that place, and settle upon the very arms and head of him that so cried, and still creep nearer and nearer, answering the noise themselves; by which our men would weigh them with their hand, and which weighed heaviest they took for the best and let the others alone, and so our men would take twenty dozen in two hours of the chiefest of them; and they were a good and well-relished fowl, fat and full as a partridge . . . which birds

for their blindness (for they see weakly in the day) and
for their cry and hooting, we called the sea owl.

[*Mutinies*]

In these dangers and devilish disquiets (whilst the al-
mighty God wrought for us and sent us, miraculously
delivered from the calamities of the sea, all blessings upon
the shore to content and bind us to gratefulness) thus
enraged amongst ourselves, to the destruction each of
other, into what a mischief and misery had we been given
up, had we not had a governor with his authority to have
suppressed the same? Yet was there a worse practice,
faction, and conjuration afoot, deadly and bloody, in
which the life of our governor with many others were
threatened and could not but miscarry in his fall. But such
is ever the will of God (who in the execution of His judg-
ments, breaketh the firebrands upon the head of him who
first kindleth them) there were, who conceived that our
governor indeed neither durst, nor had authority to put in
execution, or pass the act of justice upon anyone, how
treacherous or impious so ever. . . . They persevered therefore not only to draw unto them such a number and associates as they could work in to the abandoning of our
governor and to the inhabiting of this island. They had
now purposed to have made a surprise of the store-
house. . . .

But as all giddy and lawless attempts have always
something of imperfection, and that as well by the property of the action, which holdeth of disobedience and re-
bellion (both full of fear) as through the ignorance of
the devisers themselves; so in this (besides those defects)
there were some of the association, who not strong enough
fortified in their own conceits, brake from the plot itself,
and (before the time was ripe for the execution thereof)
discovered the whole order, and every agent and actor
thereof, who nevertheless were not suddenly apprehended,
by reason the confederates were divided and separated in
place, some with us, and the chief with Sir George
Somers.

[*Caliban, "on whose nature/ Nurture can never stick."*
IV.i.188–89]

[After the castaways have arrived in Virginia:] Certain
Indians (watching the occasion) seized the poor fellow
[one of Sir Thomas Gates's men] and led him up into the
woods and sacrificed him. It did not a little trouble the
lieutenant governor, who since his first landing in the
country (how justly soever provoked) would not by any
means be wrought to a violent proceeding against them
for all the practices of villainy with which they daily endangered our men, thinking it possible by a more tractable
course to win them to a better condition. But now being
startled by this, he well perceived how little a fair and
noble entreaty works upon a barbarous disposition, and
therefore in some measure purposed to be revenged.

[Purchas has the following marginal comment: "Can a
leopard change his spots? Can a savage remaining savage
be civil? Were not we ourselves made and not born civil
in our progenitors' days? And were not Caesar's Britons
as brutish as Virginians? The Roman swords were best
teachers of civility to this and other countries near us."]

Sylvester Jourdain: from *A Discovery of the Barmudas*, 1610.

[*Ariel: "Safely in harbor/ Is the King's ship; in the deep
nook." I.ii.226–27*]

. . . All our men, being utterly spent, tired, and dis-
abled for longer labor, were even resolved, without any
hope of their lives, to shut up the hatches and to have committed themselves to the mercy of the sea (which is said
to be merciless) or rather to the mercy of their mighty
God and redeemer. . . . So that some of them, having some
good and comfortable waters in the ship, fetched them
and drunk the one to the other, taking their last leave one
of the other, until their more joyful and happy meeting in

a more blessed world; when it pleased God out of his most gracious and merciful providence, so to direct and guide our ship (being left to the mercy of the sea) for her most advantage; that Sir George Somers . . . most wishedly happily descried land; whereupon he most comfortably encouraged the company to follow their pumping, and by no means to cease bailing out of the water. . . . Through which weak means it pleased God to work so strongly as the water was stayed for that little time (which, as we all much feared, was the last period of our breathing) and the ship kept from present sinking, when it pleased God to send her within half an English mile of that land that Sir George Somers had not long before descried—which were the islands of the Barmudas. And there neither did our ship sink, but more fortunately in so great a misfortune fell in between two rocks, where she was fast lodged and locked for further budging.

[An island paradise]

But our delivery was not more strange in falling so opportunely and happily upon the land, as our feeding and preservation was beyond our hopes and all men's expectations most admirable. For the islands of the Barmudas, as every man knoweth that hath heard or read of them, were never inhabited by any Christian or heathen people, but ever esteemed and reputed a most prodigious and enchanted place affording nothing but gusts, storms, and foul weather; which made every navigator and mariner to avoid them, as Scylla and Charybdis, or as they would shun the Devil himself; and no man was ever heard to make for the place, but as against their wills, they have by storms and dangerousness of the rocks, lying seven leagues into the sea, suffered shipwrack. Yet did we find there the air so temperate and the country so abundantly fruitful of all fit necessaries for the sustenation and preservation of man's life, that most in a manner of all our provisions of bread, beer, and victual being quite spoiled in lying long drowned in salt water, notwithstanding we were there for the space of nine months (few days over or under) not only well refreshed, comforted, and with good satiety contented but, out of the abundance thereof, provided us some reasonable quantity and proportion of provision to carry us for Virginia and to maintain ourselves and that company we found there, to the great relief of them, as it fell out in their so great extremities . . . until it pleased God . . . that their store was better supplied. And greater and better provisions we might have had, if we had had better means for the storing and transportation thereof. Wherefore my opinion sincerely of this island is, that whereas it hath been and is full accounted the most dangerous, unfortunate, and most forlorn place of the world, it is in truth the richest, healthfulest, and pleasing land (the quantity and bigness thereof considered) and merely natural, as ever man set foot upon.

Council of Virginia: from *The True Declaration of the Estate of the Colony in Virginia*, 1610.

[*Providence*]

. . . God that heard Jonas crying out of the belly of hell, He pitied the distresses of His servants. For behold, in the last period of necessity Sir George Somers descried land, which was by so much the more joyful by how much their danger was despairful. The islands on which they fell were the *Bermudos*, a place hardly accessible through the environing rocks and dangers. Notwithstanding, they were forced to run their ship on shore, which through God's providence fell betwixt two rocks, that caused her to stand firm and not immediately to be broken. . . .

Again, as in the great famine of Israel, God commanded Elias to fly to the brook Cedron, and there fed him by ravens; so God provided for our disconsolate people in the midst of the sea by fowls, but with an admirable difference. Unto Elias the ravens brought meat; unto our men the fowls brought themselves for meat. For when they whistled or made any strange noise, the fowls would come and sit on their shoulders; they would suffer themselves to be taken and weighed by our men, who would make choice of the fattest and fairest, and let fly the lean and lightest. . . .

Consider all these things together. At the instant of need, they descried land; half an hour more, had buried their memorial in the sea. If they had fell by night, what expectation of light from an uninhabited desert? They fell betwixt a labyrinth of rocks, which they conceive are moldered into the sea by thunder and lightning. This was not Ariadne's thread, but the direct line of God's providence. If it had not been so near land, their company or provision had perished by water; if they had not found hogs and fowls and fish, they had perished by famine; if there had not been fuel, they had perished by want of fire; if there had not been timber, they could not have transported themselves to Virginia, but must have been forgotten forever. *Nimium timet qui Deo non credit;* he is too impiously fearful that will not trust in God so powerful.

What is there in all this tragical comedy that should discourage us with impossibility of the enterprise? When of all the fleet, one only ship by a secret leak was endangered, and yet in the gulf of despair was so graciously preserved.

[*Order and disorder*]

[Disorder in Virginia:] The ground of all those miseries was the permissive providence of God, who, in the forementioned violent storm, separated the head from the body, all the vital powers of regiment being exiled with Sir Thomas Gates in those infortunate (yet fortunate) islands. The broken remainder of those supplies made a greater shipwrack in the continent of Virginia, by the tempest of dissension: every man, overvaluing his own worth, would be a commander; every man, underprizing another's value, denied to be commanded.

Michel de Montaigne: from *Of the Cannibals*, translated by John Florio, 1603.

[Nature vs. art: Gonzalo's ideal commonwealth,
II.i.148–73]

. . . I find (as far as I have been informed) there is
nothing in that nation [the American Indians], that is
either barbarous or savage, unless men call that barbarism which is not common to them. As indeed, we
have no other aim of truth and reason than the example
and idea of the opinions and customs of the country
we live in. There is ever perfect religion, perfect policy,
perfect and complete use of all things. They are even
savage, as we call those fruits wild which nature of herself and of her ordinary progress hath produced; whereas
indeed, they are those which ourselves have altered by
our artificial devices, and diverted from their common
order, we should rather term savage. In those are the true
and most profitable virtues and natural properties most
lively and vigorous, which in these we have bastardized,
applying them to the pleasure of our corrupted taste.
And if notwithstanding, in divers fruits of those countries
that were never tilled, we shall find that, in respect of
ours, they are most excellent and as delicate unto our
taste, there is no reason art should gain the point of
honor of our great and puissant mother Nature. We have
so much by our inventions surcharged the beauties and
riches of her works that we have altogether overchoked
her; yet wherever her purity shineth, she makes our vain
and frivolous enterprises wonderfully ashamed. . . .
    All our endeavor or wit cannot so much as reach to
represent the nest of the least birdlet, its contexture,
beauty, profit and use, no nor the web of a seely [i.e.,
trivial] spider. "All things," saith Plato, "are produced
either by nature, by fortune, or by art. The greatest
and fairest by one or other of the two first, the least

and imperfect by the last." Those nations seem therefore so barbarous unto me, because they have received very little fashion from human wit and are yet near their original naturality. The laws of nature do yet command them, which are but little bastardized by ours, and that with such purity, as I am sometimes grieved the knowledge of it came no sooner to light, at what time there were men that better than we could have judged of it. I am sorry Lycurgus and Plato had it not; for me seemeth that what in those nations we see by experience, doth not only exceed all the pictures wherewith licentious Poesy hath proudly embellished the golden age, and all her quaint inventions to fain a happy condition of man, but also the conception and desire of Philosophy. They could not imagine a genuity so pure and simple as we see it by experience; nor ever believe our society might be maintained with so little art and humane combination. It is a nation, would I answer Plato, that hath no kind of traffic, no knowledge of letters, no intelligence of numbers, no name of magistrate, nor of politic superiority; no use of service, of riches, or of poverty; no contracts, no successions, no partitions, no occupation but idle; no respect of kindred but common, no apparel but natural, no manuring of lands, no use of wine, corn, or metal. The very words that import lying, falsehood, treason, dissimulations, covetousness, envy, detraction, and pardon, were never heard of amongst them. How dissonant would he find his imaginary commonwealth from this perfection? . . .

Furthermore, they live in a country of so exceeding pleasant and temperate situation that, as my testimonies have told me, it is very rare to see a sick body amongst them; and they have further assured me they never saw any man there either shaking with the palsy, toothless, with eyes dropping, or crooked and stooping through age.

[On cannibalism itself:] I am not sorry we note the barbarous horror of such an action, but grieved that, prying so narrowly into their faults, we are so blinded in ours. I think there is more barbarism in eating men alive than to feed upon them being dead; to mangle by tortures and torments a body full of lively sense, to roast him in pieces, to make dogs and swine to gnaw and tear him in mammocks (as we have not only read but seen very lately, yea and in our own memory, not amongst ancient enemies but our neighbors and fellow citizens; and which is worse, under pretense of piety and religion) than to roast and eat him after he is dead.

Ovid: from *Metamorphoses*, Medea's speech, translated by Arthur Golding, 1567.

[*Magic and metamorphosis: Prospero's farewell to his art V.i.33–57*]

Ye airs and winds, ye elves of hills, of brooks, of woods alone,
Of standing lakes, and of the night approach ye everychone.
Through help of whom (the crooked banks much wond'ring at the thing)
I have compelled streams to run clean backward to their spring.
By charms I make the calm seas rough, and make the rough seas plain
And cover all the sky with clouds, and chase them thence again.
By charms I raise and lay the winds, and burst the viper's jaw,
And from the bowels of the earth both stones and trees do draw.
Whole woods and forests I remove; I make the mountains shake,
And even the earth itself to groan and fearfully to quake.
I call up dead men from their graves; and thee O lightsome Moon
I darken oft, though beaten brass abate thy peril soon.
Our sorcery dims the morning fair, and darks the sun at noon.

Commentaries

SAMUEL TAYLOR COLERIDGE

from *The Lectures of 1811–1812, Lecture IX*

Among the ideal plays, I will take *The Tempest*, by way of example. Various others might be mentioned, but it is impossible to go through every drama, and what I remark on *The Tempest* will apply to all Shakespeare's productions of the same class.

In this play Shakespeare has especially appealed to the imagination, and he has constructed a plot well adapted to the purpose. According to his scheme, he did not appeal to any sensuous impression (the word "sensuous" is authorized by Milton) of time and place, but to the imagination, and it is to be borne in mind that of old, and as regards mere scenery, his works may be said to have been recited rather than acted— that is to say, description and narration supplied the place of visual exhibition: the audience was told to fancy

From *Shakespearean Criticism* by Samuel Taylor Coleridge. 2nd ed., ed. Thomas Middleton Raysor. 2 vols. New York: E. P. Dutton and Company, Inc., 1960; London: J. M. Dent & Sons, Ltd., 1961. The exact text of Coleridge's lecture does not exist; what is given here is the transcript of a shorthand report taken by an auditor, J. P. Collier.

that they saw what they only heard described; the painting was not in colors, but in words.

This is particularly to be noted in the first scene—a storm and its confusion on board the king's ship. The highest and the lowest characters are brought together, and with what excellence! Much of the genius of Shakespeare is displayed in these happy combinations—the highest and the lowest, the gayest and the saddest; he is not droll in one scene and melancholy in another, but often both the one and the other in the same scene. Laughter is made to swell the tear of sorrow, and to throw, as it were, a poetic light upon it, while the tear mingles tenderness with the laughter. Shakespeare has evinced the power, which above all other men he possessed, that of introducing the profoundest sentiments of wisdom, where they would be least expected, yet where they are most truly natural. One admirable secret of his art is that separate speeches frequently do not appear to have been occasioned by those which preceded, and which are consequent upon each other, but to have arisen out of the peculiar character of the speaker.

Before I go further, I may take the opportunity of explaining what is meant by mechanic and organic regularity. In the former the copy must appear as if it had come out of the same mold with the original; in the latter there is a law which all the parts obey, conforming themselves to the outward symbols and manifestations of the essential principle. If we look to the growth of trees, for instance, we shall observe that trees of the same kind vary considerably, according to the circumstances of soil, air, or position; yet we are able to decide at once whether they are oaks, elms, or poplars.

So with Shakespeare's characters: he shows us the life and principle of each being with organic regularity. The Boatswain, in the first scene of *The Tempest*, when the bonds of reverence are thrown off as a sense of danger impresses all, gives a loose to his feelings, and thus pours forth his vulgar mind to the old Counselor:

"Hence! What care these roarers for the name of King? To cabin: silence! trouble us not."

Gonzalo replies—"Good; yet remember whom thou hast aboard." To which the Boatswain answers—"None that I more love than myself. You are a counselor: if you can command these elements to silence and work the peace of the present, we will not hand a rope more; use your authority: if you cannot, give thanks that you have lived so long, and make yourself ready in your cabin for the mischance of the hour, if it so hap.— Cheerly, good hearts!—Out of our way, I say."

An ordinary dramatist would, after this speech, have represented Gonzalo as moralizing, or saying something connected with the Boatswain's language; for ordinary dramatists are not men of genius: they combine their ideas by association, or by logical affinity; but the vital writer, who makes men on the stage what they are in nature, in a moment transports himself into the very being of each personage, and, instead of cutting out artificial puppets, he brings before us the men themselves. Therefore, Gonzalo soliloquizes,—"I have great comfort from this fellow: methinks, he hath no drowning mark upon him; his complexion is perfect gallows. Stand fast, good fate, to his hanging! make the rope of his destiny our cable, for our own doth little advantage. If he be not born to be hanged, our case is miserable."

In this part of the scene we see the true sailor with his contempt of danger, and the old counselor with his high feeling, who, instead of condescending to notice the words just addressed to him, turns off, meditating with himself and drawing some comfort to his own mind by trifling with the ill expression of the Boatswain's face, founding upon it a hope of safety.

Shakespeare had predetermined to make the plot of this play such as to involve a certain number of low characters, and at the beginning he pitched the note of the whole. The first scene was meant as a lively commencement of the story; the reader is prepared for something that is to be developed, and in the next scene he brings forward Prospero and Miranda. How is this done? By giving to his favorite character, Miranda, a sentence which at once expresses the violence and fury of the storm, such as it might appear to a witness on the land, and at the same time displays the tenderness of her feelings—the exquisite feelings of a female brought up in a desert, but with all the advantages of education, all that could be communicated by a wise and affectionate father. She possesses all the delicacy of innocence, yet with all the powers of her mind unweakened by the combats of life. Miranda exclaims:

> O! I have suffered
> With those that I saw suffer: a brave vessel,
> Who had, no doubt, some noble creatures in her,
> Dash'd all to pieces.

The doubt here intimated could have occurred to no mind but to that of Miranda, who had been bred up in the island with her father and a monster only: she did not know, as others do, what sort of creatures were in a ship; others never would have introduced it as a conjecture. This shows that while Shakespeare is displaying his vast excellence, he never fails to insert some touch or other which is not merely characteristic of the particular person, but combines two things—the person, and the circumstances acting upon the person. She proceeds:

> O! the cry did knock
> Against my very heart. Poor souls! they perish'd.
> Had I been any god of power, I would
> Have sunk the sea within the earth, or e'er
> It should the good ship so have swallow'd, and
> The fraughting souls within her.

She still dwells upon that which was most wanting to the completeness of her nature—these fellow creatures from whom she appeared banished, with only one relict to keep them alive, not in her memory, but in her imagination.

Another proof of excellent judgment in the poet, for I am now principally adverting to that point, is to be

found in the preparation of the reader for what is to
follow. Prospero is introduced, first in his magic robe,
which, with the assistance of his daughter, he lays aside,
and we then know him to be a being possessed of supernatural powers. He then instructs Miranda in the story
of their arrival in the island, and this is conducted in
such a manner that the reader never conjectures the
technical use the poet has made of the relation, by in-
forming the auditor of what it is necessary for him to
know.

The next step is the warning by Prospero that he
means, for particular purposes, to lull his daughter to
sleep; and here he exhibits the earliest and mildest proof
of magical power. In ordinary and vulgar plays we should
have had some person brought upon the stage, whom
nobody knows or cares anything about, to let the audience into the secret. Prospero having cast a sleep upon
his daughter, by that sleep stops the narrative at the
very moment when it was necessary to break it off, in
order to excite curiosity and yet to give the memory and
understanding sufficient to carry on the progress of the
history uninterruptedly.

Here I cannot help noticing a fine touch of Shakespeare's knowledge of human nature, and generally of
the great laws of the human mind: I mean Miranda's
infant remembrance. Prospero asks her—

> Canst thou remember
> A time before we came unto this cell?
> I do not think thou canst, for then thou wast not
> Out three years old.

Miranda answers,

> Certainly, sir, I can.

Prospero inquires,

> By what? by any other house or person?
> Of any thing the image tell me, that
> Hath kept with thy remembrance.

To which Miranda returns,

> 'Tis far off;
> And rather like a dream than an assurance
> That my remembrance warrants. Had I not
> Four or five women once, that tended me?

This is exquisite! In general, our remembrances of early life arise from vivid colors, especially if we have seen them in motion: for instance, persons when grown up will remember a bright green door, seen when they were quite young; but Miranda, who was somewhat older, recollected four or five women who tended her. She might know men from her father, and her remembrance of the past might be worn out by the present object, but women she only knew by herself, by the contemplation of her own figure in the fountain, and she recalled to her mind what had been. It was not that she had seen such and such grandees, or such and such peeresses, but she remembered to have seen something like the reflection of herself: it was not herself, and it brought back to her mind what she had seen most like herself.

In my opinion the picturesque power displayed by Shakespeare, of all the poets that ever lived, is only equaled, if equaled, by Milton and Dante. The presence of genius is not shown in elaborating a picture: we have had many specimens of this sort of work in modern poems, where all is so dutchified, if I may use the word, by the most minute touches, that the reader naturally asks why words, and not painting, are used? I know a young lady of much taste, who observed that in reading recent versified accounts of voyages and travels, she, by a sort of instinct, cast her eyes on the opposite page, for colored prints of what was so patiently and punctually described.

The power of poetry is, by a single word perhaps, to instill that energy into the mind which compels the imagination to produce the picture. Prospero tells Miranda,

One midnight,
Fated to the purpose, did Antonio open
The gates of Milan; and i' the dead of darkness,
The ministers for the purpose hurried thence
Me, and thy crying self.

Here, by introducing a single happy epithet, "crying," in the last line, a complete picture is presented to the mind, and in the production of such pictures the power of genius consists.

In reference to preparation, it will be observed that the storm, and all that precedes the tale, as well as the tale itself, serve to develop completely the main character of the drama, as well as the design of Prospero. The manner in which the heroine is charmed asleep fits us for what follows, goes beyond our ordinary belief, and gradually leads us to the appearance and disclosure of a being of the most fanciful and delicate texture, like Prospero, preternaturally gifted.

In this way the entrance of Ariel, if not absolutely forethought by the reader, was foreshown by the writer: in addition, we may remark, that the moral feeling called forth by the sweet words of Miranda,

Alack, what trouble
Was I then to you!

in which she considered only the sufferings and sorrows of her father, puts the reader in a frame of mind to exert his imagination in favor of an object so innocent and interesting. The poet makes him wish that, if supernatural agency were to be employed, it should be used for a being so young and lovely. "The wish is father to the thought," and Ariel is introduced. Here what is called poetic faith is required and created, and our common notions of philosophy give way before it: this feeling may be said to be much stronger than historic faith, since for the exercise of poetic faith the mind is previously prepared. I make this remark, though somewhat digressive, in order to lead to a future subject of these lectures—the poems of Milton. When adverting to those, I shall have to explain farther the distinction between the two.

Many scriptural poems have been written with so much of Scripture in them that what is not Scripture appears to be not true, and like mingling lies with the most sacred revelations. Now Milton, on the other hand, has taken for his subject that one point of Scripture of which we have the mere fact recorded, and upon this he has most judiciously constructed his whole fable. So of Shakespeare's *King Lear:* we have little historic evidence to guide or confine us, and the few facts handed down to us, and admirably employed by the poet, are sufficient, while we read, to put an end to all doubt as to the credibility of the story. It is idle to say that this or that incident is improbable, because history, as far as it goes, tells us that the fact was so and so. Four or five lines in the Bible include the whole that is said of Milton's story, and the Poet has called up that poetic faith, that conviction of the mind, which is necessary to make that seem true which otherwise might have been deemed almost fabulous.

But to return to *The Tempest*, and to the wondrous creation of Ariel. If a doubt could ever be entertained whether Shakespeare was a great poet, acting upon laws arising out of his own nature and not without law, as has sometimes been idly asserted, that doubt must be removed by the character of Ariel. The very first words uttered by this being introduce the spirit, not as an angel, above man; not a gnome, or a fiend, below man; but while the poet gives him the faculties and the advantages of reason, he divests him of all mortal character, not positively, it is true, but negatively. In air he lives, from air he derives his being, in air he acts; and all his colors and properties seem to have been obtained from the rainbow and the skies. There is nothing about Ariel that cannot be conceived to exist either at sunrise or at sunset: hence all that belongs to Ariel belongs to the delight the mind is capable of receiving from the most lovely external appearances. His answers to Prospero are directly to the question and nothing beyond; or where he expatiates, which is not unfrequently, it is to himself and upon his own delights, or upon the unnatural situation in which he is placed, though under a kindly power and to good ends.

Shakespeare has properly made Ariel's very first speech characteristic of him. After he has described the manner in which he had raised the storm and produced its harmless consequences, we find that Ariel is discontented—that he has been freed, it is true, from a cruel confinement, but still that he is bound to obey Prospero and to execute any commands imposed upon him. We feel that such a state of bondage is almost unnatural to him, yet we see that it is delightful for him to be so employed. It is as if we were to command one of the winds in a different direction to that which nature dictates, or one of the waves, now rising and now sinking, to recede before it bursts upon the shore: such is the feeling we experience, when we learn that a being like Ariel is commanded to fulfill any mortal behest.

When, however, Shakespeare contrasts the treatment of Ariel by Prospero with that of Sycorax, we are sensible that the liberated spirit ought to be grateful, and Ariel does feel and acknowledge the obligation; he immediately assumes the airy being, with a mind so elastically correspondent that when once a feeling has passed from it, not a trace is left behind.

Is there anything in nature from which Shakespeare caught the idea of this delicate and delightful being, with such childlike simplicity, yet with such preternatural powers? He is neither born of heaven, nor of earth; but, as it were, between both, like a May blossom kept suspended in air by the fanning breeze, which prevents it from falling to the ground, and only finally, and by compulsion, touching earth. This reluctance of the sylph to be under the command even of Prospero is kept up through the whole play, and in the exercise of his admirable judgment Shakespeare has availed himself of it in order to give Ariel an interest in the event, looking forward to that moment when he was to gain his last and only reward—simple and eternal liberty.

Another instance of admirable judgment and excellent preparation is to be found in the creature contrasted with Ariel—Caliban, who is described in such a manner by Prospero as to lead us to expect the appearance of a foul, unnatural monster. He is not seen at once: his voice is heard; this is the preparation; he was too offensive to be seen first in all his deformity, and in nature we do not receive so much disgust from sound as from sight. After we have heard Caliban's voice he does not enter until Ariel has entered like a water nymph. All the strength of contrast is thus acquired without any of the shock of abruptness, or of that unpleasant sensation, which we experience when the object presented is in any way hateful to our vision.

The character of Caliban is wonderfully conceived: he is a sort of creature of the earth, as Ariel is a sort of creature of the air. He partakes of the qualities of the brute, but is distinguished from brutes in two ways: by having mere understanding without moral reason; and by not possessing the instincts which pertain to absolute animals. Still, Caliban is in some respects a noble being: the poet has raised him far above contempt: he is a man in the sense of the imagination: all the images he uses are drawn from nature and are highly poetical; they fit in with the images of Ariel. Caliban gives us images from the earth, Ariel images from the air. Caliban talks of the difficulty of finding fresh water, of the situation of morasses, and of other circumstances which even brute instinct, without reason, could comprehend. No mean figure is employed, no mean passion displayed, beyond animal passion and repugnance to command.

The manner in which the lovers are introduced is equally wonderful, and it is the last point I shall now mention in reference to this, almost miraculous, drama. The same judgment is observable in every scene, still preparing, still inviting, and still gratifying, like a finished piece of music. I have omitted to notice one thing, and

you must give me leave to advert to it before I proceed:
I mean the conspiracy against the life of Alonzo. I want
to show you how well the poet prepares the feelings of
the reader for this plot, which was to execute the most
detestable of all crimes, and which, in another play,
Shakespeare has called "the murder of sleep."

Antonio and Sebastian at first had no such intention:
it was suggested by the magical sleep cast on Alonzo and
Gonzalo; but they are previously introduced scoffing and
scorning at what was said by others, without regard to
age or situation—without any sense of admiration for
the excellent truths they heard delivered, but giving themselves up entirely to the malignant and unsocial feeling
which induced them to listen to everything that was
said, not for the sake of profiting by the learning and
experience of others, but of hearing something that might
gratify vanity and self-love, by making them believe that
the person speaking was inferior to themselves.

This, let me remark, is one of the grand characteristics
of a villain; and it would not be so much a presentiment
as an anticipation of hell for men to suppose that all
mankind were as wicked as themselves, or might be so,
if they were not too great fools. Pope, you are perhaps
aware, objected to this conspiracy; but in my mind, if
it could be omitted, the play would lose a charm which
nothing could supply.

Many, indeed innumerable, beautiful passages might
be quoted from this play, independently of the astonishing scheme of its construction. Everybody will call to
mind the grandeur of the language of Prospero in that
divine speech, where he takes leave of his magic art;
and were I to indulge myself by repetitions of the kind,
I should descend from the character of a lecturer to that
of a mere reciter. Before I terminate, I may particularly
recall one short passage which has fallen under the very
severe, but inconsiderate, censure of Pope and Arbuth-
not, who pronounce it a piece of the grossest bombast.
Prospero thus addresses his daughter, directing her attention to Ferdinand:

>   The fringed curtains of thine eye advance,
>   And say what thou seest yond.

Taking these words as a periphrase of—"Look what is coming yonder," it certainly may to some appear to border on the ridiculous and to fall under the rule I formerly laid down—that whatever, without injury, can be translated into a foreign language in simple terms, ought to be in simple terms in the original language; but it is to be borne in mind that different modes of expression frequently arise from difference of situation and education: a blackguard would use very different words, to express the same thing, to those a gentleman would employ, yet both would be natural and proper; difference of feeling gives rise to difference of language: a gentleman speaks in polished terms, with due regard to his own rank and position, while a blackguard, a person little better than half a brute, speaks like half a brute, showing no respect for himself nor for others.

But I am content to try the lines I have just quoted by the introduction to them; and then, I think, you will admit, that nothing could be more fit and appropriate than such language. How does Prospero introduce them? He has just told Miranda a wonderful story, which deeply affected her and filled her with surprise and astonishment, and for his own purposes he afterwards lulls her to sleep. When she awakes, Shakespeare has made her wholly inattentive to the present, but wrapped up in the past. An actress who understands the character of Miranda would have her eyes cast down and her eyelids almost covering them, while she was, as it were, living in her dream. At this moment Prospero sees Ferdinand and wishes to point him out to his daughter, not only with great, but with scenic solemnity, he standing before her and before the spectator in the dignified character of a great magician. Something was to appear to Miranda on the sudden, and as unexpectedly as if the hero of a drama were to be on the stage at the instant when the curtain is elevated. It is under such circumstances that

Prospero says, in a tone calculated at once to arouse his daughter's attention,

> The fringed curtains of thine eye advance,
> And say what thou seest yond.

Turning from the sight of Ferdinand to his thoughtful daughter, his attention was first struck by the downcast appearance of her eyes and eyelids; and, in my humble opinion, the solemnity of the phraseology assigned to Prospero is completely in character, recollecting his preternatural capacity, in which the most familiar objects in nature present themselves in a mysterious point of view. It is much easier to find fault with a writer by reference to former notions and experience than to sit down and read him, recollecting his purpose, connecting one feeling with another, and judging of his words and phrases in proportion as they convey the sentiments of the persons represented.

Of Miranda we may say that she possesses in herself all the ideal beauties that could be imagined by the greatest poet of any age or country; but it is not my purpose now so much to point out the high poetic powers of Shakespeare as to illustrate his exquisite judgment, and it is solely with this design that I have noticed a passage with which, it seems to me, some critics, and those among the best, have been unreasonably dissatisfied. If Shakespeare be the wonder of the ignorant, he is, and ought to be, much more the wonder of the learned: not only from profundity of thought, but from his astonishing and intuitive knowledge of what man must be at all times and under all circumstances, he is rather to be looked upon as a prophet than as a poet. Yet, with all these unbounded powers, with all this might and majesty of genius, he makes us feel as if he were unconscious of himself and of his high destiny, disguising the half god in the simplicity of a child.

E. M. W. TILLYARD

The Tragic Pattern: "The Tempest"

It is a common notion that *Cymbeline* and *The Winter's Tale* are experiments leading to the final success of *The Tempest*. I think it quite untrue of *The Winter's Tale*, which, in some ways though not in others, deals with the tragic pattern more adequately than the later play. Certainly it deals with the destructive portion more directly and fully. On the other hand, *The Tempest*, by keeping this destructive portion largely in the background and dealing mainly with regeneration, avoids the juxtaposition of the two themes, which some people (of whom I am not one) find awkward in *The Winter's Tale*. The simple truth is that if you cram a trilogy into a single play something has to be sacrificed. Shakespeare chose to make a different sacrifice in each of his two successful renderings of the complete tragic pattern: unity in *The Winter's Tale*, present rendering of the destructive part of the tragic pattern in *The Tempest*.

Many readers, drugged by the heavy enchantments of Prospero's island, may demur at my admitting the tragic

From *Shakespeare's Last Plays* by E. M. W. Tillyard. London: Chatto and Windus, Ltd., 1938. Reprinted by permission of Chatto and Windus, Ltd., and Barnes and Noble, Inc.

element to the play at all. I can cite in support one of the latest studies of the play, Dover Wilson's[1] (although I differ somewhat in the way I think the tragic element is worked out). Of the storm scene he writes:

> It is as if Shakespeare had packed his whole tragic vision of life into one brief scene before bestowing his new vision upon us.

But one has only to look at the total plot to see that in its main lines it closely follows those of *Cymbeline* and *The Winter's Tale*, and that tragedy is an organic part of it. Prospero, when one first hears of him, was the ruler of an independent state and beloved of his subjects. But all is not well, because the King of Naples is his enemy. Like Basilius in Sidney's *Arcadia*, he commits the error of not attending carefully enough to affairs of state. The reason for this error, his Aristotelian ἁμαρτία, is his love of study. He hands over the government to his brother Antonio, who proceeds to call in the King of Naples to turn Prospero out of his kingdom. Fearing the people, Antonio refrains from murdering Prospero and his infant daughter, but sets them adrift in a boat. Now, except for this last item, the plot is entirely typical of Elizabethan revenge tragedy. Allow Prospero to be put to death, give him a son instead of a daughter to live and to avenge him, and your tragic plot is complete. Such are the affinities of the actual plot of *The Tempest*. And in the abstract it is more typically tragic in the fashion of its age than *The Winter's Tale*, with its debt to the Greek romances.

In handling the theme of regeneration, Shakespeare in one way alters his method. Although a royal person had previously been the protagonist, it had been only in name. Cymbeline had indeed resembled Prospero in having his enemies at his mercy and in forgiving them, but he owed his power not to himself, but to fortune and

---

[1] *The Meaning of the Tempest*, the Robert Spence Watson Memorial Lecture for 1936, delivered before the Literary and Philosophical Society of Newcastle-upon-Tyne, on October 5th, 1936.

the efforts of others. As for Leontes, he has little to do
with his own regeneration; for it would be perverse to
make too much of his generosity in sheltering Florizel
and Perdita from the anger of Polixenes. But Prospero
is the agent of his own regeneration, the parent and tutor
of Miranda; and through her and through his own works
he changes the minds of his enemies. It was by this cen-
tering of motives in Prospero as well as by subordinating
the theme of destruction that Shakespeare gave *The Tempest* its unified structure.

In executing his work, Shakespeare chose a method
new to himself but repeated by Milton in *Samson Agonis-
tes*. He began his action at a point in the story so late
that the story was virtually over; and he included the
total story either by narrating the past or by re-enacting
samples of it: a complete reaction from the method of
frontal attack used in *The Winter's Tale*.

For the re-enactment of tragedy it is possible to think
with Dover Wilson that the storm scene does this. But
it does nothing to re-enact the specific tragic plot in the
play, the fall of Prospero; and one of its aims is to sketch
(as it does with incomparable swiftness) the characters
of the ship's company. The true re-enactment is in the
long first scene of the second act where Antonio, in per-
suading Sebastian to murder Alonso, personates his own
earlier action in plotting against Prospero, thus drawing
it out of the past and placing it before us in the present.
This long scene, showing the shipwrecked king and
courtiers and the conspiracy, has not had sufficient praise
nor sufficient attention. Antonio's transformation from
the cynical and lazy badgerer of Gonzalo's loquacity to
the brilliantly swift and unscrupulous man of action is
a thrilling affair. Just so Iago awakes from his churlish
"honesty" to his brilliant machinations. Antonio is indeed
one of Shakespeare's major villains:

Antonio.   Will you grant with me
　　That Ferdinand is drown'd?

Sebastian.   He's gone.

Antonio.   Then, tell me,
  Who's the next heir to Naples?

Sebastian.   Claribel.

Antonio. She that is Queen of Tunis; she that dwells
  Ten leagues beyond man's life; she that from Naples
  Can have no note, unless the sun were post—
  The man i' the moon's too slow—till newborn chins
  Be rough and razorable; she that from whom
  We all were sea-swallow'd, though some cast again,
  And by that destiny, to perform an act
  Whereof what's past is prologue, what to come,
  In yours and my discharge.

Sebastian.   What stuff is this! how say you?
  'Tis true my brother's daughter's Queen of Tunis;
  So is she heir of Naples; 'twixt which regions
  There is some space.

Antonio.   A space whose every cubit
  Seems to cry out, "How shall that Claribel
  Measure us back to Naples? Keep in Tunis,
  And let Sebastian wake." Say this were death
  That now hath seized them; why, they were no worse
  Than now they are. There be that can rule Naples
  As well as he that sleeps; lords that can prate
  As amply and unnecessarily
  As this Gonzalo; I myself could make
  A chough of as deep chat. O, that you bore
  The mind that I do! What a sleep were this
  For your advancement! Do you understand me?

We should do wrong to take the conspiracy very seriously
in itself. We know Prospero's power, and when Ariel
enters and wakes the intended victims we have no fears
for their future safety. But all the more weight should the
scene assume as recalling the past.

Dover Wilson[2] greatly contributes to a right understanding of the play by stressing the first lines of the fifth
act, when Prospero declares to Ariel that he will pardon
his enemies, now quite at his mercy:

2 *Op. cit.,* pp. 14–18.

Ariel.   Your charm so strongly works 'em
   That if you now beheld them, your affections
   Would become tender.

Prospero.   Dost thou think so, spirit?

Ariel. Mine would, sir, were I human.

Prospero.   And mine shall.
   Hast thou, which art but air, a touch, a feeling
   Of their afflictions, and shall not myself,
   One of their kind, that relish all as sharply,
   Passion as they, be kindlier moved than thou art?
   Though with their high wrongs I am struck to the quick,
   Yet with my nobler reason 'gainst my fury
   Do I take part: the rarer action is
   In virtue than in vengeance: they being penitent,
   The sole drift of my purpose doth extend
   Not a frown further.

But when Dover Wilson would have this to represent
Prospero's sudden conversion from a previously intended
vengeance, I cannot follow him. It is true that Prospero
shows a certain haste of temper up to that point of the
play, and that he punishes Caliban and the two other
conspirators against his life with some asperity; but his
comments on them, after his supposed conversion, have
for me the old ring:

   Mark but the badges of these men, my lords,
   Then say if they be true. This misshapen knave,
   His mother was a witch, and one so strong
   That could control the moon, make flows and ebbs,
   And deal in her command without her power.
   These three have robb'd me; and this demi-devil—
   For he's a bastard one—had plotted with them
   To take my life. Two of these fellows you
   Must know and own; this thing of darkness I
   Acknowledge mine.

The last words express all Prospero's old bitterness that
Caliban has resisted him and refused to respond to his

nurture.[3] Indeed, Prospero does not change fundamentally during the play, though, like Samson's, his own accomplished regeneration is put to the test. If he had seriously intended vengeance, why should he have stopped Sebastian and Antonio murdering Alonso? That he did stop them is proof of his already achieved regeneration from vengeance to mercy. This act, and his talk to Ariel of taking part with his reason against his fury, are once again a re-enactment of a process now past, perhaps extending over a period of many years. I do not wish to imply that the re-enactment is weak or that the temptation to vengeance was not there all the time. Prospero's fury at the thought of Caliban's conspiracy, which interrupts the masque, must be allowed full weight. It is not for nothing that Miranda says that—

> never till this day
> Saw I him touch'd with anger so distemper'd.

We must believe that Prospero felt thus, partly because Caliban's conspiracy typifies all the evil of the world which has so perplexed him, and partly because he is still tempted to be revenged on Alonso and Antonio. He means to pardon them, and he will pardon them. But beneath his reason's sway is this anger against them, which, like Satan's before the sun in *Paradise Lost*, disfigures his face. When Dover Wilson calls Prospero

> a terrible old man, almost as tyrannical and irascible as Lear at the opening of his play,

he makes a valuable comparison, but it should concern Prospero as he once was, not the character who meets us in the play, in whom these traits are mere survivals.

The advantage of this technique of re-enactment was economy, its drawback an inevitable blurring of the sharp outline. The theme of destruction, though exquisitely blended in the whole, is less vivid than it is in *The*

---

[3] See the admirable discussion of "nature" and "nurture" in *The Tempest* in Middleton Murry's *Shakespeare*, pp. 396 ff.

Winter's Tale. Having made it so vivid in that play, Shakespeare was probably well content to put the stress on the theme of re-creation. And here he did not work solely by re-enactment. He strengthened Prospero's re-enacted regeneration by the figures of Ferdinand and Miranda. I argued above that, in view of his background of Elizabethan chivalrous convention, Ferdinand need not have been as insignificant as he is usually supposed. Similarly, Miranda's character has been unduly diminished in recent years. Today, under the stress of the new psychology, men have become nervous lest they should be caught illicitly attaching their daydreams of the perfect woman to a character in fiction. They laugh at the Victorians for falling unawares into this error, and Miranda may have been one of the most popular victims. Hence the anxiety not to admire her too much. E. K. Chambers has written:

> Unless you are sentimentalist inveterate, your emotions will not be more than faintly stirred by the blameless loves at first sight of Ferdinand and Miranda.

Schücking[4] goes further and considers Miranda a poor imitation of Beaumont and Fletcher's idea of the chaste female, an idea that could be dwelt on so lovingly and emphatically only in a lascivious age. In depicting her with her talk of "modesty, the jewel in my dower" and her protests that if Ferdinand will not marry her, "I'll die your maid," and in making Prospero so insistent that she should not lose her maidenhead before marriage, Shakespeare, according to Schücking, is yielding to the demands of his age against his own better judgment. But Miranda is sufficiently successful a symbolic figure for it to matter little if she makes conventional and, in her, unnatural remarks. And even this defense may be superfluous. Since Miranda had never seen a young man, it might reasonably be doubted whether she would behave herself with entire propriety when she did. Prospero, too, had made enough mistakes in his life to

4 *Character Problems in Shakespeare's Plays*, pp. 249–50.

be very careful to make no more. Further, Miranda was the heiress to the Duchy of Milan and her father hoped she would be Queen of Naples. What most strikingly emerged from the abdication of our late King was the strong "anthropological" feeling of the masses of the people concerning the importance of virginity in a king's consort. The Elizabethans were not less superstitious than ourselves and would have sympathized with Prospero's anxiety that the future Queen of Naples should keep her maidenhead till marriage: otherwise ill luck would be sure to follow.

To revert to Miranda's character, like Perdita she is both symbol and human being, yet in both capacities somewhat weaker. She is the symbol of "original virtue," like Perdita, and should be set against the devilish figure of Antonio. She is the complete embodiment of sympathy with the men she thinks have been drowned: and her instincts are to create, to mend the work of destruction she has witnessed. She is—again like Perdita, though less clearly—a symbol of fertility. Stephano asks of Caliban, "Is it so brave a lass?" and Caliban answers,

> Ay, lord; she will become thy bed, I warrant,
> And bring thee forth brave brood.

Even if *The Tempest* was written for some great wedding, it need not be assumed that the masque was inserted merely to fit the occasion. Like the goddesses in Perdita's speeches about the flowers, Juno and Ceres and the song they sing may be taken to reinforce the fertility symbolism embodied in Miranda:

Juno.   Honor, riches, marriage blessing,
                Long continuance, and increasing,
                Hourly joys be still upon you!
                Juno sings her blessings on you.

Ceres.   Earthës increase, foison plenty,
                Barns and garners never empty,
                Vines with clustering bunches growing,

Plants with goodly burthen bowing;

Spring cóme to you at the farthest
In the very end of harvest!
Scarcity and want shall shun you;
Ceres' blessing so is on you.

The touches of ordinary humanity in Miranda—her
siding with Ferdinand against a supposedly hostile father,
for instance—are too well known to need recalling. They
do not amount to a very great deal and leave her vaguer
as a human being than as a symbol. Middleton Murry
is not at his happiest when he says that "they are so
terribly, so agonizingly real, these women of Shakespeare's
last imagination." As far as Miranda is concerned, any
agonizing sense of her reality derives from the critic and
not from the play. But this does not mean that, judged
by the play's requirements (which are not those of brilliant realism), Miranda is not perfection. Had she been
more weakly drawn, she would have been insignificant,
had she been more strongly, she would have interfered
with the unifying dominance of Prospero.

Not only do Ferdinand and Miranda sustain Prospero
in representing a new order of things that has evolved out
of destruction; they also vouch for its continuation. At
the end of the play Alonso and Prospero are old and
worn men. A younger and happier generation is needed
to secure the new state to which Prospero has so pain-
fully brought himself, his friends, and all his enemies save
Caliban.

BERNARD KNOX

"The Tempest" and the Ancient Comic Tradition

In *The Tempest* Shakespeare abandons the three familiar *milieux* in which most of his plays are set (classical antiquity, medieval England, and Renaissance Europe)[1] for a nameless island which is remote even from that Tunis which is itself, according to Antonio, "ten leagues beyond man's life." This island is not only uncharted, it is one on which anything can happen; "All torment, trouble, wonder, and amazement Inhabits heere." The poet places his characters in a world which seems to be purely of his own creating; it seems in this respect significant that, in spite of prodigies of *Quellenforschung*, no satisfactory source of *The Tempest* has yet been identified.

In the so-called "romances" of Shakespeare's last period there is an accelerated flight from probability; it is a movement beyond the "probable impossibility" to the

From *English Stage Comedy*. English Institute Essays, 1954, ed. W. K. Wimsatt, Jr. New York, Columbia University Press, 1955, pp. 52–73. Reprinted by permission of Columbia University Press.
[1] Cf. Gilbert Highet, *The Classical Tradition* (Oxford, 1949), p. 194.

complete impossibility. In *The Tempest* the laws which govern objects existing in space and time as we know them are imperiously suspended. Until the solemn moment when Prospero abjures his rough magic, the action develops in a world which defies nature: "These are not naturall events, they strengthen From strange, to stranger." One wonders how Prospero can keep his promise to the bewildered Alonso—"I'le resolve you (Which to you shall seeme probable) of every These happend accidents."

A recent production by the Yale Dramatic Association presented *The Tempest* as "science fiction"; the shipwreck scene took place in a space ship, and the action which takes place away from Prospero's cell was seen on a gigantic television screen, tuned in by a Prospero who sat before a control board which buzzed and flashed green light. The point was well taken: Shakespeare has in fact done what the modern science-fictioneers do—substituted for the normal laws of the operation of matter a new set of laws invented for the occasion.

Such a substitution creates great possibilities for what Aristotle called "Spectacle," and if the Yale Dramatic Association developed those possibilities somewhat exuberantly along modern lines they at least did no worse than Dryden and Davenant in 1667, whose stage direction for Act I, scene i, reads, in part: "This Tempest . . . has many dreadful Objects in it, as several Spirits in horrid shapes flying down among the Sailers, then rising and crossing in the Air. And when the Ship is sinking, the whole House is darken'd, and a shower of Fire falls upon 'em."

But novel and fantastic effects (and in this play it is clear that Shakespeare was interested in producing them) have their dangerous side; they may, by trading too much on it, destroy that willing suspension of disbelief on which every dramatic performance depends—the audience may come to feel, with Gonzalo, "Whether this be Or be not, I'le not sweare." The dramatist, by asking too much, may lose everything. Such a defiance of the normal laws of cause and effect in the operations of nature is especially dangerous in comedy, for comedy's

appeal, no matter how contrived the plot may be, is to
the audience's sense of solid values in a real world, to
a critical faculty which can recognize the inappropriate.
Tragedy, which questions normal human assumptions,
may introduce the super- and the hypernatural more
safely than comedy, which depends on the solidity of
those assumptions for a response. A comic poet who sets
his characters in action, not in the world as we know it
but in one which defies our expectation, must compen-
sate for the strangeness of the events by making the es-
sences and relationships of the characters immediately
and strikingly familiar. To put in another way, the fantasy and originality of the setting must be balanced and
disciplined by a rigid adherence to tradition in character
and plot.

This, I suggest, is a valid formula for *The Tempest*.
It has certainly the most extraordinary and fantastic
setting, for the sorcery of Prospero is a stranger thing
than the familiar English fairy magic of *A Midsummer
Night's Dream*. But in other ways it is the most rigidly
traditional of all Shakespeare's comedies—with one exception. The exception is *The Comedy of Errors*, which
is however apprentice work, a typical Renaissance *re-
maniement* of a Plautine original. *The Tempest* is as
original as *The Comedy of Errors* is imitative; and yet
they are the beginning and end of the same road. For
the traditional foundation on which *The Tempest*'s cloud-
capped towers are raised is the ancient comedy of Plautus, Terence, and (though the name would not have
meant much to Shakespeare) Menander.

Like all proper foundations, this one is not conspicu-
ous. But there are odd corners where its outline is visible
in the superstructure. This, for example:

Prospero. [*To Ariel*] She did confine thee
   By helpe of her more potent Ministers,
   And in her most unmittigable rage,
   Into a cloven Pyne, within which rift,
   Imprison'd, thou didst painefully remaine
   A dozen yeeres: within which space she di'd,

And left thee there: where thou didst vent thy groanes
As fast as Mill-wheeles strike.

The groans of a disobedient spirit imprisoned in a
cloven pine by a "blew ey'd hag" come "as fast as Mill-
wheeles strike": the simile illustrates the unfamiliar by
appeal to an aspect of ordinary experience. Yet not,
presumably, Ariel's ordinary experience: there are no
mills in the strange economy of Prospero's island. The
simile illustrates by an appeal from one world to another,
with an anachronism the reverse of those Homeric sim-
iles which compare conditions of the heroic age to those
of the poet's own time. (Homer compares the voice of
Achilles to a trumpet, an instrument which the embattled
heroes of his poem never mention or use, almost certainly because it had not yet been invented.) The mill
wheels of Shakespeare's simile come not from his own
world but from the world of Plautine comedy, where
with monotonous frequency the rebellious slave is threatened or actually punished with an assignment to the
brutal labor of the mill. And in this fantastic context,
where Ariel ("my slave, as thou reportst thyselfe") is
reminded of his punishment for former disobedience and
threatened with even worse punishment for present disobedience, the simile gives a touch of familiarity and
proportion to the outlandish details of Ariel's nature and
status.

Here the classical precedent is for a moment distinctly
visible, but in general it does its work the more efficiently
because it is not obtrusive. Below the strange and brilliant surface composed of medieval magic and Renaissance travel tales, the initial situation, the nature and relationships of most of the characters, the development
of the action and its final solution are all conjugations
of the basic paradigms of classical comedy.

One of the most influential of these paradigms relates
to the existence in ancient society of a dividing line
stricter and more difficult to cross than any social bar-
rier has been since: the distinction between slave and
free. The free man could not imagine a misfortune worse

than slavery, nor the slave a greater blessing than freedom. Slave and free were not so much separate classes as separate worlds: Aristotle could go so far as to claim that they were separate natures. This division was the most important sociological datum of ancient society, affecting men's attitude toward each other with a power almost as great as that of natural differences of sex or color. Among other things it provided a fixed contrast of condition and standards on which comedy could be based.

Ancient tragedy at the height of its development ignores the division and deals only with free men; Attic tragedy did not deal with slaves until Euripides introduced them, and this innovation was one of the main grounds for the conservative attack on him. The place for slaves was comedy, which, says Aristotle, "is an imitation of characters of a lower type"; and the lowest type imaginable was the slave. Comic slaves could be beaten, could curse, lie, cheat, be drunken, lecherous, and cowardly to the limit of the free audience's capacity for laughter without offending its sense of propriety and human dignity. Such an exhibition might in fact be considered to have a moral effect; in Plutarch's "Life of Lycurgus" (Chap. 28) we are told that at Sparta the ephors introduced into the military dining halls Helots who had been deliberately inebriated as a spectacle to teach the young what drunkenness was like; they also made the Helots learn songs and dances that were, to quote Plutarch again, "ignoble and ridiculous."

This was, of course, not a real dramatic performance (though there is evidence of some kind of comic performance at Sparta from quite early times); at Athens the picture is clearer. It is perhaps only a coincidence that the chorus of satyrs in the only two surviving specimens of the humorous satyr play are, in the plot of the plays, temporarily enslaved, but it is evident that typical Athenian Old Comedy depended heavily on the laughter to be extracted from the low proclivities and activities of slaves. Aristophanes is not typical, but he indicates what is typical in a famous passage of self-congratulation

which sets forth his claim to have ennobled comedy.
Among other things he claims to have "liberated the
slaves, whom the poets always brought on stage howling,
all for the sake of the same old joke, so that a fellow
slave could make fun of their stripes and ask them, 'What
happened to your hide, poor devils? Were your sides
assaulted by a whiplash army that cut down the trees
on your back?' " Aristophanes did not, of course, dispense
entirely with servile humor, rather he seems to have
adapted it to subtler purposes by introducing witty contrasts between slave and free. In *The Knights,* for instance, he brings on stage all the prominent Athenian
politicians of the day as slaves in the house of a bad-
tempered old man called Demos: in this comedy De-
mosthenes' Nicias and Cleon fight, cheat, drink, spy,
play the coward, curse, bawl, lie, and rant as valiantly
as any slave ever born. Here the humorous aspects of
servile behavior are used to make a satiric point, that
the free men behave like slaves; *The Frogs* makes the
opposite point by ringing the changes on the contrast
between the master Dionysus and his slave Xanthias, who
repeatedly exchange identities—with the surprising result that the slave emerges as his master's superior in
wit, courage, and, incidentally, literary taste, for Xanthias
cannot abide Euripides.

In the comedy of the fourth century the magnificent
fantasy and political wit of Aristophanes are sadly lacking, but the theme of contrast between slave and free
remains. In the domestic comedy of Menander and his
contemporaries (the models of the Roman comic poets)
the theme crystallizes into a variety of stock patterns,
which have exerted enormous influence on comedy ever
since.

In this comedy the master design is always more or
less the same. A domestic problem involving the free
members of the household (usually, in Menander, a marriage or a seduction—sometimes both) is eventually
solved through complicated intrigues which involve the
slave members of the household. The comedy proceeds
on two social levels which interpenetrate, often on two

plot levels as well, which also interpenetrate. The slave characters (and a host of technically free but hardly distinguishable lower-class types such as parasites, butlers, cooks, and pimps) have their own problems (the attainment of freedom, a free meal or a free drink), the solution of which is artfully made to depend on the solution of the problem of the free characters. A typical paradigm is the plot in which a clever slave, by intelligent initiative and intrigue (often directed against his less intelligent fellow slaves) solves his master's problem (which may range from finding a wife to marrying off a child) and, as a reward for his services, gains his private objective, his liberty.

This is a slave who has the intelligence of, and eventually attains the status of, a free man; but there is another type of slave who is a convenient vehicle for the traditional servile humor. This one provides the sullen bad temper, the cursing, the drunkenness, the indecency, thievishness, and cowardice which are the traditional characteristics of the comic slave. He may have the same ambition as his cleverer fellow, but not the same capacity; he forms grand designs, but through stupidity (often through the direct intervention of the clever slave) he fails miserably, and is humiliated and punished with blows or a stint at the mill.

While the slaves, in aspiration and action, trespass on the confines of the free world, the freeborn may find themselves, as foundlings, kidnapped children, or prisoners of war, temporary denizens of the slave world; their identification and restoration to freedom (and usually marriage) is the play's denouement, and usually coincides with, and balances, the liberation of the clever slave or the restoration of the stupid slave to his proper station, or both. Together with these contrasts of condition there are deeper contrasts of nature; free men can think and act like slaves and slaves rise superior in intelligence or emotion to their masters. One of the most searching and profound of Roman comedies is Lessing's favorite, *The Captives* of Plautus, in which master and slave, both enslaved as prisoners of war, exchange iden-

tities so that the master (as the slave) can be released
to take the ransom demand home, while the slave remains in slavery (as the master), risking and, as it turns
out, suffering terrible punishment when the truth is discovered. The nobility displayed by the slave is, charac-
teristically enough, justified at the end of the play by the
discovery that he was really born free, and his liberation
is balanced by the punishment of the slave who originally
kidnapped and sold him into slavery. In this and in
practically all Roman comedy, the finale is a restoration
of the characters to their proper status; in the typical
pattern, the restoration of one of the two young lovers
to freedom makes possible their marriage, and the stern
father releases the clever and independent slave who has
been instrumental in bringing about the happy conclusion.

When the dramatists of the Renaissance began to imi-
tate the Roman comedies, slavery was a thing of the past
in Europe (though not a few Elizabethan worthies made
their fortunes by introducing it into the West Indies),
but the ancient comic design was easily adapted to the
conditions of a society which, like that of Elizabethan
England, was based, however insecurely, on hierarchical
social categories. Shakespearean comedy abounds in brilliant adaptations of the basic formula: the cruel reduction
to his proper station suffered by Malvolio, who had
"greatnesse thrust" upon him; the exposure of Parolles
"the gallant militarist" as a "past-saving slave"; above
all the magnificent interpenetration of the two worlds of
court and tavern in *Henry IV*. Falstaff acts the role of
the King in the Boar's Head, runs his sword through Hot-
spur's corpse at Shrewsbury, and sets out for London
crying, "The Lawes of England are at my command-
ment," only to be brusquely restored to his proper station as a "Foole and Jester." Prince Hal, like some
foundling, as his father suggests, begins as "sworn brother
to a leash of Drawers," sounding "the very base-string
of humility," but in the end restores himself to his proper
station, "to mock the expectation of the world."

But in *The Tempest*, a Utopia which Shakespeare invented for himself (as Gonzalo invents his in the play),

there is no need to translate the classic form: it can be used literally. Prospero is master (and incidentally an irritable old man with a marriageable daughter) and Ariel and Caliban are slaves. Prospero as sorcerer has the power to enslave and release the free men too: this contrast is relevant for all the characters of the play—one of its main components is what Brower has called "the slavery-freedom continuity." "The 'slaves' and 'servants' of the play," he points out, 'suffer various kinds of imprisonment, from Ariel in his 'cloven pine' to Ferdinand's mild confinement, and before the end of Act IV everyone except Prospero and Miranda has been imprisoned in one way or another. During the course of Act V all the prisoners except Ferdinand (who has already been released) are set free. . . ."[2]

After the long expository scene between Prospero and Miranda (itself a typical Plautine delayed prologue) we are presented with an interview between master and intelligent slave:

> All haile, great Master, grave Sir, haile: I come
> To answer Thy best pleasure; be't to fly,
> To swim, to dive into the fire: to ride
> On the curld clowds: to thy strong bidding, taske
> Ariel, and all his Qualitie.

This is servile enough, and comparable to many a hyperbolic declaration of availability made by Roman comic slaves; its comic tone is pointed up by the fact that the moment Ariel is asked to make good some of these fine promises, he rebels. "Is there more toyle?" he asks,

> Since thou dost give me pains,
> Let me remember thee what thou hast promis'd
> Which is not yet perform'd me.

Prospero.   How now? moodie?
> What is't thou canst demand?

Ariel. My Libertie.

[2] R. A. Brower, *The Fields of Light* (Oxford, 1951), p. 110.

Some critics have been disturbed at the vehemence of
Prospero's reaction; and it is true that phrases such as
"Thou liest, malignant Thing"—"my slave, as thou reportst thy selfe"—and "Dull thing, I say so" sound more
suited for Caliban than delicate Ariel. Yet it is not really
surprising that Prospero should display what Wilson calls
"ebullitions of imperious harshness" toward a slave who,
after such an enthusiastic declaration of willingness to
serve him, balks at the first mention of "more worke."

Prospero does more than chide; he threatens punishment. Sycorax punished Ariel with confinement in a
cloven pine—"it was a torment To lay upon the damn'd"
—but Prospero threatens to go one step farther: "I will
rend an Oake And peg—thee in his knotty entrailes. . . ."
Ariel begs for pardon and promises to be "correspondent
to command." He is rewarded with a fresh promise of
freedom—"after two daies I will discharge thee"—and
sent about his master's business with renewed imperious-
ness:

> goe take this shape
> And hither come in 't: goe: hence
> With diligence.

"*Exit*," reads the stage direction.

From this point on Ariel is correspondent to command, and his first service is to bring Ferdinand into the
presence of Miranda. It is the traditional role of the intelligent slave to further his master's marriage projects,
and Ariel fully regains Prospero's favor and gets a renewed promise of the traditional reward. "Delicate Ariel,
Ile set thee free for this." In fact, Ariel gains a remission
of part of his stated time: "Ile free thee Within two dayes
for this."

Throughout the rest of the play Ariel acts as Prospero's eyes and ears, but, as befits the clever slave, with
a certain initiative too. He rescues Alonso and Gonzalo
from the conspirators, and his words suggest that, though
he has a general commission to protect Gonzalo at any

rate, the methods have been left to him. "Prospero my Lord, shall know what I have done." His mischievous action against Caliban and the two Neapolitans is apparently his own idea, for Prospero later asks him where they are, and Ariel gives a full report of the chase he has led them. Yet the comic aspects of the relationship between master and slave are not neglected in the swift action of the play's central section. Ariel, ordered to produce spirits for the masque, replies:

> Before you can say come, and goe,
> And breathe twice: and cry so, so:
> Each one tripping on his Toe,
> Will be here with mop, and mowe.

This sounds remarkably like the half-ironical servile exaggeration of the Plautine slave promising miracles of speed. Charmides orders his slave to go from Athens to Piraeus—*I, i, ambula, actutum redi,* "Go on, go on, start walking, come back right away"—and gets the answer, *Illic sum atque hic sum,* "I'm there and back again." And that same Ariel who asks "Doe you love me Master? no?" at the end of the jingle quoted above, can also admit that he fears his master's temper.

Prospero. Spirit: We must prepare to meet with Caliban.

Ariel. I my Commander, when I presented *Ceres*
I thought to have told thee of it, but I fear'd
Least I might anger thee.

The comic aspects of Ariel's slavery are balanced by those of Prospero's mastery. This is not the only reference to Prospero's short temper. "Why speakes my father so ungently?"—"he's compos'd of harshnesse"—"your fathers in some passion"—"never till this day Saw I him touch'd with anger, so distemper'd"—these observations only confirm the impression made by Prospero's outbursts of fury against his slaves. There is more than a touch in him of the Plautine old man, the irascible *senex* (*severus, difficilis, iratus, saevus,* as Donatus describes him),[3] who may in the end turn out to have a heart of gold, but who for the first four acts has only a noticeably short temper and a rough tongue.

This anger of Prospero is of course much more than a reminiscence of the irascibility of the stock comic figure: he is a man who has been grievously wronged, and who now, with his enemies at his mercy, intends to revenge himself. That this has been his intention is made perfectly clear in the speech in which that intention is forever renounced:

> Thogh with their high wrongs I am strook to th' quick
> Yet, with my nobler reason, gainst my furie
> Doe I take part: the rarer Action is
> In vertue, then in vengeance.

And this renunciation takes place when the slave rises superior to his master, setting an example of noble compassion:

Ariel. . . . your charm so strongly works 'em
   That if you now beheld them, your affections
   Would become tender.

Prospero. Dost thou thinke so, Spirit?

Ariel. Mine would, Sir, were I humane.

Prospero. And mine shall.

This is a magnificently imaginative version of the scenes in which the comedy slave surpasses the master in qualities which are traditionally those of the free man—in intelligence, courage, self-sacrifice. Here the nonhuman slave surpasses his human master in humanity.

As the play draws to a close, the recognition of Ariel's services and the renewed promises of liberation increase in frequency to become an obsessive burden:

[3] Cf. George F. Duckworth, *The Nature of Roman Comedy* (Princeton, 1952), p. 242, n. 14.

>   thou
> Shalt have the ayre at freedome: for a little
> Follow, and doe me service.
>   quickly Spirit,
> Thou shalt ere long be free.
>   I shall misse
> Thee, but yet thou shalt have freedome.
> Bravely (my diligence) thou shalt be free.

"The reluctance of the sylph to be under the command even of Prospero," says Coleridge, "is kept up through the whole play, and in the exercise of his admirable judgment Shakespeare has availed himself of it in order to give Ariel an interest in the event, looking forward to that moment when he was to gain his last and only reward—simple and eternal liberty." He might have added that what Shakespeare "has availed himself of" is a dramatic design as old as European comedy.

Ariel, the slave whose nature is free, is balanced by Ferdinand, the free man and prince, who is enslaved. Accused as "spy" and "traitor," he is subdued by Prospero's magic: but there is nothing magical about the entertainment he is promised.

> Ile manacle thy necke and feete together:
> Sea water shalt thou drinke: thy food shall be
> The fresh-brooke Mussels, wither'd roots, and huskes
> Wherein the Acorne cradled. Follow.

This is a Shakespearean version of the chains and prison diet with which the ancient comic slave is so often threatened, and of which he so often complains. And Ferdinand's next appearance shows him performing servile tasks:

>   I must remove
> Some thousands of these Logs, and pile them up,
> Upon a sore injunction.

The work he is doing is in fact Caliban's work ("*Enter*

Caliban with a burthen of wood" is the stage direction
for the preceding scene), and Ferdinand himself describes it as "wodden slaverie." But whereas Caliban has
just declared his independence, and Ariel longs to be
free, Ferdinand the free man is for the moment content
to be a slave:

> all corners else o' th' Earth
> Let liberty make use of: space enough
> Have I in such a prison.

The service which he so willingly accepts is of course
not that of his master, but that of his mistress:

> The verie instant that I saw you, did
> My heart flie to your service, there resides
> To make me slave to it, and for your sake
> Am I this patient Logge-man.

And the multiple wit of these variations on the theme
is dazzlingly displayed when he and Miranda plight their
troth:

Miranda.   to be your fellow
> You may denie me, but Ile be your servant
> Whether you will or no.

Ferdinand. My Mistris (deerest)
> And I thus humble ever.

Miranda. My husband then?

Ferdinand. I, with a heart as willing
> As bondage ere of freedome: heere's my hand.

He accepts marriage (that is, bondage) with a heart "as
willing as bondage ere of freedome" (as willingly as
Ariel, for example, would accept his liberty), but this
acceptance, overheard by Prospero, is the signal for his
release from the "wodden slaverie" in which he is now
bound.

Ferdinand, as we have seen, is contrasted to Ariel, but Ariel's real opposite is Caliban, "my slave, who never Yeelds us kinde answere." Caliban's employment is menial: while Ariel treads "the Ooze of the salt deepe," Caliban "do's make our fire Fetch in our wood, and serves in Offices That profit us." It is remarkable that on an island where spirits can be made to produce banquets and perform masks, Prospero should need the services of Caliban to "fetch in firing . . . scrape trenchering" and "wash dish," but so it is. "We cannot misse him."

Caliban, besides being a "Tortoys," "Hag-seed," a "delicate Monster," a "Moone-calfe," a "debosh'd Fish," and a "borne Devill," is also a slave, a poisonous, lying, and abhorred slave, to quote Prospero. His first speech (offstage)—"There's wood enough within"—and the onstage curses which follow it are enough to suggest a familiar frame of reference for the first appearance of this outlandish figure: he is the surly, cursing slave of the old tradition.

Caliban's curses are highly original in expression—"language as hobgoblin as his person," says Dryden justly. Shakespeare has created a special vocabulary of invective appropriate to the savage apprehension of nature, but the expressions have the same dramatic characteristics as their venerable ancestors. The cursing seems to be a thing in and for itself—it violates plausibility, for one thing. Why should Prospero put up with it, and counter it with threats of punishment that sound curiously like it? And Caliban is made to refer to another aspect of this improbability; "his Spirits heare me, And yet I needes must curse." He "needes must curse" because his cursing is vital to the comic essence of his nature; the scene in which he exchanges curses for Prospero's threats of punishment is a traditional feature of the comedy of master and slave.

Caliban is a sullen slave (a Sceparnio), a cursing slave (a Toxilus), and he is also a lecherous one. The only touch of low sexual humor in *The Tempest* is Caliban's unrepentant laughter when reminded of his attempt on

Miranda's virtue: but that one laugh is enough to remind us that he has an ancestry reaching back through scurrilous Plautine slaves and Aristophanic comic actors wearing a leather *phallos* to the ithyphallic satyrs of the Greek vase paintings.

Caliban's meeting with Trinculo and Stephano is a servile parallel and parody of Miranda's meeting with Ferdinand; both mistress and slave are overcome with wonder at the vision of their counterparts in Neapolitan society. Miranda's worshiping remark, "I might call him A thing divine," is echoed in Caliban's "that's a brave God, and beares Celestiall liquor"; while Ferdinand's "My Language? Heavens" finds a base echo in Stephano's "where the divell should he learne our language?" Stephano and Trinculo—"two *Neapolitanes* scap'd"—are to Ferdinand as Caliban is to Miranda; creatures of a lower order. And Stephano the "drunken butler" is a familiar figure; the slave in charge of his master's wine who drinks most of it himself is a standard character of the old comedy. In one of the better-known Plautine plays, the *Miles Gloriosus*, there is a scene with not one but two drunken butlers, one dead drunk on his back inside the house, the other drunk on his feet outside.

But the drunkenness of Stephano is surpassed by that of Caliban. His extravagant admiration of Stephano, as Trinculo perceives, is more than savage simplicity: "The poore Monster's in drinke." In his drunken fit he thinks of the primary objective of all slaves, his freedom. Unlike Ariel, he cannot hope to win it by delicate service; he can gain his freedom only by working against his master or by running away from him. He deserts Prospero, "the Tyrant that I serve," for Stephano, and the service of this new master turns out to be perfect freedom, which he proceeds to celebrate in song and dance: "Freedome, high-day, high-day, freedome." It is the traditional servile drunken exhibition and it is grotesquely funny, but it is only the other side of the coin which shows us Ariel, moody, demanding his liberty. Ariel and Caliban are opposite as earth and air, but they are both

enslaved, and in this they are alike. One suspects that
Caliban speaks something close to the truth when he tells
Stephano that Prospero's power depends on one thing
only, his "Bookes":

>   without them
>   Hee's but a Sot, as I am; nor hath not
>   One Spirit to command: they all do hate him
>   As rootedly as I.

"They say there's but five upon this Isle," says Trinculo. "We are three of them, if th' other two be brain'd
like us, the State totters." Of the three of them, the one
with the most brains is Caliban. With servile flattery and
cunning he supplants Trinculo in Stephano's graces, securing a series of reprimands and eventually a beating
for his fellow slave.

>   Beate him enough: after a little time
>   Ile beate him too.

He is now Stephano's "lieutenant," but he knows what
must be done to guarantee his new-found dignity: he
must encompass Prospero's death. And so the "foule
Conspiracy" is formed. The slaves indulge their exagger-
ated fantasies of freedom and sovereignty: "Monster, I
will kill this man: his daughter and I will be King and
Queene, save our Graces: and *Trinculo* and Thy selfe
shall be Vice-royes." It is a servile parody of the more
serious conspiracy of the free men, Antonio and Sebastian.

The drunken butler dreams of a kingdom; he is not
the first. It is instructive to compare his plans with those
of Gripus, the Plautine slave who has fished a treasure
out of the sea and intends to hang on to it:

When I'm once free, I'll equip myself with property, an
estate, a house. I'll go into trade with great ships; I'll be
considered a King among Kings. . . . I'll build a great city,
and call it Gripus, after myself, a monument to my fame

and doings. And in it I'll set up a great Kingdom . . . And
yet, King though I am, I must make my breakfast on sour
wine and salt, no relish for my bread.

This comic incongruity between the present and the imagined future, between station and ambition, is carried to
hilarious lengths in the climactic appearance of Caliban
and his associates. They "do smell all horse-pisse," but
Stephano's royal dignity is undisturbed. "Wit shall not
goe unrewarded while I am King of this Country," he
says, and Trinculo hails him in the titles of the old ballad,
"O King *Stephano*, O Peere: O worthy *Stephano*." Standing at the entrance to Prospero's cell King Stephano
talks like a tragic hero: "I do begin to have bloody
thoughts." And Caliban's urgent warnings are rejected in
royal style: "Monster, lay to your fingers . . . or Ile turne
you out of my Kingdome."

A few seconds later Stephano's kingdom melts into
thin air. And on his last appearance he and Trinculo are
ordered off with Caliban to perform menial tasks; no
distinction is made between them.

> Goe Sirha, to my Cell,
> Take with you your Companions: as you looke
> To have my pardon, trim it handsomely.

The stupid slaves, their wild ambitions foiled and their
presumption suitably punished, are restored to their
proper place and function.

Prospero has already been recognized as "sometime
Millaine" and restored to *his* proper station—"thy dukedom I resigne"—the marriage of Ferdinand and Miranda
is arranged; all that remains is to free the clever slave—
"to the elements Be free, and fare thou well"—and the
play, except for a version of the conventional Plautine
request for applause, is over, the traditional paradigm
complete. Gonzalo is given the speech in which the loose
ends are tied together and the pattern of restoration
spelled out:

> In one voyage
> Did *Claribell* her husband finde at *Tunis,*
> And *Ferdinand* her brother, found a wife,
> Where he himselfe was lost: *Prospero* his Dukedome
> In a poore Isle:

So far we are still within the recognizable limits of the ancient plan, but Gonzalo's closing words (though they continue the metaphor of liberation) can serve to remind us that this plan is only the bare outline of a poetic structure which in feeling and imagination as far surpasses Plautine comedy as "great'st do's least":

> —*Prospero* his Dukedome
> In a poore Isle: and all of us, our selves,
> When no man was his owne.

REUBEN A. BROWER

The Mirror of Analogy: "The Tempest"

> *The Mind, that Ocean where each kind*
> *Does streight its own resemblance find;*
> *Yet it creates, transcending these,*
> *Far other Worlds, and other Seas . . .*
> ANDREW MARVELL

Of *The Tempest*, we may say what Ferdinand said of
the masque,

> This is a most majestic vision, and
> Harmonious charmingly.

The harmony of the play lies in its metaphorical design,
in the closeness and completeness with which its rich and
varied elements are linked through almost inexhaustible
analogies. It is hard to pick a speech at random without
coming on an expression that brings us by analogy into
direct contact with elements that seem remote because of
their place in the action or because of the type of experience they symbolize. Opening the play at the second act
we read,

From *Fields of Light* by Reuben A. Brower. New York: Oxford University Press, 1951. Copyright 1951 by Oxford University Press, Inc. Reprinted by permission.

Four legs and two voices; a most delicate monster!

The last phrase is comic enough as used of Caliban and
as issuing from the lips of Stephano, a "most foul"
speaker. But "delicate" evokes a more subtle incongruity
by recalling characters and a world we might suppose
were forgotten. Stephano is parodying Prospero when
he rebukes Ariel as "a spirit too delicate / To act her
[Sycorax's] earthy and abhorr'd commands" and when
he says,

> delicate Ariel,
> I'll set thee free for this!

We have in Stephano's words not only the familiar Shakespearean balancing of comic and serious, but a counter-
pointing of analogies that run throughout the play. "Delicate" as the antithesis of "earth" points to the opposition
of Ariel and Caliban and to the often recurring earth-air
symbolism of *The Tempest*. "Delicate" used of this remarkable island creature echoes also the "delicate temperance" of which the courtiers spoke and "the air" that
"breathes . . . here most sweetly." "Monster"—almost another name for Caliban—balances these airy suggestions
with an allusion to "the people of the island . . . of monstrous shape" and thereby to the strain of fantastic sea
lore in *The Tempest*, which is being parodied in this
scene.

So viewed, Shakespeare's analogies may perhaps seem
too much like exploding nebulae in an expanding though
hardly ordered universe. But Shakespeare does not "mul-
tiply variety in a wilderness of mirrors"; he makes use of
a few fairly constant analogies that can be traced through
expressions sometimes the same and sometimes extra-
ordinarily varied. And the recurrent analogies (or continuities) are linked through a key metaphor into a single
metaphorical design. Shakespeare is continually prodding
us—often in ways of which we are barely conscious—
to relate the passing dialogue with other dialogues into
and through a super-design of metaphor.

In concentrating on how the design is built up, I am

not forgetting that it is a metaphorical design in a *drama*, that we are interested in how Shakespeare has linked stages in a presentation of changing human relationships. Toward the énd of the chapter I hope to show how wonderfully the metaphorical design is related to the main dramatic sequence of *The Tempest*, especially in the climactic speeches of Acts IV and V.

The play moves forward, we should remember, from a scene of tempest to a final promise of "calm seas, auspicious gales," and through a series of punishments or trials to a series of reconciliations and restorations. Although, as Dr. Johnson might say, there is a "concatenation of events" running through Prospero's "project" and though the play has a curiously exact time schedule, there is often little chronological or logical connection between successive dialogues or bits of action. To be sure Shakespeare has the Elizabethan conventions on his side, but the freedom of his dramatic composition in *The Tempest* never seems merely conventional or capricious because the linkage of analogy is so varied and so pervasive.

The surest proof 'of the pervasiveness of Shakespeare's design lies in the mere number of continuities that can be discovered in the play. But some are more important than others because they can be traced through more expressions or in more scenes and because they express analogies more closely related to the key metaphor. The six main continuities, roughly labeled to indicate their character, are: "strange-wondrous," "sleep-and-dream," "sea-tempest," "music-and-noise," "earth-air," "slavery-freedom," and "sovereignty-conspiracy."

All of these continuities appear during the second scene of Act I, which is an exposition of Shakespeare's metaphorical and dramatic designs for the entire play. Near the close of the scene, Ariel's two songs offer wonderfully concentrated expressions of both designs. "Come unto these yellow sands" calms the "fury" of the waves and Ferdinand's "passion," thus charting in brief the course of the action. "Full fathom five" is anticipatory in a very different fashion. It presents in miniature the main lines of the metaphorical design and sounds the key note of "sea change," Shakespeare's most direct expression of the key metaphor of *The Tempest*. [See I.ii.1–186.]

As we trace the first two continuities ("strange-wondrous," "sleep-and-dream"), the reader can appreciate how unobtrusively they emerge from the developing dramatic pattern. Prospero's narrative, with which the scene opens, tells us of the past and describes the present situation while symbolizing the quality of *The Tempest* world. Prospero explains that his enemies have come to this shore "by accident most strange," and Miranda, who falls to sleep at the end of his tale, accounts for her lapse by saying,

> The strangeness of your story put
> Heaviness in me.

Prospero's tale was strange indeed: it included a ruler "rapt in secret studies," a "false uncle" who "new created / The creatures" of the state, the miraculous voyage of Prospero and Miranda (who was "a cherubin") and their safe arrival "by Providence divine." This "strangeness" is best defined by Alonso's remarks near the end of the play:

> These are not natural events; they strengthen
> From strange to stranger...
>
> This is as strange a maze as e'er men trod;
> And there is in this business more than nature
> Was ever conduct of . . .

They are "unnatural" in a broad seventeenth-century sense of the term; that is, outside the order which includes all created things. The theme is almost constantly being played on: "strange," "strangely," or "strangeness" occur altogether some seventeen times, and similar meanings are echoed in "wondrous," "monstrous," "divine."

Of all the analogies of the play this is probably the vaguest, the nearest in effect to the atmospheric unity of nineteenth-century Romantic poetry. But a more precise

metaphor of strangeness appears, the "strangeness" of
"new created creatures." From the "accident most strange"
of the shipwreck we come to Alonso's ponderous woe:

> O thou, mine heir
> Of Naples and of Milan! what strange fish
> Hath made his meal on thee?

and then to Trinculo's discovery of Caliban—"A strange
fish!" With a similar comic antiphony, Miranda finds
Ferdinand "a thing divine," and Ferdinand replies, "O
you wonder"; while a little later Caliban hails Trinculo
as his god and cries, "Thou wondrous man." The full
significance of these strange births will appear later.

The vague "strangeness" of the island world is closely
allied to a state of sleep, both continuities appearing in
Miranda's remark about the "heaviness" that came over
her while listening to Prospero's story. The feeling that
we are entering on an experience of sleep-and-dream
arises beautifully out of the dramatic and rhythmic texture of the opening dialogue between father and daughter.
The movement of these speeches with their oddly rocking
repetitions is in key with the sleepy incredibility of the
events about to be described: "Canst thou remember...
thou canst ... I can ... thy remembrance ... my remembrance ... thou remember'st ... Twelve year since, Miranda, twelve year since ..." Throughout the story Prospero is continually reminding Miranda to "attend" to the
telling, and it seems perfectly natural that at the end she
should be "inclin'd to sleep." (Note in passing how neatly
Shakespeare has broken a long narrative into dialogue
and also given a distinct impression of Prospero's firm-
ness and of Miranda's innocent dependence.) Miranda's
images of the past come back to her "rather like a dream,"
and Prospero seems to be drawing their story from a
world of sleep, "the dark backward and abysm of time."

With the next scene (the mourning King and his courtiers) we meet one of Shakespeare's typical analogical
progressions. The sleep which affects the courtiers is, like
Miranda's, a strange "heaviness." Their dialogue runs

down, psychologically and rhythmically, through three echoes of Miranda's words:

Gonzalo. Will you laugh me asleep, for I am very heavy?...

Sebastian. Do not omit the heavy offer of it ...

Alonso. Thank you. Wondrous heavy.

Sebastian. What a strange drowsiness possesses them!

The conversation that follows between the conspirators shows how Shakespeare uses an analogy to move to a new level of action and experience and to make them harmonious with what precedes and follows. Sebastian and Antonio begin by talking about actual sleep and waking: why are they not drowsy like the others? Then Antonio shifts to talking of sleepiness and alertness of mind, and from that to imagining that he sees "a crown dropping" upon Sebastian's head. The wit becomes more complex as Sebastian describes Antonio's talk as "sleepy language"—without meaning—though indicating that it does have meaning, "There's meaning in thy snores." This dialogue, which readers are liable to dismiss as so much Elizabethan wit, has its place within the play's metaphorical pattern. The plotting takes on a preposterous dreamy-sleepy character like that of Prospero's narrative and Miranda's recollections. Through such verbal trifling Shakespeare maintains the continuous quality of his imagined world.

References to similar wakings and sleepings, to dreams and dreamlike states, abound from here to the end of the play, where the sailors are "brought moping . . . even in a dream," and the grand awakening of all the characters is completed. But up to that point confusion between waking and sleep is the rule, being awake is never far from sleep or dream. In *The Tempest* sleep is always imminent, and more than once action ends in sleep or trance.

The witty talk of the conspirators glides from conceits of "sleep" to conceits of "the sea," to talk of "standing water" and "flowing" and "ebbing." The "good Gonzalo," in consoling the King, speaks in similar figures:

> It is foul weather in us all, good sir,
> When you are cloudy.

Recurrent expressions of "sea and tempest," like those of "sleep and dream," are numerous and have a similar atmospheric value of not letting us forget the special quality of life on Prospero's island. But they also have far more important effects, for many of them become metaphors which are more precisely and more variously symbolic and which link more kinds of experience together.

By tracing two groups of "tempest" expressions, metaphors of "sea-swallowing" and images of "clouds," we may understand how these more complex analogies are built up. We may also see how Shakespeare moves from narrative fact to metaphor, from image or metaphor referring only to narrative fact to metaphor rich in moral and psychological implications. As in creating the analogies of "strangeness" and "sleep," Shakespeare starts from a dramatic necessity: the audience must be told what the situation was in the storm scene with which the play opens, and they must learn through an actor (Miranda) how they are to take it. (See I.ii.1–186.) Although there is a hint of magic in Miranda's vision of the tempest, she pictures it as a violent actuality:

> Had I been any god of power, I would
> Have sunk the sea within the earth, or e'er
> It should the good ship so have swallow'd and
> The fraughting souls within her.

As if there were an inner rhythm in these responses, this metaphor, like others we have been tracing, recurs in the plotting episode. Antonio is speaking of his sister Claribel, left behind in Tunis:

>   she that from whom
> We all were sea-swallow'd, though some cast again,
> And by that destiny to perform an act
> Whereof what's past is prologue, what to come
> In yours and my discharge.

In this new context "sea-swallowed" does several things at once. It brings back Miranda's horrified impression; but the magical nature of the storm now being known, the phrase reminds us that there was no "sea-swallowing," no actual sinking of "fraughting souls." Next, with a curiously Shakespearean "glide and a jump" via the pun on "cast," "sea-swallowed" merges into another metaphor (they are now "cast" as actors in destiny's drama). "Sea-swallowing" has become a metaphor that expresses destiny's extraordinary way of bringing Sebastian to the throne.

The irony of Antonio's words, which is clear to the audience, is made explicit later in the solemn speech in which Ariel explains the purpose of the tempest:

> You are three men of sin, whom Destiny—
> That hath to instrument this lower world
> And what is in 't—the never-surfeited sea
> Hath caused to belch up you . . .

Few passages could show better how Shakespeare carries his analogies along and at the same time completely renews them. The "belching up" recalls the wreck and the casting ashore and the earlier connection with destiny. But the sea's action is now described in much grosser terms and with grim sarcasm, while the oddly compact grammar makes "the never-surfeited sea" very nearly a synonym for "Destiny." The violence though increased is now religious and moral; the imagery has become expressive of the strenuous punishment and purification of "three men of sin."[1] So by the continuity of his varying metaphor Shakespeare has expressed an unbroken transition from actual storm to the storm of the soul. This sequence, which expresses both physical and metaphysical transformations, points very clearly to the key metaphor of *The Tempest*.

The recurrent cloud images present a similar sequence as they take on various symbolic meanings in the course of the play. "Cloud" does not actually occur in the open-

1 Alonso, Antonio, Sebastian.

ing storm scene, but when Trinculo sees "another storm
brewing" and speaks of a "black cloud," we are reminded
of the original tempest. The cloud undergoes an appropriate change in Trinculo's speech; it "looks like a foul
bombard that would shed his liquor." This comic cloud is
very different from "the curl'd clouds" on which Ariel
rides, though they too are associated with storms. The
clouds of Caliban's exquisite speech are those of Ariel
and the deities of the masque:

>   and then, in dreaming,
> The clouds methought would open and show riches
> Ready to drop upon me . . .

Clouds—here linked with magical riches—become in
Prospero's "cloud-capp'd towers" speech a symbol for
the unsubstantial splendor of the world. One of the sub-
ordinate metaphors there, the "melting into air" and the
"dissolving" of the clouds, is picked up in Prospero's
later words about the courtiers:

>   The charm dissolves apace;
> And as the morning steals upon the night,
> Melting the darkness, so their rising senses
> Begin to chase the ignorant fumes that mantle
> Their clearer reason.

This dissolution of night clouds (suggested also by
"fumes") is a figure for the change from madness to
sanity, from evil ignorance to the clear perceptions of
reason. Although the cloud images of the play are so
varied, they have a common symbolic value, for whether
they are clouds of tempest or of visionary riches or of the
soul, they are always magically unsubstantial. The reader
is led to feel some touch of likeness among experiences
as different as a storm at sea, a bit of drunken whimsy,
a vision of heavenly and earthly beauty, and a spiritual
regeneration. The cloud sequence, as an arc of metaphor,
is in perfect relation to the gradual dramatic movement
from tempest and punishment to fair weather and recon-

ciliation, the images having meanings more and more remote from any actual storm.

The "cloudlike" change in the distracted souls of the guilty nobles was induced (as if in reminiscence of Plato) by *Solemn music*—

> A solemn air and the best comforter
> To an unsettled fancy.

Many of the expressions referring to music, like the stage direction above, are not explicitly metaphorical, but along with the continuities of "sleep" and "strangeness" they help maintain the magical character of the action. The music is always the music of spirits and always a sign of more than natural events.

The one fairly constant musical metaphor[2] in *The Tempest* is the symbolic opposition of confused noises, especially storm sounds, and harmonious music. The key word and the central impression of the opening scene is certainly "noise"[3] in the modern sense. The impression is carried over in the first words of the next scene:

> If by your art, my dearest father, you have
> Put the wild waters in this roar, allay them.

Miranda's request is soon answered by Ariel's first song, "the wild waves" are "whist." The *solemn and strange music* heard when the *strange Shapes* bring a banquet to the courtiers makes Alonso say, "What harmony is this? my good friends, hark!" Gonzalo replies: "Marvelous sweet music!" By contrast, when Ariel enters shortly

---

[2] The music and tempest metaphors have been traced in a very different fashion and with quite different aims by G. Wilson Knight in *The Shakespearian Tempest*. My analysis (which I had worked out before reading Professor Knight's essay) has a more limited purpose: to show a continuity of analogy and a development of metaphor parallel to that of the other continuities I have traced.

[3] The scene is full of expressions such as: *A tempestuous noise of thunder and lightning heard*, "roarers," "command these elements to silence," *A cry within*, "A plague upon this howling! they are louder than the weather, or our office," "insolent noisemaker," *A confused noise within*, et cetera.

after, in order to inform the "three men of sin" of their punishment by the storm, there is an offstage sound of *Thunder and lightning.* The masque vision which Ferdinand finds "harmonious charmingly" is rudely interrupted by *a strange, hollow, and confused noise* which symbolizes the stormy anger expressed by Prospero in the speeches that follow. When in the next scene he prepares to forgive his enemies, he abjures the "rough magic" by which he

> call'd forth the mutinous winds,
> And 'twixt the green sea and the azur'd vault
> Set roaring war . . .

As the *solemn music* is played the clouds of ignorance "dissolve," and so the musical metaphor, like the sea metaphor, has moved from outer to inner weather.

The music analogy has some close links with the earth-air continuity which we glanced at in the introductory chapter of the book. Ferdinand, following Ariel's "yellow sands" song, asks, "Where should this music be? i' th' air, or th' earth?" And a little later:

> This is no mortal business, nor no sound
> That the earth owes: I hear it now above me.

The connection of air and music can never be long forgotten: Ariel and his spirits of "thin air" are the musicians of the island.

The earth-air, Caliban-Ariel antithesis coincides at points with what we might call a slavery-freedom continuity, for Caliban is in Prospero's words both "slave" and "earth." Ariel too is called a "slave"[4] by Prospero, and for the time of the play he is as much a slave as Caliban. He is always asking for his freedom, which is at last granted, his release being symbolically expressed in the airy rovings of his final song. He flies into perpetual summer and, like air, becomes merged with the elements.

---

[4] Both are called "slaves" in Act I. ii, the scene of metaphorical exposition.

By contrast, the "high-day, freedom!" of which Caliban sings is ironically enough simply a change of masters.

The "slaves" and "servants" of the play suffer various kinds of imprisonment, from Ariel in his "cloven pine" to Ferdinand's mild confinement, and before the end of Act IV everyone except Prospero and Miranda has been imprisoned in one way or another. During the course of Act V all the prisoners except Ferdinand (who has already been released) are set free, each of them by Prospero's special command.

A sovereignty-conspiracy analogy parallels very closely the slavery-freedom analogy, some of the same persons, e.g., Ferdinand and Caliban, appearing as both slaves and conspirators. "That foul conspiracy/ Of the beast Caliban, and his confederates" is of course a parody version of the "Open-ey'd Conspiracy" of Sebastian and Antonio. Ferdinand, too, is charged fantastically by Prospero with plotting against his island rule. Talk of kings and royalty turns up in many scenes, being connected usually with the denial of kingship, as in "good Gonzalo's" speech on his golden-age commonwealth where "he would be king" and yet have "no sovereignty." Though no single explicit metaphor for conspiracy or usurpation is often repeated, Shakespeare rings many changes on the theme as he moves from plot to plot. Prospero's brother, we recall, is said to have "new created the creatures" of state. Alonso's seizure of power is called a "substitution": "crediting his own lies," he began to believe "he was indeed the duke," and from merely playing a part he went on to become "absolute Milan." The figure is picked up in the somnolent dialogue of Sebastian and Antonio:

> I remember
> You did supplant your brother Prospero.

In the second of the scenes in which Caliban and his fellows plot to overthrow the island "tyrant," Sebastian's "supplant" is recalled with a difference:

Caliban. I would my valiant master would destroy thee; I do
not lie.

Stephano. Trinculo, if you trouble him any more in his tale,
by this hand, I will supplant some of your teeth.

The figure recurs a little later in a more serious context:

> . . . you three
> From Milan did supplant good Prospero.

In Act V after various supplantings, serious and comic,
accomplished or merely projected, all true kings are restored and all false ones dethroned.

The two continuities, sovereignty-conspiracy and
slavery-freedom, are also alike in the fact that their metaphorical force is expressed through scenes that are just
one step removed from allegory. The more serious of the
restorations and releases convey similar kinds of moral
meaning. Ferdinand's release from "wooden slavery" sig-
nifies that he is a true lover and a true prince. In being
freed from madness Alonso has escaped from "heart-
sorrow" and regained his rightful rank and a "clear life
ensuing." Both continuities convey an impression of topsy-
turvydom in the order of things, an unnatural interchange
of status among creatures of every kind. Both express a
return to stability after a disturbance of degree.

What then is the key metaphor through which the
various continuities are linked, and how are they connected through it? Shakespeare's most direct expression
of his key metaphor is "sea change," the key phrase of
Ariel's song. But what does Shakespeare mean by "sea
change"? Ariel sings of "bones" being made into "coral"
and of "eyes" becoming "pearls." "A change into something rich and strange," we now understand, is a change
"out of nature." "Sea change" is a metaphor for "magical
transformation," for metamorphosis. The key metaphor
of the play is "change" in this special sense, and "change"
is the analogy common to all of the continuities we have
been tracing. (I am not forgetting that they are also expressive of many other relationships, or that Shakespeare

is often playing with two or three metaphors at once, as in the various figures of "sea-swallowing." But all are at least expressive of change, or changeableness.)

Through the first rather vague analogies we traced, of "strangeness" and "sleep-and-dream," numerous events and persons in the play are qualified as belonging to a realm where anything may happen. Expressions of "strangeness" and "sleep," like many of the references to sea and music, suggest "far other Worlds and other Seas," where magical change is to be expected. A more particular metaphor of change is expressed through the stress on the "strangeness" of "new creations" and on the confusion between sleep and dream and waking. The island is a world of fluid, merging states of being and forms of life. This lack of dependable boundaries between states is also expressed by the many instances of confusion between natural and divine. Miranda says that she might call Ferdinand

> A thing divine; for nothing natural
> I ever saw so noble.

Ferdinand cannot be sure whether she is a goddess or a maid, and Caliban takes Trinculo for a "brave god." There is a further comic variation on this theme in Trinculo's difficulty in deciding whether to classify Caliban as fish or man, monster or devil.

But "change" is most clearly and richly expressed through the sequence of tempest images (especially "cloud" and "sea-swallowed") and through the noise-music antithesis. All kinds of sounds, harmonious and ugly, like the manifestations of sea and storm, are expressive of magical transformation. "The fire and cracks/ Of sulfurous roaring" (imagery in which both storm and sound analogies are blended) "infects" the courtiers' "reason," and *solemn music* induces the "clearing" of their understanding. The "music" and the "tempest" continuities, taken together as metaphors of "sea change," are perhaps the most extensive of all the analogies in their organizing power. They recur often, they connect a wide

diversity of experiences, and they express in symbolic
form some of the main steps in the drama, in particular,
the climactic moments of inner change: Ariel's revelation
to the courtiers of their guilt, Alonso's first show of remorse, and the final purification.

The earth-air or Caliban-Ariel antithesis may seem to
have very little to do with metamorphosis. But the relation of this theme to the key metaphor is clear and important. Air, Ariel, and his music are a blended symbol
of change as against the unchanging Caliban, "the thing
of darkness." He can be punished, but hardly humanized;
he is, says Prospero,

> A devil, a born devil, on whose nature
> Nurture can never stick; on whom my pains,
> Humanely taken, are all lost, quite lost.

The other continuities parallel to earth-air, of slavery-
freedom and conspiracy-sovereignty, are frequently expressive of major and minor changes of status among the
inhabitants and temporary visitors on Prospero's island.

But the interconnection of Shakespeare's analogies
through the key metaphor cannot be adequately described, since we are able to speak of only one point of
relationship at a time. We can get a better sense of the
felt union of various lines of analogy in *The Tempest*
by looking at the two passages where Shakespeare expresses his key metaphor most completely, the "Full
fathom five" song and Prospero's "cloud-capp'd towers"
speech.

Rereading Ariel's song at this point, we can see how
many of the main continuities are alluded to and related
in the description of "sea change" and how the song anticipates the metaphorical design that emerges through
the dialogue of the whole play. The total metaphorical
pattern is to an amazing degree an efflorescence from this
single crystal:

> Full fathom five thy father lies;
> Of his bones are coral made:

Those are pearls that were his eyes:
Nothing of him that doth fade,
But doth suffer a sea change
Into something rich and strange.
Sea nymphs hourly ring his knell:
         Burthen: "Ding-dong!"
Hark! now I hear them—Ding-dong, bell.

In addition to the more obvious references to the deep
sea and its powers and to the "strangeness" of this drowning, there are indirect anticipations of other analogies.
"Fade" prefigures the "dissolving cloud" metaphor and
the theme of tempest changes, outer and inner. "Rich,"
along with "coral" and "pearls," anticipates the opulent
imagery of the dream-world passages and scenes, the
"riches ready to drop" on Caliban and the expressions
of wealth[5] and plenty in the masque. The song closes
with the nymphs tolling the bell, the transformation and
the "sea sorrow" are expressed through sea music. Ferdinand's comment reminds us that the song has connec-
tions with two other lines of analogy:

The ditty does remember my drown'd father.
This is no mortal business, nor no sound
That the earth owes:—I hear it now above me.

The song convinces Ferdinand that he is now King of
Naples (the first of the interchanges of sovereignty), and
it is a "ditty" belonging not to the "earth," but to the
"air."

The sense of relationship between the many continuities is still more vividly felt in the lines of Prospero's
most memorable speech:

You do look, my son, in a mov'd sort,
As if you were dismay'd: be cheerful, sir:
Our revels now are ended. These our actors,
As I foretold you, were all spirits and
Are melted into air, into thin air:

---

[5] "Rich" and "riches" occur no less than five times in the masque.

And, like the baseless fabric of this vision,
The cloud-capp'd towers, the gorgeous palaces,
The solemn temples, the great globe itself,
Yea, all which it inherit, shall dissolve
And, like this insubstantial pageant faded,
Leave not a rack behind. We are such stuff
As dreams are made on, and our little life
Is rounded with a sleep.

In Prospero's words Shakespeare has gathered all the
lights of analogy into a single metaphor which sums up
the metaphorical design and the essential meaning of
The Tempest. The language evokes nearly every continuity that we have traced. "Melted into air," "dissolve,"
"cloud," and "rack" bring us immediately to Ariel and
tempest changes, while "vision," "dream," and "sleep"
recall other familiar continuities. "Revels," "gorgeous palaces," and "pageant" (for Elizabethans closely associated
with royalty) are echoes of the kingly theme; and "solemn" is associated particularly with the soft music of
change. The "stuff" of dreams is at once cloud-stuff
(air) and cloth, both images being finely compressed in
"baseless fabric." Taken with "faded" these images refer
obliquely to the garments so miraculously "new-dyed
. . . with salt water," one of the first signs of "sea
change" noted by Gonzalo. Within the metaphor of tem-
pest-clearing and of cloudlike transformation, Shakespeare has included allusions to every important analogy
of change in the play.

But it is through the twofold progress of the whole
figure that the change metaphor is experienced and its
most general meaning fully understood. We read first:
that like the actors and scenery of the vision, earth's
glories and man shall vanish into nothingness. Through a
happy mistake we also read otherwise. By the time we have
passed through "dissolve," "insubstantial," and "faded,"
and reached "leave not a rack behind," we are reading
"cloudcapped towers" in reverse as a metaphor of tower-
like clouds. "Towers," "palaces," "temples," "the great
globe," "all which it inherit" are now taken for cloud forms.

Through a sort of Proustian[6] merging of icon and subject, we experience the blending of states of being, of substantial and unsubstantial, or real and unreal, which is the essence of *The Tempest* metamorphosis.

Similar meanings are expressed through the closing dream figure, which grows equally out of the metaphorical context of the speech and the play. "Rounded," we should take with Kittredge as "surrounded," but without losing the force of round, as in Donne's "surrounded with tears." "Our little life" is more than sentimental, it is our little life (microcosm) in contrast with "the great globe" (macrocosm). There may also be an over-image in "surrounded" of the world in classical myth and geography with its encircling ocean, sleep being the stream that "rounds" the lesser world. In relation to the metaphorical design of the play, "rounded with a sleep" and the notion of life ending in dreams express again the sense of confusion between sleep and dream and waking. This metaphor which completes the figure of cloud-change is Shakespeare's most perfect symbol for the closeness of states that to our daylight sense are easily separable. Although the vision here expressed goes far beyond the play, it is still a natural extension of the dramatic moment and a fulfillment of the metaphor that has been implicit since the noisy opening lines of *The Tempest*.

But if Shakespeare's total metaphor is in a sense present everywhere, it is also a design that develops in close relation to the main dramatic movement of the play. As we have noted more than once, a particular metaphor will be varied to fit a new dramatic situation and so serve to express the situation more fully and to anticipate the next step in the development of the drama. The best example of this adaptation of metaphor comes in a speech in which Shakespeare seems to be playing capriciously with his noise-music theme. At first sight the passage seems inconsistent with the symbolic contrast between storm noise and music:

[6] This merging in Proust was brought to my attention by J. I. Merrill in [an unpublished honors thesis done at Amherst].

Alonso.   O, it is monstrous! monstrous!
   Methought the billows spoke and told me of it;
   The winds did sing it to me; and the thunder,
   That deep and dreadful organ pipe, pronounc'd
   The name of Prosper: it did bass my trespass.

It is admittedly odd that the confused noise of the tempest should, in Alonso's soul, compose a harmony—however gloomy—but the paradox fits in perfectly with the developing structure of the play. Alonso has just been told by Ariel that the storm had a purpose as an instrument of Destiny. Since at this moment remorse first appears in the play and the inner clearing begins, it is exactly right that the storm sounds should seem harmonious and so point forward to the events of the fourth and fifth acts. No use of metaphor in *The Tempest* reveals more clearly Shakespeare's exact sense of the movement of his drama, of the changing human relations and feelings he is presenting.

In building up his metaphorical design, Shakespeare prepares us for the moment in *The Tempest* when the major shift in dramatic relationships takes place. The moment comes in the speech in which Prospero describes the behavior of the King and the courtiers as they slowly return from madness to sanity. The first important step toward this climax, Alonso's acknowledgment of his guilt, was expressed through a metaphor combining both sea and musical changes. The next step, Ferdinand's release from his tempest-trials and from dreamlike enchantment, is expressed through the masque, which is an elaborate dramatization of metamorphosis, Ariel's "meaner fellows," "the rabble," being now transformed into majestic Olympian goddesses. Once again, familiar continuities appear, and again they are transformed to fit a new occasion. "Earth," for example, is no longer "barren place and fertile," but the earth enriched by human cultivation and symbolized now by Ceres—not by Caliban, who is "nature resisting nurture." Iris summons this new Earth in the gorgeous speech beginning "Ceres, most bounteous lady, thy rich leas . . . ," lines in which we hear a quite new majesty of tone and movement. The couplet form sets the dialogue apart from human speech, while the longer periods, the added stresses, the phrasal balancings are especially appropriate to "that large utterance of the early gods." (Here is one of many instances of how Shakespeare adapts his sound patterns to his metaphorical and dramatic designs.) Prospero's visionary speech that ends "the revels" is not simply a concentration of metaphor without reference to the dramatic development. It announces the changes to come, it gives a rich expression of their meaning, and it anticipates the dreamlike flux of the psychological events of the last act.

If we now read Prospero's words in Act V, in which he describes the great changes as they take place, we see many references back to Shakespeare's metaphorical preparation for this moment. We also realize that various lines of action and various lines of analogy are converging almost simultaneously. The speech opens with Prospero's farewell to his art, after which he turns his thoughts to "restoring the senses" of the courtiers, whom Ariel has just gone to release:

A solemn air and the best comforter
To an unsettled fancy, cure thy brains,
Now useless, boil'd within thy skull! There stand,
For you are spell-stopp'd.
Holy Gonzalo, honorable man,
Mine eyes, even sociable to the show of thine,
Fall fellowly drops. The charm dissolves apace;
And as the morning steals upon the night,
Melting the darkness, so their rising senses
Begin to chase the ignorant fumes that mantle
Their clearer reason. O good Gonzalo!
My true preserver, and a loyal sir
To him thou follow'st, I will pay thy graces
Home, both in word and deed. Most cruelly
Didst thou, Alonso, use me and my daughter:
Thy brother was a furtherer in the act;
Thou'rt pinch'd for 't now, Sebastian. Flesh and blood,
You, brother mine, that entertain'd ambition,

Expell'd remorse and nature; who, with Sebastian—
Whose inward pinches therefore are most strong—
Would here have kill'd your king; I do forgive thee,
Unnatural though thou art! Their understanding
Begins to swell, and the approaching tide
Will shortly fill the reasonable shores
That now lie foul and muddy. Not one of them
That yet looks on me, or would know me. Ariel,
Fetch me the hat and rapier in my cell: [*Exit Ariel.*
I will discase me, and myself present,
As I was sometime Milan. Quickly, spirit;
Thou shalt ere long be free.

If this is a climactic moment, what changes in dramatic
relationships are taking place, what is happening dramat-
ically? The "men of sin," like Ferdinand, have come to
the end of the trials which began with the storm and continued through various "distractions." Now, as Prospero
explains, they are undergoing a moral as well as a mental
regeneration, they are "pinch'd" with remorse and are
being forgiven. The twofold regeneration is further dram-
atized in the speeches that follow: "th' affliction of
Alonso's mind amends," he resigns Prospero's dukedom
and "entreats" him to pardon his "wrongs."

But these are the prose facts, the bare bones of the
changes in dramatic relationships. We cannot feel the
peculiar quality of what is taking place or grasp its meaning apart from the metaphorical language through which
it is being expressed. And the expressions acquire their
force and precision from the whole metaphorical preparation we have been tracing. The courtiers' senses are
restored by "an airy charm," by magic similar to that
which was worked by Ariel and his spirits. The allusions
to "heavenly music" and "a solemn air," in contrast to
the "rough magic" that Prospero has abjured, remind us
that these changes will be musically harmonious, like
the songs of Ariel, and not noisy and confused like the
storm sent to punish these men and reveal their "monstrous" guilt. Toward the end of the speech, the imagery
recalls the tempest metaphor, but it is altered so as to

express the mental and moral change that is taking place. The return of understanding is like an approaching tide that covers the evidence of a storm (both "foul" and "muddy" have storm associations from earlier occurrences).

But the metaphor that best expresses this clearing is the one for which the preparation has been most complete:

> The charm dissolves apace;
> And as the morning steals upon the night,
> Melting the darkness, so their rising senses
> Begin to chase the ignorant fumes that mantle
> Their clearer reason.

"Dissolving" and "melting" and "fumes" take us back at once to the grand transformations of the masque speech, to the earlier cloud transformations both serious and comic; and they take us back further to the association of clouds with magical tempests, inner storms, and clearing weather. We read of the moral and psychological transformations with a present sense of these analogies. They are qualified for us as a dreamlike dissolution of tempest clouds, as events in the "insubstantial" region where reality and unreality merge.

It is through such links that Shakespeare concentrates at this climactic moment the fullest meaning of his key metaphor. There is of course no separation in the reader's experience between the dramatic fact and the metaphorical qualification. The images that recur in Prospero's speech take us back to felt qualities, but to felt qualities embedded in particular dramatic contexts. "Melting," for example, carries us to the spiritlike dissolution of "spirits . . . melted into air, into thin air"; but it also reminds us of the masque pageantry and of Prospero's calming of Ferdinand's fears. We hear Prospero's soothing and mysterious tone in both the earlier and later uses of the word. The dramatic links and the analogical links are experienced at once, which is to say that metaphorical design and dramatic design are perfectly integrated.

We can now realize that metamorphosis is truly the key metaphor to the *drama,* and not the key metaphor to a detachable design of decorative analogies. Through the echoes in Prospero's speech of various lines of analogy, Shakespeare makes us feel each shift in dramatic relationships as a magical transformation, whether it is the courtiers' return to sanity, or Prospero's restoration to his dukedom, or Ariel's flight into perpetual summer. While all of the "slaves" and "prisoners" are being freed, and while all of the "sovereigns" are being restored, the sense of magical change is never wholly lost. The union of drama and metaphor in *The Tempest* is nowhere more complete than in the last act of the play.

The larger meaning of Shakespeare's total design, which was anticipated in the cloud and dream metaphor of Prospero's visionary speech, is most clearly and fully expressed in these final transformations. In a world where everything may become something else, doubts naturally arise, and in the swift flow of change the confusion about what is and what is not becomes fairly acute. When Prospero "discases" himself and appears as Duke of Milan, Gonzalo says with understandable caution:

> Whether this be,
> Or be not, I'll not swear.

And Prospero answers:

> You do yet taste
> Some subtilties o' the isle, that will not let you
> Believe things certain.

Whereas in the earlier acts the characters had often accepted the unreal as real (spirits, shipwrecks, drownings, visions), they now find it difficult to accept the real as truly real. The play concludes with their acceptance of the unexpected change to reality. But for the spectator there remains the heightened sense of the "thin partitions" that "do divide" these states. The world that common sense regards as real, of order in nature and society and of sanity in the individual, is a shimmering transformation of disorder. "We shall all be changed, in a moment, in the twinkling of an eye." (This or something like it is as near as we can come to describing the total attitude conveyed by *The Tempest*.)

Thus *The Tempest* is, like Marvell's "Garden," a Metaphysical poem of metamorphosis,[7] though the meaning of change is quite different for the two writers. It is worth noting too that Shakespeare "had Ovid in his eye," a fact that is obvious from the echoes of Golding's famous translation. There could be no better proof of Shakespeare's maturity than the contrast between the "sweet witty" Ovidianism of "Venus and Adonis" and the metaphorical design of *The Tempest*, which gives philosophic meaning to a drama of Ovidian metamorphosis. We remember "a lily prison'd in a jail of snow" as an isolated "beauty," but hardly as an apt symbol of the amorous relations of Venus and Adonis, or as symbolic of some larger meaning in their story. (Indeed a "jail of snow" is rather inept for the fervid goddess of the poem.) "Those were pearls that were his eyes" revives Ariel's sea music, Ferdinand's melancholy, and a world of fantasy and transshifting states of being. The increased concentration in meaning of the image from *The Tempest* is a sign of a growth in the command of language which is command of life for a poet. As Arnold said of Wordsworth, Shakespeare now "deals with more of *life*" and "he deals with *life*, as a whole, more powerfully." His maturity and power appear in the variety of experience so perfectly harmonized through the imaginative design of *The Tempest*.

7 See the excellent analysis of the poem in M. C. Bradbrook and M. G. Lloyd Thomas: *Andrew Marvell* (Cambridge, 1940), pp. 59–64.

LORIE JERRELL LEININGER

The Miranda Trap

Sexism and Racism
in Shakespeare's *Tempest*

Shakespeare's *Tempest* was first performed before King
James I at Whitehall in November of 1611. It was presented a second time at the court of King James early in
1613, as part of the marriage festivities of James's daughter Elizabeth, who, at the age of sixteen, was being married to Frederick the Elector Palatine. The marriage
masque within *The Tempest* may have been added for this
occasion. In any case, the Goddess Ceres' promise of a
life untouched by winter (*"Spring come to you at the
farthest / In the very end of harvest!"* IV.i.114–15)[1] and
all the riches the earth can provide (*"Earth's increase,
foison plenty"*) was offered to the living royal couple as
well as to Ferdinand and Miranda.

Elizabeth had fallen dutifully in love with the bridegroom her father had chosen for her, the youthful ruler of
the rich and fertile Rhineland and the leading Protestant
prince of central Europe. Within seven years Frederick
was to become "Frederick the Winter King" and "The
Luckless Elector," but in 1613 he was still the living
counterpart of Ferdinand in *The Tempest*, even as Eliz-

From *The Woman's Part: Feminist Criticism of Shakespeare*, eds.,
Carolyn R. S. Lenz, Gayle Green, and Carol T. Neely. Urbana, Illinois:
University of Illinois Press, 1980. Reprinted by permission of University
of Illinois Press, pp. 285–94.

abeth was the counterpart of Miranda. Like Miranda, Elizabeth was beautiful, loving, chaste, and obedient. She believed her father to be incapable of error, in this sharing James's opinion of himself. Miranda in the play is "admired Miranda," "perfect," "peerless," one who "outstrips all praise"; Elizabeth was praised as "the eclipse and glory of her kind," a rose among violets.[2]

What was the remainder of her life to be like? Elizabeth, this flesh-and-blood Miranda, might have found it difficult to agree that "We are such stuff / As dreams are made on; and our little life / Is rounded with a sleep" (IV.i.156–58). The future held thirteen children for her, and forty years as a landless exile. Her beloved Frederick died of the plague at the age of thirty-six, a plague spreading through battle camps and besieged cities in a Europe devastated by a war which appeared endless—the Thirty Years War, in which whole armies in transit disappeared through starvation and pestilence. The immediate cause of this disastrous war had been Frederick and Elizabeth's foolhardy acceptance of the disputed throne of Bohemia. Politically inept, committed to a belief in hierarchical order and Neoplatonic courtliness, the new king and queen failed to engage the loyalty of the Bohemians or to prepare adequately for the inevitable attack by the previously deposed king.

While the happiness of the young lovers in The Tempest depended upon their obedience to Miranda's father, the repeated political and military failures of Elizabeth and Frederick were exacerbated by their dependence upon the shifting promises of King James. Elizabeth experienced further tragedy when two of her sons drowned, the eldest at the age of fifteen in an accident connected with spoils from the New World, the fourth son in a tempest while privateering in the New World. There was no Prospero-figure to restore them to life magically.

The Princess Elizabeth, watching The Tempest in 1613, was incapable of responding to clues which might have warned her that being Miranda might prove no unmixed blessing: that even though Miranda occupies a place next to Prospero in the play's hierarchy and appears to enjoy all of the benefits which Caliban, at the base of that hierarchy, is denied, she herself might prove a victim of the play's hierarchical values. Elizabeth would be justified in seeing Miranda as the royal offspring of a ducal father, as incomparably beautiful (her external beauty mirroring her inward virtue, in keeping with Neoplatonic idealism), as lovingly educated and gratefully responsive to that education, as chaste (her chastity symbolic of all human virtue), obedient and, by the end of the play, rewarded with an ideal husband and the inheritance of two dukedoms. Caliban, at the opposite pole, is presented as the reviled offspring of a witch and the Devil, as physically ugly (his ugly exterior mirroring his depraved inner nature), as racially vile, intrinsically uneducable, uncontrollably lustful (a symbol of all vice), rebellious, and, being defined as a slave by nature, as justly enslaved.

Modern readers have become more attentive than Elizabeth could have been in 1613 to clues such as Prospero's address to Miranda, "What! I say, / My foot my tutor?" (I.ii.469–70). The crucial line is spoken near the end of the scene which begins with Prospero's and Ariel's delighted revelation that the tempest was raised through Prospero's magic powers and then continues with the demonstration of Prospero's ability to subjugate the spirit Ariel, the native Caliban, and finally the mourning Prince Ferdinand to his will. Miranda's concern is engaged when Prospero accuses Ferdinand of being a spy, a traitor and usurper; Prospero threatens to manacle Ferdinand's head and feet together and to force him to drink salt water. When Ferdinand raises his sword to resist Prospero's threats, Prospero magically deprives him of all strength. Miranda, alarmed, cries,

> O dear father,
> Make not too rash a trial of him, for
> He's gentle, and not fearful. (I.ii.467–69)

Prospero's response is,

> What! I say,
> My foot my tutor?
>
> (I.ii.469–70)

Miranda is given to understand that she is the foot in the family organization of which Prospero is the head. Hers not to reason why, hers but to follow directions: indeed, what kind of body would one have (Prospero, or the play, asks) if one's foot could think for itself, could go wherever it pleased, independent of the head?

Now it is true that Prospero is acting out a role which he knows to be unjust, in order to cement the young couple's love by placing obstacles in their way. Miranda, however, has no way of knowing this. Prospero has established the principle that stands whether a father's action be just or unjust: the daughter must submit to his demand for absolute unthinking obedience.

But might not being a "foot" to another's "head" prove advantageous, provided that the "head" is an all-powerful godlike father who educates and protects his beloved daughter? Some ambiguous answers are suggested by the play, particularly in the triangular relationship of Prospero, Miranda, and Caliban.

When Prospero says to Miranda,

> We'll visit Caliban my slave, who never
> Yields us kind answer,

Miranda's response is,

> 'Tis a villain, sir,
> I do not love to look on.
>
> (I.ii.308–09)

Miranda fears Caliban, and she has reason to fear him. The play permits either of two interpretations to explain the threat which Caliban poses. His hostility may be due to his intrinsically evil nature, or to his present circumstances: anyone who is forced into servitude, confined to a rock, kept under constant surveillance, and punished by supernatural means would wish his enslavers ill.[3] Whatever Caliban's original disposition may have been when he lived alone on the isle—and we lack disinterested evidence—he must in his present circumstances feel hostility toward Prospero and Miranda. Miranda is far more vulnerable to Caliban's ill will than is her all-powerful father.

Prospero responds to Miranda's implicit plea to be spared exposure to Caliban's hostility with the *practical* reasons for needing a slave:

> But, as 'tis,
> We cannot miss him: he does make our fire,
> Fetch in our wood, and serves in offices
> That profit us. What, ho! slave! Caliban!
>
> (I.ii.310–13)

A daughter might conceivably tell her loving father that she would prefer that they gather their own wood, that in fact no "profit" can outweigh the uneasiness she experiences. Miranda, however, is not free to speak, since a father who at any time can silence his daughter with "What! My foot my tutor?" will have educated that "foot" to extreme sensitivity toward what her father does or does not wish to hear from her. Miranda dare not object to her enforced proximity to a hostile slave, for within the play's universe of discourse any attempt at pressing her own needs would constitute both personal insubordination and a disruption of the hierarchical order of the universe of which the "foot/head" familial organization is but one reflection.

Miranda, admired and sheltered, has no way out of the cycle of being a dependent foot in need of protection, placed in a threatening situation which in turn calls for more protection, and thus increased dependence and increased subservience.

Miranda's presence as the dependent, innocent, feminine extension of Prospero serves a specific end in the play's power dynamics. Many reasons are given for Caliban's enslavement: the one which carries greatest dramatic weight is Caliban's sexual threat to Miranda. When Prospero accuses Caliban of having sought "to violate / The honor of my child" (I.ii. 348–49), Caliban is made to concur in the accusation:

> O ho, O ho! Would't had been done!
> Thou didst prevent me; I had peopled else
> This isle with Calibans.   (I.ii.349–51)

We can test the element of sexual politics at work here by imagining, for a moment, that Prospero had been cast adrift with a small son instead of a daughter. If, twelve years later, a ship appeared bearing King Alonso and a marriageable daughter, the play's resolution of the elder generation's hatreds through the love of their offspring could still have been effected. What would be lost in such a reconstruction would be the sexual element in the enslavement of the native. No son would serve. Prospero needs Miranda as sexual bait, and then needs to protect her from the threat which is inescapable given his hierarchical world—slavery being the ultimate extension of the concept of hierarchy. It is Prospero's needs—the Prosperos of the world—not Miranda's, which are being served here.

The most elusive yet far-reaching function of Miranda in the play involves the role of her chastity in the allegorical scheme. Most critics agree that the chastity of Miranda and Ferdinand in the fourth act symbolizes all human virtue ("Chastity is the quality of Christ, the essential symbol of civilization"[4]), while Caliban's lust symbolizes all human vice.

The first result of this schematic representation of all virtue and vice as chastity and lust is the exclusion from the field of moral concern the very domination and enslavement which the play vividly dramatizes. The exclusion is accomplished with phenomenal success under the guise of religion, humanism, and Neoplatonic idealism, by identifying Prospero with God (or spirit, or soul, or imagination), and Caliban with the Devil (or matter, body, and lust). Within the Christian-humanist tradition, the superiority of spirit over matter, or soul over body, was a commonplace: body existed to serve soul, to be, metaphorically, enslaved by soul. In a tradition which included the *Psychomachia*, medieval morality plays, and Elizabethan drama, the "higher" and "lower" selves existing within each person's psyche had been represented allegorically in the form of Virtues and Vices. A danger inherent in this mode of portraying inner struggle lay in the possibility of identifying certain human beings with the Vice-figures, and others (oneself included) with the representatives of Virtue. Such identification of self with Virtue and others with Vice led to the great Christian-humanist inversion: the warrant to plunder, exploit and kill in the name of God—Virtue destroying Vice.

It was "only natural" that the educated and privileged be identified with virtue and spirit, and that those who do society's dirty work, and all outsiders, be identified with vice and matter. Ellen Cantarow has analyzed the tendency of allegory to link virtue with privilege and sin with misfortune, making particular power relationships appear inevitable, "natural" and just within a changeless, "divinely ordained" hierarchical order;[5] Nancy Hall Rice has analyzed the manner in which the artistic process of embodying evil in one person and then punishing or destroying that person offers an ersatz solution to the complex problem of evil, sanctioning virulent attacks on social minorities or outcasts;[6] and Winthrop D. Jordan has discussed the tendency of Western civilization to link African natives, for example, with preconceived concepts of sexuality and vice. Jordan speaks of "the ordered hierarchy of [imputed] sexual aggressiveness": the lower one's place on the scale of social privilege, the more dangerously lustful one is perceived as being.[7]

Thus in *The Tempest*, written some fifty years after England's open participation in the slave trade,[8] the island's native is made the embodiment of lust, disobedience, and irremediable evil, while his enslaver is presented as a God-figure. It makes an enormous difference in the expectations raised, whether one speaks of the moral obligations of Prospero-the-slave-owner toward Caliban-his-slave, or speaks of the moral obligations of Prospero-the-God-figure toward Caliban-the-lustful-Vice-figure. In the second instance (the allegorical-symbolic), the only requirement is that Prospero be punitive toward Caliban and that he defend his daughter Miranda's chastity—that daughter being needed as a pawn to counterbalance Caliban's lust. In this symbolic scheme, Miranda is deprived of any possibility of human freedom, growth or thought. She need only *be* chaste—to exist as a walking emblem of chastity. This kind of symbolism is damaging in that it deflects our attention away from the fact that real counterparts to Caliban, Prospero, and Miranda exist —that real slaves, real slave owners, and real daughters existed in 1613 for Shakespeare's contemporaries and have continued to exist since then.

To return to one of those daughters, Miranda's living counterpart Elizabeth Stuart, at whose wedding festivities *The Tempest* was performed: it appears likely that King James's daughter and her bridegroom were influenced in their unrealistic expectations of their powers and rights as future rulers by the widespread Jacobean attempt to equate unaccountable aristocratic power with benevolent infallibility and possibly by the expression of that equation in *The Tempest*. In our own century the play apparently continues to reflect ongoing societal confusions that may seduce women—and men—into complicity with those who appear to favor them while oppressing others. Can we envision a way out? If a twentieth-century counterpart to Miranda were to define, and then confront, *The Tempest*'s underlying assumptions—as, obviously, neither the Miranda created by Shakespeare nor her living counterpart in the seventeenth century could do—what issues would she need to clarify? Let us invent a modern Miranda, and permit her to speak a new Epilogue:

"My father is no God-figure. No one is a God-figure. My father is a man, and fallible, as I am. Let's put an end to the fantasy of infallibility.

"There is no such thing as a 'natural slave.' No subhuman laborers exist. Let's put an end to *that* fantasy. I will not benefit from such a concept presented in any guise, be it Aristotelian, biblical, allegorical, or Neopla-

tonic. Three men are reminded of Indians when first they
see Caliban; he might be African, his mother having been
transported from Algiers. I will not be used as the excuse
for his enslavement. If either my father or I feel threatened
by his real or imputed lust, we can build a pale around our
side of the island, gather our own wood, cook our own
food, and clean up after ourselves.

"I cannot give assent to an ethical scheme that locates
all virtue symbolically in one part of my anatomy. My
virginity has little to do with the forces that will lead to
good harvest or to greater social justice.

"Nor am I in any way analogous to a foot. Even if I
were, for a moment, to accept my father's hierarchical
mode, it is difficult to understand his concern over the
chastity of his *foot*. There is no way to make that work.
Neither my father, nor my husband, nor any one alive has
the right to refer to me as his foot while thinking of himself as the head—making me the obedient mechanism of
his thinking. What I do need is the opportunity to think for
myself; I need practice in making mistakes, in testing the
consequences of my actions, in becoming aware of the
numerous disguises of economic exploitation and racism.

"Will I succeed in creating my 'brave new world' which
has people in it who no longer exploit one another? I cannot be certain. I will at least make my start by springing
'the Miranda-trap,' being forced into unwitting collusion
with domination by appearing to be a beneficiary. I need
to join forces with Caliban—to join forces with all those
who are exploited or oppressed—to stand beside Caliban
and say,

> As we from crimes would pardon'd be,
> Let's work to set each other free."

NOTES

1. This quotation and subsequent ones are from *The Tempest*,
Arden Shakespeare, ed. Frank Kermode (Cambridge, Mass.:
Harvard University Press, 1958).

2. "The eclipse and glory of her kind" is the closing line of Sir
Henry Wotton's poem, "On His Mistress, The Queen of Bohemia," in *The Poems of Sir Walter Raleigh . . . with those of
Sir Henry Wotton and other Courtly Poets from 1540–1650*, ed.
John Hannah (London: Bell and Sons, 1892), pp. 95–96. "A
rose among violets" is a paraphrase of the third verse of that
poem; the compliment was often quoted.

3. That the spirit Ariel, the figure contrasted to Caliban in the
allegorical scheme, is a purely imaginary construct for whom no
human counterparts exist helps to obscure the fact that human
counterparts for Caliban did indeed exist. A community of free
blacks had been living in London for over fifteen years at the
time of the writing of *The Tempest*. The first Indian to have
been exhibited in England had been brought to London during
the reign of Queen Elizabeth's grandfather, Henry VII. For a
full discussion of the historical background see Chapter II of
my dissertation, "The Jacobean Bind: A Study of *The Tempest,
The Revenge of Bussy D'Ambois, The Atheist's Tragedy, A
King and No King* and *The Alchemist*, the Major Plays of 1610
and 1611, in the Context of Renaissance Expansion and Jacobean
Absolutism," University of Massachusetts/Amherst, 1975. For
more on the effects of the ambiguity surrounding the definition
of Caliban as an abstract embodiment of evil and as an inhabi-
tant of a newly discovered island see Chapter III of the same
work, which considers *The Tempest* in relation to seventeenth-
and twentieth-century imperialism.

Four critics, among others, who have dealt with the colonial
aspects of *The Tempest* and have focused upon Caliban and his
enslavement as moral concerns are O. Mannoni, *Prospero and
Caliban: The Psychology of Colonization*, trans. Pamela Powes-
land (New York: Praeger, 1956); Philip Mason, *Prospero's
Magic: Some Thoughts on Class and Race* (London: Oxford
University Press, 1962), pp. 75–97; Roberto Fernández Retamar,
Caliban," *Massachusetts Review*, 15 (Winter-Spring 1974), 7–72;
and Kermode, "Introduction," *The Tempest*. While Kermode
observes that Shakespeare, and more generally Renaissance
writers, held contradictory attitudes toward Indians, viewing
them on one hand as inhabitants of a golden age, with no
meum or *tuum*, and on the other hand as human beasts in whom
one could place no trust, he nevertheless arrives at the conclusion that "the confusion of interests characteristic of the
subject is harmoniously reflected in Shakespeare's play" (p.
xxxi)—a "harmony" more likely to be acceptable to those who
are at ease with the historical reality of conquest and enslavement than by those who, like Caliban's living counterparts, have
been conquered, enslaved, or colonized. It is puzzling that even

216 LORIE JERRELL LEININGER

an article as sensitive as Harry Berger, Jr.'s "Miraculous Harp: A Reading of Shakespeare's *Tempest*," in *Shakespeare Studies*, 5 (1969), 253–83, in its exploration of the contradictory elements in Prospero's character—his tendency to see himself as a god, his limited knowledge of human nature, his pleasure in dominating others, and his preference for, and success in, dealing with projected embodiments of pure evil—falls short of focusing upon the dramatization of enslavement itself as an ethical concern. I explore this question, posed in general terms, in my "Cracking the Code of *The Tempest*," *Bucknell Review*, 25 (Spring 1979), issue on "Shakespeare: Contemporary Critical Approaches," ed. Harry R. Garvin and Michael D. Payne.

4. Irving Ribner, "Introduction" to Shakespeare's *Tempest*, ed. George Lyman Kittredge, rev. Ribner (Waltham, Mass.: Blaisdell, 1966), p. xv.

5. Ellen Cantarow, "A Wilderness of Opinions Confounded: Allegory and Ideology," *College English*, 34 (1972), 215–16.

6. Nancy Hall Rice, "Beauty and the Beast and the Little Boy: Clues about the Origins of Sexism and Racism from Folklore and Literature," Diss. University of Massachusetts/Amherst 1974, p. 207.

7. Winthrop D. Jordan, *The White Man's Burden: Historical Origins of Racism in the United States* (New York: Oxford University Press, 1974), p. 196.

8. See, for example, accounts of the 1562–68 slaving voyages of Sir John Hawkins (one with Sir Francis Drake) which appear in Richard Hakluyt's *Principall Navigations Voiages and Discoveries of the English Nation* (London, 1589; facs. rpt. Cambridge: Cambridge University Press, 1965), Part Two, 521–22, 526–29, 531–32, 553–54, 562–64.

SYLVAN BARNET

"The Tempest" on the Stage

> These our actors,
> As I foretold you, were all spirits and
> Are melted into air, into thin air.

Although performances of plays are illusive and elusive, we do have some evidence about even the earliest productions of Shakespeare—for instance in original stage directions—and we have detailed descriptions of many later productions.

Shakespeare's company played chiefly at the Globe Theatre, an open-air playhouse that served the London public, and although there is every likelihood that *The Tempest* was produced there, in fact no document specifies that it was. The earliest reference to a performance tells us that the *The Tempest* was given before King James I on November 1, 1611, at the Banqueting House in Whitehall. The second reference (May 20, 1613) is to yet another performance at court, asserting that the play was staged as part of the wedding celebrations of Princess Elizabeth, daughter of Charles I. Court performances, especially performances of the highly allegorical dramatic works called masques, customarily made great use of spectacular effects, some of which would be particularly suited to *The Tempest*. Consider, for example, descriptions of nautical effects. Ben Jonson's *Masque of Blackness*, staged in the Banqueting House in 1605, began when a curtain decorated with a landscape painting dropped to the floor

217

(the hall was not equipped to elevate the curtain): "An
artificial sea was seen to shoot forth, . . . raised with waves
which seemed to move, and in some places the billow to
break." Jonson's next production at court, *Masque of
Beauty* (1608), required an "island floating on a calm
water." As the introduction to the present volume indicates, *The Tempest* itself in some ways resembles a
masque, and Prospero stages what is in effect a masque,
when in IV.i.118ff. he conjures up Iris, Ceres, and Juno
in "a most majestic vision." An original stage direction
says that Juno "descends," but this action would cause no
difficulty even at the Globe, which was equipped to let a
deity descend in a throne from above the stage. Still, perhaps when *The Tempest* was staged at court some visual
effects were heightened or added. For instance, a production in the Banqueting House would have used artificial
illumination, making possible lighting effects that could
not have been achieved at the open-air Globe Theatre and
that perhaps could not have been equaled even in the
indoors Blackfriars Theatre used by Shakespeare's company in the winter. On the other hand, nothing specified in
The Tempest was beyond the facilities available at the
Globe.

Whatever the original productions were like, we can
roughly classify most subsequent productions as either
plain or fancy, that is, either relatively simply staged productions of the text or, on the other hand, relatively elab-
orately staged productions of a text altered to accommodate
the machinery necessary to produce spectacular effects.
Justifications can be offered for both kinds. Briefly, advocates of fancy, spectacular productions point to the court
records we have just noticed, and argue that the production of *The Tempest* must have resembled other court
productions. Advocates of plain production, on the other
hand, argue that the records merely record but do not
describe productions of *The Tempest,* and, moreover, that
The Tempest was surely not written simply to be produced only twice at court. Shakespeare must have written
the play for regular production at the Globe (though,

again, there are no extant references to any production there.

This much can certainly be said, based on the evidence of the stage directions in the first printed version of the play (and reprinted in the present text): Shakespeare valued auditory and visual effects. Thus, the play begins with "Thunder and lightning," and a little later in the first scene we encounter a stage direction that says, "Enter mariners wet." In the next scene Prospero says to Ariel, "Go make thyself like a nymph o' th' sea. Be subject / To no sight but thine and mine, invisible / To every eyeball else," and a few lines later we get this stage direction: "Enter Ariel like a water nymph." If Ariel is "invisible to every eyeball" other than Prospero's and Ariel's, why the costume of a sea nymph? Because, obviously, Shakespeare wanted to feast the spectators' eyes with unusual visual material. Later (III.iii.52) we get a stage direction calling for spectacle and magic: "Thunder and lightning. Enter Ariel, like a harpy; claps his wings upon the table; and with a quaint device the banquet vanishes." Although a later stage direction calls for "Shapes" to enter and carry out the table, thus indicating that only the food on the table vanishes, not the table itself, the effect nevertheless must have been wonderful, and whatever the "quaint device" was—perhaps a table whose top flipped over—we seem to be in a world of masquelike machinery. Less complex, but no less indicative of Shakespeare's use of visual effects, is the stage direction at the beginning of the last act: "Enter Prospero in his magic robes." It seems reasonable to assume that these robes were something extraordinary.

Fancy versions of *The Tempest* were common in the late seventeenth century, and in the first half of the eighteenth. "Versions" is perhaps too generous; these adaptations were so extensive that they should be considered independent works rather than productions of Shakespeare's play. In 1667 William Davenant's and John Dryden's *The Tempest: or the Enchanted Island* was staged, a play which added (to balance Miranda) Hippolito, a handsome young man who had never seen a woman. There were other additions, too: Miranda was given a younger sister, Dorinda, who would marry Hippolito; Caliban also was given a sister, Sycorax; and Ariel was paired with a female sprite, Milcha, who was pursued by two new comic sailors. Other changes included a good many cuts, especially in Prospero's lines. Shakespeare's play was thus made more symmetrical—more orderly, so to speak—and at the same time more fanciful, thus suiting the taste of an age that regarded itself as rational or classical and also as willing to enjoy the most extreme flights of a poet's imagination.

In 1674 Thomas Shadwell, adapting the adaptation, converted the piece into an opera. He added songs, a chorus of devils, and ballets of winds and Tritons, and in 1695 this opera was done with music by Henry Purcell. But the Davenant-Dryden version, too, continued to be immensely popular. It was produced at the Theatre Royal, Drury Lane, almost every year between 1701 and 1756, virtually driving Shakespeare's play from the stage. In 1745–46, however, Shakespeare's original play was given six performances at Drury Lane, and though the Davenant-Dryden version was again revived, its days were numbered. In 1757 David Garrick put on Shakespeare's play, cutting only 432 lines and (more remarkable, in an age that felt free to "improve" Shakespeare) adding only 14. Although this relatively faithful version of Shakespeare's play was regularly staged during much of the rest of the eighteenth century, in 1787 John Philip Kemble, the noted classical actor, restored Hippolito and Dorinda. Because Dorinda's role was larger than Miranda's, it was much preferred by actresses in the last decade of the century. Operatic treatments, too, continued in the early nineteenth century, but in 1838 William Charles Macready, manager of Covent Garden, played Prospero in a text remarkably close to Shakespeare's. Still, it should be noted that although Macready rejected the accretions, his production employed a good deal of machinery, beginning with a huge ship, and continuing with Ariel flying around.

Charles Kean's production in 1857, which cut much of Shakespeare's text, was remarkable for its mechanically contrived spectacular effects, especially the storm and the other magic. It was boasted of this production: "The scenic appliances are of a more extensive nature than have been attempted in any theater in Europe." But whereas Davenant and Dryden believed that they had to refine Shakespeare's rather primitive plays for a more sophisticated age, the Victorian and Edwardian producers could with some reason believe they were fulfilling Shakespeare's intention when they provided as much splendor and magic as the theater (equipped with gaslight in 1817, and with limelight twenty years later) could produce. When electricity was introduced, in the third quarter of the nineteenth century, even more wonderful illusions became possible. This was an age when the theaters concentrated on splendid visual effects, and if the effects went far beyond anything that was possible in Shakespeare's own day it can nevertheless be argued that Shakespeare, with his thunder and lightning, his unusual costumes for Ariel and for Prospero, his masque of goddesses, and even his "wet" mariners, had himself sought to provide both realism and marvelous spectacles.

Probably the most notable Edwardian spectacular production was staged by Herbert Beerbohm Tree in 1904, when Tree played Caliban. An amazingly realistic shipwreck, in the Kean tradition, was followed by a blackout, then by the expository scene between Prospero and Miranda, and then by a scene, behind a gauze, of nymphs in a purple light playing on the water (they were suspended by wires) and on the sand. The light gradually turned amber, and the sands became gold, to the strains of "Come unto These Yellow Sands." Tree transposed some scenes, and made some heavy cuts, reducing the last act to less than half its original length, but he added elaborate pantomimes. Thus, he deleted the material that follows Prospero's speech beginning "Ye elves of hills, brooks, standing lakes, and groves" (V.i.33–57), in which Prospero breaks his staff and vows to drown his book. Tree then added lightning, thunder, another vision of nymphs singing about their yellow sands, and a final pantomime. In a souvenir playbill Tree describes the end:

Caliban creeps from his cave, and watches the departing ship bearing away the freight of humanity which for a brief spell has gladdened and saddened his island home, and taught him to "seek for grace." For the last time Ariel appears, singing the song of the bee. . . . The voice of the sprite rises higher and higher until it is merged into the note of the lark—Ariel is now as free as a bird. Caliban listens for the last time to the sweet air, then turns sadly in the direction of the departing ship. The play is ended. As the curtain rises again, the ship is seen on the horizon, Caliban stretching out his arms towards it in mute despair. The night falls, and Caliban is left on the lonely rock. He is a King once more.

But if most nineteenth-century productions strove to make Shakespeare real by means of elaborate sets and illusionistic lighting effects, the period also saw the rise of a counter-movement. As early as 1811 Ludwig Tieck, the German critic and translator of Shakespeare, pleaded for an Elizabethan-like theater in which the plays could be staged as they had been staged in Shakespeare's day. In 1894 William Poel founded the Elizabethan Stage Society, dedicated to restoring Elizabethan stage conditions. Poel saw that the use of cumbersome sets (encouraged by the proscenium stage) destroyed the continuity of Shakespeare's scenes; since elaborate sets could not be quickly struck, directors tended to delete or transpose scenes that in the text intervened between scenes requiring a given massive set. Moreover, Poel believed that attempts at illusionism were futile. In 1897 he staged *The Tempest* on what was thought to be an Elizabethan stage erected in the hall of the Mansion House. Bernard Shaw, in a review of the production, gives us a good idea of Poel's aims:

Mr. Poel says frankly, "See that singers' gallery up there! Well, let's pretend that it's the ship." We agree; and the thing is done. But how could we agree to such a pretence with a stage ship? Before it we should say, "Take that thing away: if our imagination is to create a ship, it must not be contradicted by something that apes a ship so vilely as to fill us with denial and repudiation of its imposture."

The singing gallery makes no attempt to impose on us: it disarms criticism by unaffected submission to the facts of the case, and throws itself honestly on our fancy, with instant success.

Poel dressed his players in Elizabethan costume, basing Prospero's costume on a print in a renaissance book about magic, and basing the costumes for the magical "Shapes" on prints illustrating court masques. He made some cuts—notably the bawdry—but because the stage itself provided a permanent set, and because the spectators were expected to imagine the locales, he did not have to cut scenes that otherwise, requiring a change of set, would have been deleted. Poel's efforts to present Shakespeare without illusion were to have an enormous effect on the staging of Shakespeare, but they did not immediately banish Victorian spectacular, illusionistic productions. As we have seen, one of the most spectacular, Tree's, was given in 1904.

It is worth noting, by the way, that Tree played Caliban. This role has, of course, been played in several ways, sometimes as a drunken beast, sometimes as a noble savage, sometimes as the missing link (an 1890s interpretation based on Darwinism), and, recently, as a detribalized victim of colonial power. In the late seventeenth century, and in the eighteenth, Caliban was chiefly a minor comic figure, but with the rise of Romanticism he could become a "natural" man, a creature of sensibility. In 1806, in Kemble's production, he was not only a comic lout but also a pitiful victim; in 1811–12, Samuel Taylor Coleridge, in a series of lectures, spoke of Caliban as a "noble being; a man in the sense of the imagination, all the images he utters are drawn from nature, and are highly poetical." A viewer of Macready's production of 1838 saw in Caliban one who "arouses our sympathies" because he resists a tyrannical oppressor. The late nineteenth-century Darwinian versions persisted into the first third of the twentieth century, in their way helping to make Caliban sympathetic, for, though a beast, he supposedly aspired to become a man. Beerbohm Tree, calling attention to Caliban's "love of music and his affinity with the unseen world," said that in Caliban "we discern in the soul which inhabits this elemental man the germs of a sense of beauty, in the dawn of art."

In our own time, Caliban has been variously presented —for example, as an American Indian, as a militant black, and (in Peter Brook's production at Stratford-upon-Avon in 1963 and especially in his production at the Round House in London in 1968) as a prehistoric man, the incarnation of bestial sexuality. In a production at the Mermaid Theatre in London, in 1970, Jonathan Miller, advancing a view that could not have been imagined before the middle of our century, saw the play as being about the destructive effects of colonialism, and he therefore depicted Caliban (played by a black actor) as the uneducated field hand, juxtaposed against Ariel (also played by a black actor), the cunning house slave. Prospero, of course, was the brutal local governor. (In 1945 in the United States, by the way, Canada Lee became the first black actor to play Caliban, but the production did not advance a view about colonialism.) Miller dressed his courtiers in black and introduced an attendant dwarf, thus evoking the world of Velasquez, i.e., the world of the Spanish conquistadores. Miller has said that the underlying idea is the tragic destruction consequent upon a white assault on a tribal culture. Gone was Beerbohm Tree's Caliban, who at the end extended his hands toward the departing ship "in mute despair"; instead, Miller's *Tempest* ended with Caliban shaking his first in rage, and Ariel— ever the alert opportunist—picking up the staff that their master had abandoned. But this view already shows signs of having worn thin: several productions in the last decade have returned to Caliban the noble savage, and, on the other hand, to Caliban as part of Prospero's own passionate (or even monstrous) nature.

Probably the most memorable Prospero of modern times has been John Gielgud, who has performed the role in four productions: 1930, 1940, 1957, and 1974. The last two productions especially evoked comment. The scenery in the 1957 production at Stratford-upon-Avon, and later at Drury Lane, directed by Peter Brook, was on the whole bleak, though some scenes showed a stifling tropical jungle. There was lots of magic—trapdoors and dissolving gauzes—but the masque was eerie rather than beautiful, and the costumes (except for Ferdinand's, which was orange, green, and white) were relatively drab. Except at the end, when he was again the duke, Gielgud wore not an elaborate magician's robe but a simple saronglike garment. To several reviewers he was a haunted figure out of El Greco, a man filled with anguish, struggling to rise above the memory of the "high wrongs" he had endured. He finally conquered his passions, and, at the end, armed with a sword, set out for Milan, not as one who would live in easy retirement but as one who would continue to struggle against evil. In 1974, directed by Peter Hall at the National Theatre, Gielgud again played a Prospero whose mind was beating through most of the play, though the harshness (which Brook wanted in 1957) was somewhat modified by the music of the great organ voice for which Gielgud is famous, and the settings were magical and dreamlike. At the end of this version, when he appeared not in silks but in ordinary Elizabethan attire, the audience perceived a resemblance to Shakespeare. In other ways, too, Hall sought to emphasize the Renaissance origin of the work. The production employed Inigo Jones-like symbolism: half of Calibans' face was monstrous, the other half that of the noble savage, and the stage balanced Prospero's cave (civilization) against Caliban's (primitivism).

Finally, a few words must be devoted to Peter Brook's *Tempest* of 1968, at the Round House in London, a converted station house for trains at the end of the line. This production, like the Davenant-Dryden adaptation that ruled the stage in the late seventeenth century and the first half of the eighteenth, made the play into something utterly new. Brook began with actors and audience milling on the floor (there was no stage, except for some low platforms and for some scaffolding under a white tent that hung from the high ceiling), and then the actors (in work clothes, except for Prospero, who wore a white karate suit,

and Ariel, who wore a kimono) started to do warm-up
exercises. Next, the actors stiffened their faces into masks,
uttered unintelligible sounds, and the play began. Some of
the audience sat on boxes or chairs along three sides of the
auditorium, others sat on the scaffolding. The gist of
Shakespeare's plot was retained, but with much cutting
(Alonso, Antonio, Gonzalo, and Sebastian were dropped);
the surviving lines were chiefly muttered or intoned without pauses at the ends of lines or sentences. Caliban's
mother, Sycorax (mentioned in Shakespeare's text but not
a character in the play) was presented, a monstrous giant,
and Caliban's birth—the birth of evil—was staged. Caliban furiously rejects Prospero's attempts to teach (i.e.,
subjugate) him, rapes Miranda, is captured, escapes, and
engages in an orgy (including sex with his mother). Prospero is captured and raped. Ariel's arrival disperses Caliban and the other rapists, and after some improvision
Miranda and Ferdinand marry. Various characters speak
lines of what was once Prospero's epilogue. At the end,
there is no change of light, and no curtain. This description, necessarily brief, perhaps is long enough to support
the view that seventeenth-century (per)version by Davenant and Dryden has its modern equivalent.

Suggested References

The number of possible references is vast and grows alarmingly. (The *Shakespeare Quarterly* devotes one issue each year to a list of the previous year's work, and *Shakespeare Survey* —an annual publication—includes a substantial review of recent scholarship, as well as an occasional essay surveying a few decades of scholarship on a chosen topic.) Though no works are indispensable, those listed below have been found helpful.

1. Shakespeare's Times

Byrne, M. St. Clare. *Elizabethan Life in Town and Country.* Rev. ed. New York: Barnes & Noble, 1961. Chapters on manners, beliefs, education, etc., with illustrations.

Joseph, B. L. *Shakespeare's Eden: The Commonwealth of England 1558–1629.* New York: Barnes & Noble, 1971. An account of the social, political, economic, and cultural life of England.

Schoenbaum, S. *Shakespeare: The Globe and the World.* New York: Oxford University Press, 1979. A readable, handsomely illustrated book on the world of the Elizabethans.

Shakespeare's England. 2 vols. London: The Oxford University Press, 1916. A large collection of scholarly essays on a wide variety of topics (e.g., astrology, costume, gardening, horsemanship), with special attention to Shakespeare's references to these topics.

Stone, Lawrence. *The Crisis of the Aristocracy, 1558–1641,* abridged edition. London: Oxford University Press, 1967.

2. Shakespeare

Barnet, Sylvan. *A Short Guide to Shakespeare.* New York: Harcourt Brace Jovanovich, 1974. An introduction to all of the works and to the dramatic traditions behind them.

Bentley, Gerald E. *Shakespeare: A Biographical Handbook.* New Haven, Conn.: Yale University Press, 1961. The facts about Shakespeare, with virtually no conjecture intermingled.

Bush, Geoffrey. *Shakespeare and the Natural Condition.* Cambridge, Mass.: Harvard University Press, 1956. A short, sensitive account of Shakespeare's view of "Nature," touching most of the works.

Chambers, E. K. *William Shakespeare: A Study of Facts and Problems.* 2 vols. London: Oxford University Press, 1930. An invaluable, detailed reference work; not for the casual reader.

Chute, Marchette. *Shakespeare of London.* New York: Dutton, 1949. A readable biography fused with portraits of Stratford and London life.

Clemen, Wolfgang H. *The Development of Shakespeare's Imagery.* Cambridge, Mass.: Harvard University Press, 1951. (Originally published in German, 1936.) A temperate account of a subject often abused.

Granville-Barker, Harley. *Prefaces to Shakespeare.* 2 vols. Princeton, N. J.: Princeton University Press, 1946–47. Essays on ten plays by a scholarly man of the theater.

Harbage, Alfred. *As They Liked It.* New York: Macmillan, 1947. A long, sensitive essay on Shakespeare, morality, and the audience's expectations.

Kernan, Alvin B., ed. *Modern Shakespearean Criticism: Essays on Style, Dramaturgy, and the Major Plays.* New York: Harcourt Brace Jovanovich, 1970. A collection of major formalist criticism.

————. "The Plays and the Playwrights." In *The Revels History of Drama in English,* general editors Clifford Leech and T. W. Craik. Vol. III. London: Methuen, 1975. A book-length essay surveying Elizabethan drama with substantial discussions of Shakespeare's plays.

Schoenbaum, S. *Shakespeare's Lives.* Oxford: Clarendon Press, 1970. A review of the evidence, and an examination of many biographies, including those by Baconians and other heretics.

————. *William Shakespeare: A Compact Documentary Life.* New York: Oxford University Press, 1977. A readable presentation of all that the documents tell us about Shakespeare.

Traversi, D. A. *An Approach to Shakespeare.* 3rd rev. ed. 2 vols. New York: Doubleday, 1968–69. An analysis of the plays, beginning with words, images, and themes, rather than with characters.

Van Doren, Mark. *Shakespeare.* New York: Holt, 1939. Brief, perceptive readings of all the plays.

3. Shakepeare's Theater

Beckerman, Bernard. *Shakespeare at the Globe, 1599–1609.* New York: Macmillan, 1962. On the playhouse and on Elizabethan dramaturgy, acting, and staging.

Chambers, E. K. *The Elizabethan Stage.* 4 vols. New York: Oxford University Press, 1945. A major reference work on theaters, theatrical companies, and staging at court.

Cook, Ann Jennalie. *The Privileged Playgoers of Shakespeare's London, 1576–1642.* Princeton, N.J.: Princeton University Press, 1981. Sees Shakespeare's audience as more middle-class and more intellectual than Harbage (below) does.

Gurr, Andrew. *The Shakespearean Stage 1579–1642.* 2nd edition. Cambridge: Cambridge University Press, 1980. On the acting companies, the actors, the playhouses, the stages, and the audiences.

Harbage, Alfred. *Shakespeare's Audience.* New York: Columbia University Press, 1941. A study of the size and nature of the theatrical public, emphasizing its representativeness.

Hodges, C. Walter. *The Globe Restored.* London: Ernest Benn, 1953; New York: Coward-McCann, Inc., 1954. A well-illustrated and readable attempt to reconstruct the Globe Theatre.

Hosley, Richard. "The Playhouses." In *The Revels History of Drama in English,* general editors Clifford Leech and T. W. Craik. Vol. III. London: Methuen, 1975. An essay of one hundred pages on the physical aspects of the playhouses.

Kernodle, George R. *From Art to Theatre: Form and Convention in the Renaissance.* Chicago: University of Chicago Press, 1944. Pioneering and stimulating work on the symbolic and cultural meanings of theater construction.

Nagler, A. M. *Shakespeare's Stage.* Tr. by Ralph Manheim. New Haven, Conn.: Yale University Press, 1958. A brief introduction to the physical aspect of the playhouse.

Slater, Ann Pasternak. *Shakespeare the Director*. Totowa, N.J.: Barnes & Noble, 1982. An analysis of theatrical effects (e.g., kissing, kneeling) in stage directions and dialogue.

Thomson, Peter. *Shakespeare's Theatre*. London: Routledge & Kegan Paul, 1983. A discussion of how plays were staged in Shakespeare's time.

4. Miscellaneous Reference Works

Abbott, E. A. *A Shakespearean Grammar*. New edition. New York: Macmillan, 1877. An examination of differences between Elizabethan and modern grammar.

Bevington, David. *Shakespeare*. Arlington Heights, Ill.: A. H. M. Publishing, 1978. A short guide to hundreds of important writings on the works.

Bullough, Geoffrey. *Narrative and Dramatic Sources of Shakespeare*. 8 vols. New York: Columbia University Press, 1957–1975. A collection of many of the books Shakespeare drew upon with judicious comments.

Campbell, Oscar James, and Edward G. Quinn. *The Reader's Encyclopedia of Shakespeare*. New York: Crowell, 1966. More than 2,600 entries, from a few sentences to a few pages on everything related to Shakespeare.

Greg, W. W. *The Shakespeare First Folio*. New York: Oxford University Press, 1955. A detailed yet readable history of the first collection (1623) of Shakespeare's plays.

Kökeritz, Helge. *Shakespeare's Names*. New Haven, Conn.: Yale University Press, 1959. A guide to the pronunciation of some 1,800 names appearing in Shakespeare.

———. *Shakespeare's Pronunciation*. New Haven, Conn.: Yale University Press, 1953. Contains much information about puns and rhymes.

Muir, Kenneth. *The Sources of Shakespeare's Plays*. New Haven, Conn.: Yale University Press, 1978. An account of Shakespeare's use of his reading.

The Norton Facsimile: The First Folio of Shakespeare. Prepared by Charlton Hinman. New York: Norton, 1968. A handsome and accurate facsimile of the first collection (1623) of Shakespeare's plays.

Onions, C. T. *A Shakespeare Glossary*. 2d ed., rev., with enlarged addenda. London: Oxford University Press, 1953. Definitions of words (or senses of words) now obsolete.

Partridge, Eric. *Shakespeare's Bawdy*. Rev. ed. New York: Dutton; London: Routledge & Kegan Paul, 1955. A glossary of bawdy words and phrases.

Shakespeare Quarterly. See headnote to Suggested References.

Shakespeare Survey. See headnote to Suggested References.

Shakespeare's Plays in Quarto. A Facsimile Edition. Ed. Michael J. B. Allen and Kenneth Muir. Berkeley, Calif.: University of California Press, 1981. A book of nine hundred pages, containing facsimiles of twenty-two of the quarto editions of Shakespeare's plays. An invaluable complement to *The Norton Facsimile: The First Folio of Shakespeare* (see above).

Smith, Gordon Ross. *A Classified Shakespeare Bibliography 1936–1958*. University Park, Pa.: Pennsylvania State University Press, 1963. A list of some 20,000 items on Shakespeare.

Spevack, Marvin. *The Harvard Concordance to Shakespeare*. Cambridge, Mass.: Harvard University Press, 1973. An index to Shakespeare's words.

Wells, Stanley, ed. *Shakespeare: Select Bibliographies*. London: Oxford University Press, 1973. Seventeen essays surveying scholarship and criticism of Shakespeare's life, work, and theater.

5. *The Tempest*

Auden, W. H. "The Sea and the Mirror: A Commentary on Shakespeare's *The Tempest*," *The Collected Poetry*. New York: Random House, Inc., 1945.

————. *The Dyer's Hand and Other Essays*. New York: Random House, Inc., 1962, 128–34, 524–27.

Bamber, Linda. *Comic Women, Tragic Men*. Stanford, Calif.: Stanford University Press, 1982.

Berger, Harry. "Miraculous Harp: A Reading of Shakespeare's *Tempest*," *Shakespeare Studies*, 5 (1969), 253–83.

Cantor, Paul A. "Prospero's Republic: The Politics of Shakespeare's *The Tempest*." In *Shakespeare as Political Thinker*. Eds. John Alvis and Thomas West. Durham, N.C.: Carolina Academic Press, 1981, 239–55.

Champion, Larry S. *The Evolution of Shakespeare's Comedy.* Cambridge, Mass.: Harvard University Press, 1970.

Frye, Northrop. *A Natural Perspective.* New York: Columbia University Press, 1965.

James, D. G. *The Dream of Prospero.* Oxford: Clarendon Press, 1967.

Kernan, Alvin B. *The Playwright as Magician.* New Haven, Conn.: Yale University Press, 1979.

Knight, G. Wilson. *The Crown of Life.* New York and London: Oxford University Press, 1947.

————. *The Shakespearian Tempest.* New York and London: Oxford University Press, 1932.

Leavis, F. R. "The Criticism of Shakespeare's Late Plays," *The Common Pursuit.* London: Chatto & Windus, 1952.

Semon, Kenneth J. "Shakespeare's *Tempest:* Beyond a Common Joy," *ELH,* 40 (1973), 24–43.

Still, Colin. *Shakespeare's Mystery Play: A Study of "The Tempest."* London: Cecil Palmer, 1921. Revised as *The Timeless Theme.* London: Nicholson & Watson, Ltd., 1936.

Strachey, Lytton. "Shakespeare's Final Period," *Books and Characters.* London: Chatto & Windus, 1922. Reprinted in *Literary Essays.* London: Chatto & Windus, Ltd., 1922. Reprinted in *Literary Essays.* London: Chatto & Windus, Ltd., 1948.

Tillyard, E. M. W. *Shakespeare's Last Plays.* London: Chatto & Windus, Ltd., 1938. Part of the material on *The Tempest* is reprinted above.

Traversi, Derek A. *Shakespeare: The Last Phase.* New York: Harcourt, Brace & Company, Inc., 1955.

Wilson, J. Dover. *The Meaning of "The Tempest."* Robert Spence Watson Memorial Lecture, published by the Literary and Philosophical Society of Newcastle upon Tyne, 1936.